EX LIBRIS

VINTAGE **CLASSICS**

THE BLACKBIRDER

Dorothy B. Hughes (1904-93) was born in Kansas City, Missouri, and lived most of her life in New Mexico. A journalist and a poet, she began publishing hard-boiled crime novels in 1940, three of which were made into successful films: *The Fallen Sparrow* (1943), *Ride the Pink Horse* (1947) and *In a Lonely Place* (1950). In her later years, Hughes reviewed crime novels for the *LA Times*, the *New York Herald Tribune* and other papers. She was named a Grand Master by the Mystery Writers of America.

DOROTHY B. HUGHES

The Blackbirder

VINTAGE BOOKS
London

Published by Vintage 2015

12

Copyright © Dorothy B. Hughes 1943

Dorothy B. Hughes has asserted her right under the Copyright, Designs
and Patents Act, 1988 to be identified as the author of this work.

First published in the USA by Duell, Sloan and Pearce in 1943

First published in Great Britain by Penguin Books in 1990

Vintage
Random House, 20 Vauxhall Bridge Road,
London SW1V 2SA

www.vintage-classics.info

A Penguin Random House Company

global.penguinrandomhouse.com

A CIP catalogue record for this book is available from the British Library

ISBN 9781784870492

Printed and bound in Great Britain by
Clays Ltd, Elcograf S.p.A.

FOR CHRISTINE, MY FRIEND

1

The waiter was looking at her. Not just looking. He was watching. Under black caterpillar eyebrows, his cold little black eyes were crawling on her face.

She whispered, 'That waiter is looking at me.' For a moment she thought she had said it out loud, that Maxl had heard her. Her lips had moved but she hadn't spoken, only to herself. She mustn't let Maxl guess that she had noticed the waiter. Maxl might have ordered the man to watch.

She smiled now across the red-checkered tablecloth, across the stone mugs of beer, at the boy opposite her. He had black eyes too but not like the waiter's horny ones. Maxl's were bright and guileless under his rimmed spectacles. He had black curly hair and a narrow face, small bones under his blue serge shoulders. He was a German, one of the Aryans, the pure Nordics. He boasted that. He looked like a Serb, a Croat, an Armenian. He looked like a great many pure Aryan, pure Nordic, pure nonsense Germans. Like too many of the leaders. Once she had thought Maxl a good-looking young man. That was in Paris.

She smiled at him. Her smile looked real. She had learned to form it that way. She said, 'I'm sorry, Maxl. I didn't notice what you were saying. My mind was somewhere else.'

Those who had escaped quite often found their minds wandering elsewhere. Even when they were in New York, in an old time New York rathskeller, their minds often wandered. She had got out of Paris. So had Maxl.

He repeated eagerly. 'How did you get into the States?' When he remembered, his accents were as clipped, as British, as London's own. He'd been educated at Eton, at Heidelberg, at the Sorbonne.

She didn't know if he was Nazi. He'd been an acquaintance in Paris before the Germans marched in three years ago. She hadn't discussed ideologies with him during the witless, halcyon days that preceded the march. But she hadn't sought his aid when she was trying to get out of Paris. She hadn't been sure. If he were on Their side, he might have thwarted her. If he were not, she might have been concentrated along with him.

She said, 'It was difficult, yes.'

'But how?'

The waiter's eyes were unwavering. Perhaps his big red ears could hear across the room. Perhaps her meeting with Maxl tonight hadn't been accidental. He had been standing there in the thronging lobby of Carnegie Hall while she came pushing slowly down the stairs after the Russian Relief concert. She had seen him before he saw her, before he seemed to see her. She had seen him and something had lurched inside of her. For a moment she had stood motionless, but the surging phalanx behind her pushed her on relentlessly, down into the lobby. After that one moment she hadn't been frightened. He wouldn't notice her. Even if he did he wouldn't recognize Julie Guille in the small and shabby, faded girl. Automatically she had pushed her hair across her cheek. One step farther and she could turn her shoulder, shuffle with the crowd out into the night, safe. One step more. And he saw her, called out a sharp, surprised, 'Julie!' She had known it would be that way. She had known when she saw his motionless, dark head there below that he would recognize her, that she would not be allowed to creep into the night unseen. Her luck had held steadfast for too many months now.

She hadn't answered that first call. She'd turned the shoulder, pressed hard against the overcoat of the unknown dawdling in front of her. But the dark coat was too sluggish, those ahead of him too lethargic, the currents too twisted. The door was only a few paces ahead but it was blocked by too many coats. Maxl had cut slantwise through the crowd, he was beside her, surprise and pleasure on his narrow face. 'Julie! Imagine our meeting here. Like this . . .'

She was caught. And the smile on her face was as guileless as the one on his. She prattled, 'Maxl! You in New York? Should I mention a small world?' The door was there now but she didn't step through it. Maxl's yellow pigskin glove restrained her arm.

'You must have a drink with me. Talk over other days— the good days . . .'

The walk on this side of 57th Street was crowded. Buses and cabs blocked the street. The pigskin glove swerved her to the corner. Unbelievably, there was an empty cab. She didn't know if the meeting were accidental. If it were, it would direct suspicion if she refused. No one was suspicious of her in New York. No known person.

That simply she came to be sitting across from him in a Yorkville rathskeller. And now he was asking questions.

She folded her hands in front of her, looked at them, not back there at the burly man in the white apron. She said,

'I managed to get to Lisbon.' She wouldn't say any more of those dragging months. 'There was a refugee ship. Finally it docked at Havana.' How many ports had it put in and been refused? The glaring sun of Africa. The spiced South American docks. Finally haven. 'I waited there. A friend of mine'—her very blue eyes faced his defiantly—'a Cuban gentleman helped me.'

Maxl was grieved for her. 'If I'd only known. I could have helped you, Julie. It is so easy. If you had only come to me.' He drank his beer tenderly. 'But I thought you'd have no trouble.'

'Why?' Her voice was sharp and she hushed it at once. She wanted to warn Maxl to speak softly too but she was afraid to let him know she had noticed the listening, watching waiter. Because it might not be chance that he had brought her to this place. He might know why the waiter kept his eyes unblinking on her.

Maxl's shoulders moved. 'You are an American.'

'Perhaps technically. Not actually. My father accepted French citizenship long before his death. I was reared in France. I have no citizenship. And I came from occupied France. No one to vouch for me.'

'Your aunt—'

She spoke on top of him. Her voice was too quiet. 'Don't speak of her.'

Maxl looked a little surprised. He broke off at once.

She waited until she could control her voice. She asked curiously then, 'You say it is simple. But you are a German.'

'A refugee,' he said smugly.

She pressed it. 'A German would not be admitted. How did you come into this country?'

He looked sharply at her and her eyes were wide

4

innocence. He laughed irrepressibly, bumped his mug on the table. Her glance jumped to the waiter in fear but he didn't move. Another one came, another one brought the fresh mug of beer. She refused. She wanted to get out of here.

Maxl did lower his voice just a bit now. 'If you can pay for it, it is easy. There are planes every week from Old Mexico into New Mexico.' His laugh was contagious. 'A regular tram line. You pay for your seat, in you go!' He shrugged. 'Or if you like—out you go. So simple.' He winked.

She touched her tongue to her upper lip. 'Who runs this? Not—not the Gestapo?'

'Oh no!' Now he looked over his shoulder as if he sensed a listener. Now he did drop his voice. 'It is not run for governments—not for any governments, nor by any governments. It is a business venture. In Mexico and New Mexico. I ask no questions. A passenger does not question the carrier which transports him. Certainly not.' The line of his mouth was greedy. 'It is a good business, this blackbirding. A big business.' Again he winked. His thumb and forefinger made a round. 'I wouldn't mind having a little slice of it.' His eyes were slits of obsidian. 'It is like the American prohibition. No taxes to pay. You pay no tax when there is no business, no registered business. Certainly *not!* The receipts—some are very large—are all for you.'

She said quietly, 'You learned a lot, Maxl.'

His thin chest swelled. 'Maxl isn't stupid, Julie. Reckless perhaps. Not stupid. I stayed about Santa Fe—'

'That is their headquarters?' She had spoken too quickly. Wariness was a thin film over his spectacles.

'Did I say that? Santa Fe is the capital city of this New

5

Mexico. In the records is there listed: plane service across the border, north and south? I think not.' There was a little suspicion. 'You have heard nothing of this?'

'Nothing.' Nothing as definite as this. Only the whispers where refugees gathered. Only a name—The Blackbirder. She let a small sigh blow from her lips. 'If I should have to leave this country quickly . . .'

He looked up, his nose pointed like a pin.

It wasn't taking much of a chance; he had come in the wrong way too. He couldn't betray her; they checkmated. It was worth the risk to learn more. 'If it should be learned that I entered illegally . . .' Carefully she said it, 'I don't want to be locked up.' She took a moment to stifle her beating heart.

He smiled blandly, tapped the red swirls on his dark green tie. 'You come to Maxl. I will fix you right.'

But his eyes retained suspicion. That was all for now. She knew. It would do no good to push further at this moment. Another time. She said, 'You're a good friend, Maxl.' She reached for her worn brown handbag and the waiter's white apron quivered. He brought his hands like great thick red paws to the front of it. She knew then she must get away and quickly. She said, 'I must go home. I have to be at work early.' Deliberately she spoke out, not trying to keep her voice down now. 'I work at the Free French offices mornings, until I can find a better paying job.' A warning. The Free French would miss her.

Maxl said, 'You are not afraid?'

'Afraid?' She couldn't help but make the word quiver.

He paid their waiter, not rising until the man crabbed away.

'That it is discovered how you came into the country?'

She spoke slowly. 'Yes, I am afraid. But I must risk it. I am all alone here. If anything should happen to me'—her words rushed—'I mean if I were taken sick, or run over, you know— there would be someone to inquire for me. I take the risk that I will not be so alone.' She swallowed. 'They are kind people, my own people. I don't believe they'd ever give me away, even if they found out. They wouldn't, Maxl. They'd help me.' Only she could never ask their help. She could never involve them. They had too large a burden. She must walk alone.

Maxl needn't know that. If he and the waiter were . . . She realized then. She realized and her hands in the brown coat pockets were like snow. The watching waiter was no longer in the room.

2

They stood on the sidewalk and the air of a too early spring night was cold as her hands and her heart. She said, 'Good-by, Maxl. I'll see you again soon.' She would have to try to find a new place to live. He'd written her address in his little black morocco notebook there at the table, before she noticed the waiter. He'd written her own name, Juliet Marlebone, not Julie Guille, and under it her address and the telephone number.

He said, 'I'll see you home, Julie.' The shoulders of his fuzzy black greatcoat clicked back. He was recalling the Parisian gentlemen. He hadn't been a Parisian gentleman. He'd been a shabby German scholar, studying at the Sorbonne. He might have been a refugee from the Reich. He might have been the vanguard of the Reich.

She tinkled lightly, 'Gentlemen don't see ladies home in

7

New York, Maxl. The distances are too great.' She hoped he wouldn't notice that her teeth were chattering, or that he would think it was because the night was cold. Her worn brown coat wasn't as comfortable as his heavy dark one. 'I've learned that in my seven months here.'

He took her arm. 'I will see you home in a taxicab.' He raised his arm manfully to one idling at the corner.

She couldn't jerk away and run toward Lexington. It wouldn't do any good if there were a reason for his determination. And if there were none, it would be foolish to arouse suspicions in a harmless Maxl. She let him help her into a cab, sit beside her. She spoke the address, an apartment off the Drive on West 78th Street. She didn't like the wide back of the taxi driver. His ears squared out from under a greasy cap. She didn't remember the ears of the watching waiter. She'd been too occupied with the caterpillar eyebrows, the skinned head with a stubble of black bristling on it.

She didn't try to answer Maxl's exuberances on the crosstown drive. Murmurs were enough. He wasn't telling her how a shabby student who had fled a Naziized continent became a lordly bourgeois with cab money and an expensive greatcoat.

The cab didn't maneuver. It went swiftly through the quiet side streets to Fifth, down to the 79th Street Transverse, across, down again, and across. It stopped at the dark worn brick front of her apartment. She said, 'Thank you, Maxl,' holding out her brown fabricked hand, but he walked with her, up the four worn steps to the front entrance door. She had her key in hand and her teeth together. She didn't know yet if there had been a purpose in this meeting. He said, 'Allow me.' She stood tensed as he took the key from her, opened the vestibule door. But he returned the key and stepped back. He removed his hat, bowed. He said, 'I will telephone you and we will have dinner soon, Julie? Perhaps Sunday night?'

She said, 'Yes, telephone me.' Perhaps she could move tomorrow, Saturday, be lost to him again. Perhaps there was no reason for this fear of him. Perhaps he hadn't noticed the waiter. Perhaps he had been genuinely pleased to see her at Carnegie, lonely in a strange land, proud to show his new prosperity to one who had known him poor. She softened. She smiled and took his outstretched hand. 'I'd be delighted, Maxl. Telephone me.'

She stepped into the dim smell of old tiles, closed the door. She looked through the half-lighted pane, watched Maxl descend the steps and walk toward the cab. He stopped and his hand went into his pocket She smiled. He wasn't as prosperous as his pretense. He was going to pay off and go by subway from here. She liked him better.

She turned and climbed the three flights to her walkup apartment. Third floor, left front. A small, soiled-looking room, a stained bath, a cubbyhole called a kitchenette. It was cheap and it looked cheap. Once she hadn't known that anyone could live in such a fashion. Paul still wouldn't know. The very unpleasantness made this a haven. No one would seek the niece of Paul Guille, rightfully the Duc de Guille, here. No one from the past must find her. Maxl had. By accident or design. It didn't matter. She must move on to another such place before he sought her again.

She turned on the rose-shaded lamp, walked to the front windows to draw the blinds. The taxi was gone.

Maxl wasn't gone. Under the street lamp he looked as if he'd started to run down the steep incline leading to the

Drive. He looked as if he'd fallen and forgotten to get up. She knew it was Maxl. She could almost feel the fuzz on his black coat.

She pulled the shade down, down, down, and suddenly took her brown gloved fingers away from it as if it burned. She stood there very stiff, knowing something but not able to say to herself what it was. Then a shaft opened in her mind and she did know. It was something she had to do. She had to go downstairs again to help Maxl. He wasn't dead. This was America, not Gestapo-ridden Europe. He couldn't just lie there on the walk. She must go to him. Even if his attackers were outside hovering, she must do it. It was the creed of refugees; help one another.

She left the lamp burning. She made no sound descending the three flights but there were sounds about her, rustles and whispers, bumps and creaks. She reached the front door, put her gloved hand on the knob. She hesitated. Whether it was Nazis or anti-Nazis who had attacked him, she was on the wrong side. She had been with him.

She opened the door and crept down the steps. She turned toward the Drive, moved on dragging feet. A few steps to his shadow on the pavement. She bent over him and she stood again quickly. He was dead.

She had known that he would be dead. He wouldn't have lain face down on the sidewalk in his new coat if he weren't dead. She must run, now, quickly; not return to the dingy room. Fortunately, she hadn't removed her wraps or laid down her purse. Run, run fast. But before she ran she had to get that little black morocco book from his inner pocket. Because her name was in it. When the police found Maxl, found that book, they would come for her. He lay on the sidewalk in front of her apartment house, and in his book was the address of her apartment house right under her name.

When the police came for her, they would interrogate her. Why was she in this country? There was no reason she dared give. Had she friends, family? None. How was she here? She had no passport for Juliet Marlebone. Señora Eloysa Vigil y de Vaca's passport had been returned to Havana long ago. She could be locked up. Terror beat her hands together. She could be deported to Paris. Terror shook every fiber of her body.

Run, run fast. Even now the police might be on the way. Someone behind one of these blank brick walls might have heard a shot. She hadn't heard a shot. Someone might have seen Maxl fall, might have given the alarm. She stooped down swiftly over him.

She had to lift him to reach that pocket. He was dead weight. She couldn't budge him. Frantically she rammed her arm between the unyielding sidewalk and his hulk; she snaked her gloved fingers within the greatcoat, into the inner pocket. It took so long. She closed on the book, painfully edged it up and out. The killer hadn't taken it. He hadn't known it was there. Or he didn't want it. It was nothing but a little book with names and addresses in it. She didn't look at it, she only felt it, thrust it down into her bag. She rose up quickly and plunged, half running, half stumbling toward the Drive. She didn't look back. She was afraid to look back.

3

The sound was her breath. It was coming and going fast, an animal sound. She turned the corner of the Drive into the snagged teeth of the wind. She put her head down into it and forced her way on to 79th Street. She turned sharp there and started back up the hill toward Broadway. The hill held her back, the wind had followed her. It was like trying to hasten in a dream. She could hear the hunted sound of her breath. The lights of a cab were approaching and she shrank close to the dark hull of the buildings. But she didn't stop walking. She kept on, slowly as in a nightmare, with her heart pumping faster, faster. The cab didn't stop. It rolled down the street, turning north at the Drive.

She crossed West End without looking right or left, particularly not looking right. Someone might be on the corner of 78th Street. Her legs ached pushing them up the hill. The crosstown blocks were always long, now they were endless. She might have been on a squirrel tread, moving but not advancing. And then she reached the crest, Broadway.

There were lights here, not as many as once there had been, the street lamps dimmed, the store windows darkened by war conditions. But more light than on the side ways. She slid her left arm out of the coat sleeve, looked down at her wrist watch. Ten minutes to two o'clock. It had been after one when Maxl left her at the door. The hours since hadn't added to one hour.

She stood there under the dull street light not looking at the watch. The palms of her gloves were dark; she touched them together, dark, sticky darkness. She had held them tensed, palm to palm, while she braced the wind and the hill and night shadow. She rubbed them frantically; the stain matted. On the right sleeve of her brown coat the dark stuff had crawled like a monstrous spider. It seemed to be crawling still. She was shaking so much that she couldn't move, but she did, darting across the half street, cowering into the downtown subway entrance. On the damp stairs she pulled the gloves from her hands inside out. Her breath was sobbing when she scrubbed them against the right sleeve of her coat. She could throw them away but not her coat, the night was too cold.

She ran on down the steps, opened her purse and her coin purse, found a nickel, went through the turnstile. There was no one on the platform, not on the downtown or uptown side. She scurried to the bench, sat there, wishing she were numb, not palsied. Her fingers felt sticky now. A silent scream ached in her throat as she saw the dark red gumming them. They'd been clean before they delved into her purse. The notebook there inside. She fumbled the gloves back on her hands, wiped them over the purse. She opened it furtively, clicked it shut. The color of blood was inside. There were smudges on the front of her coat where the purse had lain. If she pressed it there again, that one stain was hidden.

Someone was clatting down the stairs. She froze, not daring to look. She heard the nickel's click, the thud of the turning stile. The steps moved away. From under the brim of her hat, her eyes slanted. A man, a night worker. His back turned to her, the early morning tabloid in his hands.

She rubbed her gloved fist against her coatsleeve. The worst was on the under side where her arm had slid into Maxl's inner pocket. If she held her arm close to her side, it wouldn't be noticed much. If she kept her gloved hands in her pockets, they wouldn't show. The stains didn't look like blood.

They had the smell of blood.

The roar of the local came from the tunnel. She stood, waited until the train had stopped before hurrying to it.

She entered a different car from the tabloid man. There were only a few persons in the lighted interior, two men with the inevitable tabloids before their faces; one man asleep, his head swaying forward and back and side with the motion of the train. She stood in the darkened vestibule, pressed against the steel wall for support, watching blindly the dark rush of tunnel. She didn't know where she was going. She didn't know where she could go. There was less than five dollars in her purse. Even if she'd had more than that a hotel was out of the question. Without luggage, matted with blood, a girl couldn't walk into a hotel in the middle of the night. The railroad terminals—she didn't dare. She'd be watched. There were signs: No Loiterers. There were all-night movie theaters but she was afraid, afraid of a lighted foyer, of a ticket seller's memory.

She couldn't leave town until morning. She must have more money; she must get rid of the blood-stained clothes first. Lucky she'd been foresighted about putting her funds into a savings bank. There'd be no questions asked when she withdrew it. A large check offered by a haggard young girl would be questioned. Particularly one with blood on her garments. Her face mirrored in the half-lighted pane of the door was more than haggard. It was the face of a tortured ghost.

Where could she go until morning? Where could she hide? The train pulled into Times Square. Without volition she left it. The vast underground cavern was curiously empty at this morning hour. She wasn't lost in a throng as she would be during the day and early evening. She was someone to be remembered by the other stragglers. She took the next train that came along. It didn't matter where she was going. She was too tired to remain longer on her feet. She crept into the lighted interior, sat in a corner, hugging her purse and arms close against her, tucking her gloved hands under her elbows. There were two other nightweary passengers. They didn't look at her.

She rode to the end of the line. She didn't know where she was: Brooklyn, Flatbush, Queens—it didn't matter. When the guard came through, she said, 'I slept through my station.' She moved wearily, paid another nickel, and began the long ride uptown.

She rode until her watch said seven o'clock. Sometimes she dozed from sheer weariness but she was afraid. The jerk of the train entering a station was the jerk of the arm of the law. Always it woke her. She was sly in her terror, leaving trains at odd stations, waiting, sometimes an hour, for the next car. Only once was she spoken to and that by a drunk. He might have caused a scene, remembered her later, but she wasn't alone on the platform then. Two men stared at him and he swaggered away.

At six there were more persons coming into the trains. She stood then and whenever anyone looked at her, she left the train at the next station. When her watch said seven, she waited for Times Square again. She shuttled to Grand Central, climbed the stairs, entered the women's room on the upper level. She didn't look at anyone; there weren't very many women there. Her face in the mirror was gray; even her lips were gray. Under her eyes were slate-gray circles.

She used a machine for towel and soap, laid the packet on the ledge, and stripped the gloves from her hands. The palms were stiff now. She thrust them into her bag quickly and closed it. She scrubbed her hands, her face, her hands again. She could still feel the stickiness on her fingertips.

She reopened her bag, forced her fingers inside, found lipstick and a comb. Her dark hair was lank about her face. She tucked it behind her ears, pulled off her hat suddenly and thrust it up beneath the crown. The hat didn't look right but it was better that way.

She couldn't sponge at her coat, it might run red; she couldn't remove articles from her purse, examine them for caked blood. She wasn't alone here. She was afraid to lock herself inside a private dressing room; someone might become suspicious of the stains. She washed her hands again before she left the room.

She went up the ramp to 42nd Street. At the door she bought the two tabloids and the Herald *Tribune*. She put the papers under her arm, crossed the yet quiet traffic of the street, went down into the Automat. She had to open her purse again but she knew the bills in the zipper compartment were unstained. She laid the dollar on the counter, swept the two quarters and ten nickels into her ungloved hand, carried them to her tray.

Out of sheer weariness she dared the steam table for scrambled eggs and bacon. Toast and fruit juice went with it on the special. For a nickel the slot filled her cup with strong steaming coffee. She carried her tray to the farthest corner. She wasn't hungry for food but she was weak. She finished the last crust before she opened the papers.

There wasn't much in the *Herald Tribune*, a small item, the body of Maximilian Adlebrecht found on West 78th Street early this morning. Identified from letters on him. The tabloids were more lurid but they didn't know much more. Not in these early editions. The man was shot twice in the back at close range. She hadn't heard shots. The body was described as about twenty-four years old, well-dressed, twenty-five dollars in a billfold, no robbery. The janitor of her house had found him about three A.M., turned in the alarm. The janitor with an unpronounceable Polish name was being held for further questioning. There was nothing about a dark girl who lived in that apartment house.

The day in New York didn't begin until nine o'clock. She could do nothing until then. An hour to wait. She was awake now although her eyes felt as if pins held them open. She sat there while the room filled, refilled, over and again, ignoring each pointed look at her continued occupation of a chair. She sat behind the opened newspapers, reading every readable word. She read for an hour. When she left, the *Tribune* and the News remained on her chair. She carried the less bulky *Mirror* folded beneath her purse. It helped hide the stains that were not coffee stains.

She went up and out into the morning, into crowded streets now. Despite the cold she walked leisurely up to Fifth, turned downtown, looking into shop windows. She walked to 37th Street, crossed Fifth, and turned back uptown. At nine-twenty she entered Kresge's. She hadn't wanted to be the first customer. There was almost three dollars left in bills and in change. She held the bills in her hand. For one dollar and two cents she bought a brown, imitation-leather purse. For fifty-nine cents, she bought brown fabric gloves. She went up to the women's room. Behind the locked toilet door, she took the blood-matted gloves, thrust them into the new paper sack. She opened her old purse. The handkerchief was blood-stained; she thrust it in with the discarded gloves. The coin purse, a pencil, the little black notebook, stiff to her touch, she transferred. Her lipstick and golden compact were clean. The handkerchief had protected them.

The old purse was larger than the new. The old wouldn't fit into that paper sack. She took the center doublespread of the newspaper, folded it about the purse.

Again on Fifth Avenue she walked uptown. The paper sack she crumpled under the discarded newspapers in the first metal trash container. The newspaper-covered purse she laid in another container. She walked west and south to the savings bank.

She made out the withdrawal slip. Nineteen hundred dollars, leaving one hundred dollars in order that there would be no questions asked, no closing of the account. She hadn't wanted to touch this two thousand until she knew what the future would bring. Until she had found Fran. It was necessary now.

The cashier asked, 'In cash?' and she nodded. 'Small bills or large?'

She said quickly, 'Half in small, half large.' She mustn't offer a large denomination until she was safely away from this city. She mustn't attract any attention.

She pushed the sum deep into her purse and left the bank, caught a Sixth Avenue bus and rode to 34th Street. Safer to buy clothes in a mammoth department store. No questions asked. No remembrance of a girl with coffee stains matted on her coat.

As soon as she was within the store she removed the coat, folded it inside out, carried it over her arm. She wasn't frightened now. She was hidden in the crowd. She had her ration books in her purse. She selected a navy coat, a navy gabardine suit, a tailored blouse, a frilled blouse, a blue pullover sweater. Underclothes, stockings, nightclothes, a tailored robe. Everything new from the skin out. Hat, shoes, gloves, a new large navy bag. Cosmetics, brush and comb.

She went from counter to counter, unhurried. When her arms were loaded she checked her parcels, returned for more. She had spent almost two hundred dollars before she bought the luggage, one large suitcase, one small. She didn't buy the more expensive ones but it was almost fifty dollars more. She had to watch her money. Nineteen hundred to see her through. It seemed a vast sum but it wasn't. Because she was going to some far-off place called Santa Fe and she didn't want to be inconspicuous there. She was going as Julie Guille and she hoped someone would recognize the name. Someone who watched for refugees. Someone who was blackbirding.

She took her bags unwrapped to the mezzanine, retrieved her purchases, put what she could inside. She couldn't carry all the load. She checked the week-end bag with some parcels in it, and she carried the large suitcase and the large box which held her coat. She bumped her way down the stairs and out through the revolving doors.

On 34th Street again she found a cab, rode the short trip to the Pennsylvania Station. She went to the women's waiting-room, to the inner room, and put a coin in a dressing-room slot. Behind closed doors she changed suit, blouse, hat and shoes. There wasn't time for more. She crammed the brown ones, the Kresge bag and gloves, into the suit box. She tied the string around its bulge. Her large suitcase she checked. The box she put into a locker. She threw the key into a waste container.

She wasn't tired now and she wasn't afraid. She didn't look the same. She had the courage needed for what must be done. She left the station, walked to the corner of 34th and caught an uptown bus. At 42nd she left it, started eastward across town. No one looked at her. The westward didn't know she was passing, the eastward walkers didn't know she was among them. There was no curiosity on city faces. Even if police officers were watching for Juliet Marlebone they wouldn't recognize her now. Her description would be without identifying marks save for shabby brown clothes. Hundreds of girls had blue eyes, small faces, dark curling hair.

The bank stood foursquare on the corner of Madison. She hadn't been in it since she rented the box almost seven months ago. No one in so large a bank would remember the girl who had rented it. If the police had her name, they could be waiting here. But they couldn't have it yet. She and Maxl had spoken to no one during the evening. Even if it had been part of a plan, even if Maxl had been deliberately lying in wait for her, he would have talked of her as Julie Guille. He hadn't known her real name until last night when she had given it with her phone number. She had had to spell it out—Marlebone. In Paris she had been Julie Guille. It was simpler that way. She lived with the Guilles; Paul and Lily were her guardians.

She slipped into the bank, took a breath. She counted the steps descending to the vaults. This was the moment. Experience had taught her over and over how to behave in possible as well as in actual danger. This was only possible. She was aloof, seemingly certain of herself. She stated her name softly, giving it a French accent, 'Marlebone.' She passed the guard with no tremor. Alone in the diminutive room she laid the small box on the table. Her gloved fingers opened it, removed the shabby zipper bag. From it she took the soiled lump of cloth, unrolled it.

There was no aesthetic impulse to her senses, no breathless impact on her eyes, when the blaze of diamonds lay on her palm. Two missing from the delicate, exquisite necklace. Two she had sold, one in a stifling room of a Havana hotel, one in the furtive back streets of downtown New York. Stones for bread. She had no regrets. She wrapped the necklace again in the fold of cloth, pressed it within the depths of the large navy handbag. The zipper bag she replaced empty in the metal box. This was not the time to court identification by relinquishing the box. She followed routine, replacing it, nodded briskly to the guard.

He said, 'Nice day, isn't it, Miss?' He was a prim little Irishman with faded brick hands. He said, 'When you were coming down the stairs I was thinking it was my own daughter. She's overseas, a nurse. She used to wear her hair like to yours—on the shoulders that way. It's dark, too.'

Her hair. There was yet time. She walked more quickly up the stairs, into the cold sunshine. Again to Fifth. She chose an expensive department store. It was restful, the shampoo, the drying, but she didn't sleep. A short swirling haircut. She didn't need a permanent; there was enough curl in her hair. She couldn't have endured that time waste.

She wasn't at all afraid when she stepped out on the Avenue again. It was nearing four o'clock. She didn't stop to eat. She returned to the great department store, stood in line to retrieve the weekend bag and the other parcels. The girl behind the counter hadn't looked at her when she'd turned them in; if it was the same girl she didn't look now. There were too many faces on the daily treadmill.

Julie walked back to the Pennsylvania for the large suitcase, opened it in the waiting-room and put the parcels inside. A cab took her to Grand Central. A redcap took her bags. To his question, 'What train?' she answered, 'I'm not certain about my reservations.' She walked down the marble stairs to the great concourse, her head high. Her elegant heels tapped to the pullman window. No one could see the ghost of a gray girl in stained brown clothes that had flitted here in the early dawn.

Expense or no she must have a compartment, must be able to lock a door behind her. It didn't matter what train. The harassed clerk didn't look at her. He grunted, 'You're lucky. Roomette cancellation on the Century—these Washington big shots . . .' Lucky. She'd forgotten that with wartime restrictions it might be impossible to find a place on an outgoing train. She held her teeth together.

She bought her ticket only to Chicago. If questions were asked, if the police discovered who had been with Maxl, Chicago should be large enough to cover her.

She told the porter, 'The Century.'

There was almost an hour to spare; the train didn't leave until six. She had time for a sandwich and tea in Liggett's. She didn't want more now, she was too tired. She could eat early on the train. She bought magazines, the afternoon papers, *World-Telegram, Sun, Post, PM*. She didn't let her eyes look at the headlines, not that Maxl's death would be headline material with wholesale slaughter to the East and to the West. She bought a carton of Pall Malls, a box of chocolates. Any young girl on pleasure bent.

There was yet the final barrier. Her heart was louder than her heels approaching the gate. Were there plain-clothes men now watching the departing trains, watching for a small thin girl with long dusky hair, dressed in worn brown? She moved with the mask of pleasant assurance, a taller girl in navy blue suit, dark hair curled above her face under her navy blue Breton, color on her lips and cheeks.

No one halted her. Her red cap met her on the walk,

she smiled with her generous tip. The porter helped her up the train steps; she brushed past a gray-flanneled man in the entry, went into her own square, locked the door. Until she sank down in the seat, she didn't know how her knees trembled. She pulled off the hat, put her head against the rest, and closed her eyes. Safe. A little bit safe for a little while.

2

The train moved out of city caverns into the suburban countryside. Julie opened her eyes. Now was the opportunity to study that small address book. She opened her handbag, put her fingers on the leather, withdrew them. She snapped the bag. She didn't have to look now; she could wait. She could have these few hours, if not of Lethe, at least of respite. She wished she dare throw the book from the train. It could be found, her name burning from the page. Burn. She could burn it, page by page. That would rid her of it forever. But it might prove valuable; it might hold Santa Fe names and addresses which she would need. She would wait.

Her eyes closed again. She must sleep. Wearied as she was she couldn't descend into depths of sleep; she was but dozing when the rap came at her door. The conductor. She took her ticket from her bag before unlocking to the summons. She stepped back quickly, and then she smiled.

It was only the tall man in gray flannels. She hadn't noticed his physical appearance in the corridor. Now she filed it. Lean body about six feet, lean cheeks, blond hair with a swatch of gray through it, darker brows, gray eyes, good straight nose and mouth. She said, 'I thought you were the conductor.'

'Awfully sorry.' His voice was British, as Maxl's had been

when he remembered London. He smiled at her. 'I thought this was my compartment.' His eyes looked her over, went around her small cubicle, before he went away. He limped slightly, favoring his left leg.

She locked the door and sucked breath into her lungs. It hadn't been the police. Certainly not. The police couldn't have located her yet. She had covered her trail today. She sat down again and took up the papers. There wasn't much more than what had been in the morning editions. Maxl's address was printed, a large commercial hotel. No one there knew where he had gone the night before. No one remembered seeing him leave. He had been wise; you were anonymous in a large hotel. She would go to a large hotel in Santa Fe. Someone—the inevitable someone—had heard a taxi stop on West 78th Street about one o'clock. The police asked the driver to report. He hadn't as yet. No mention of a girl on West 78th Street. Nor was there a report from Yorkville. If it were a pro-Nazi rathskeller, it wouldn't call attention to itself by volunteering information. Juliet Marlebone hadn't figured in it as yet.

She must remember. She was no longer Juliet Marlebone. She was Julie Guille. She hadn't ever wanted to return to Julie Guille. She hadn't ever expected to resume that name, that self. It made her a little sick knowing that she must. Only in these straits would she ever have assumed Paul's name again. Only to remain free, to be able to draw breath, come and go. She must remain free until she found Fran. There hadn't been time to think of him in these last frantic hours; now, remembering again, she was suddenly sick inside of her. The answer to her letter might come this very day. It would gather dust at the Free French offices. She would have to write again, wait again. It would be more difficult now, but she couldn't risk remaining in this country. She would have to operate from a safer point. If she were to be involved in Maxl's murder, if she were locked up, she couldn't help Fran. Somehow she would find him. She must find him. Her fingers pressed against her cheeks. She must find Fran. She mustn't be locked up. She couldn't bear to be locked up again. She would go mad.

Again a rap at the door. This time the conductor, his voice called through, 'Tickets.' He and his assistant checked, said, 'Chicago,' echoed, 'Chicago,' wrote something, returned a receipt. They were impersonal as the landscape outside the window. They didn't see her. Never could they identify her.

It was seven o'clock. She rang for the porter, said, 'I'd like to eat here. Could you send a waiter?'

Special privileges were not wisdom in flight, but better to risk the identification of porter and waiter than to face the dining car. She wasn't hungry but she ordered, ate while twilight rushed past the window into darkness. Her eyes were leaden. She wouldn't double the identification risk by asking more privilege. She would wait until the porter came to her compartment. She locked the door after the dining-car waiter and she slept, uncomfortably, until the buzzer woke her. She had been dreaming. She couldn't remember of what; it was shadowed. She only knew that it was unpleasant.

She stood outside in the narrow corridor while the porter made up the berth. It seemed long. She could hear a portable radio behind the next door; it wasn't giving the news, only dance music. When someone was approaching she swerved quickly, pretended to be engrossed in the moving dark outside the window.

The porter stepped outside again. She said, 'Will you call

me in the morning, please?' and then she locked herself into the small safe cubicle for the night. She undressed rapidly. With care she opened her handbag, took out the little black book. It had a smell. She dampened the corner of a Pullman towel, scrubbed at the leather, kneading the rough linen over and over on those covers. It wouldn't smell again. She fingered the pages slowly. Unfamiliar names. Girls' names. Manhattan telephone numbers. And then Santa Fe numbers, street names in Spanish. Suddenly five letters crackled on the page. Popin. It couldn't be the same. It must be the same. Popin. Tesuque 043J3.

Popin had smuggled Fran's letter into Mexico from the internment camp. Fran had been afraid to write where he was; she knew only it was somewhere in the United States. Tesuque, Mexico? She was on her way to New Mexico. She replaced the book in her purse, laid it under her pillow, her fingers and her mind clinging to it. She felt stronger now, more certain. There was some connection between Popin and New Mexico. Her flight in this direction was inspired. If she could locate him, make arrangements with him, he could send Fran to her quickly. She didn't know him; he was no more than a name in Fran's letter. But someone in New Mexico must know of Popin.

She felt the purse again as she climbed into the narrow bed. Her fingers pressed against the hard lump. She had forgotten the Guille diamonds. She slid from bed, opened her weekend case, took out the canvas money belt. One of her purchases of the day. She folded the larger bills into it, threaded the necklace beside them, and buttoned the flap. The money belt she fastened about her, beneath her nightclothes. Again she climbed into the bed. This time she pushed the purse under the covers, touching her knees. A hand might reach under a pillow without disturbing a sleeper. But if covers were disarranged, one would wake. She had learned that from a woman wise in her trade, a woman who had helped her escape from an unknown village in Nazi-ridden France and no questions asked. Julie extinguished the bed light, closed her eyes. The train's motion rocked her quickly to sleep.

2

Morning was gray; the entrance to Chicago shoddy, grim. She followed the red cap up the dirty walk into the shabby station. There was a dismal lunch room and she had her bags carried there. She hadn't had time for breakfast on the train. She bought a Chicago paper at the cashier's desk, sat at the counter, ordered orange juice and coffee. After the other passengers had gone their separate ways, she would make inquiries about trains farther west. Someone brushed her paper, took the stool beside her. She glanced over. It was the man who had mistaken her compartment for his, the gray man. He would have spoken but her face balked that. She kept her shoulder turned, studied the paper while she breakfasted. Nothing about Maxl here. The Chicago press must consider it a second-rate murder, a minor affair. Not a line.

She felt the gray man pass her, saw his gray legs as he stopped at the cashier's cage. She kept her face in the paper; before stirring, she lowered it to look through the plate glass. As far as she could tell, the man was gone. He wasn't following her. But he'd used up fifteen minutes of her time.

She paid her check, went into the soiled, cavernous lobby. It might not be necessary but it might be wise. It was what an innocent person would do without thinking. She bought two postcards, two for five, and two one-cent stamps. She would take a few minutes to write them. The women's waiting-room was like the station, old and tired, soiled despite constant scrubbings. It might once have been grandeur; now it sat in decayed, obsolescent doom. There was no pen or ink. She used her pencil.

She had noted the apartment manager's name, scrawled on rent receipts. She had seen him only when she rented the apartment and when she paid monthly. There was no lease required in that shabby house, her rent had about ten days to run. Of Mr Something like Tolfre she could recall only shrunken skin, a drooping mustache, and a basement look. She wondered what he could recall of her. She had given her name, Miss Marlebone, on that first day, but he didn't address her when she paid her rent, the first of each month in advance. She had been there but three months. She didn't know a single inhabitant of the place by sight.

She wrote in a simple schoolgirl hand, one she had never used before. *Dear Mr Tolfre—I have a job in—*

Milwaukee. On the railroad folders it lay north of Chicago. She knew it was a largish city.

—Milwaukee. My uncle came for me and I had to leave at once. When I have the money I will send for my other things.

Two cheap dresses, a pair of shoes, underthings, a few books, comb and brush. Ten-cent store toiletries. A cheap umbrella and heelless rubbers. No letters. Nothing with a name.

Will you please keep them for me until then?

Very truly yours,

Juliet Marlebone.

She made the signature as illegible as possible. It might have been better to scrawl the whole but a schoolgirl's hand looked innocent. If the police questioned about a dark girl on West 78th Street, Mr Tolfre would have this to show. They couldn't locate her in Milwaukee; she wouldn't be there.

The other card she addressed to Mme. Durel at the Free French Relief office. Her handwriting was unknown there, her work had been filing, placement.

Dear Madame Durel—
I am on my way to Milwaukee where my uncle has found work for me. I am sorry not to bid you good-by but it was necessary to leave at once. Thank you for your kindness.

Juliet Marlebone.

They would not miss her there. So many refugees needed work even for the small sum. If by any chance the police did draw these two ends together, the post-cards would tally. Mme. Durel had been kind. Perhaps she had suspected that Juliet's entrance into the States hadn't been legal. She had not pried. She knew nothing save that Juliet Marlebone had lived in Paris before the war, that her parents were dead, and that she needed help. An uncle might be a surprise to Mme. Durel. 'I am all alone,' Juliet had told her. Perhaps in kindness she would think that Juliet's uncle hadn't wanted her on his hands until he had a job for her. Perhaps she might suspect that it wasn't an uncle with whom Juliet had gone to Milwaukee. But she wouldn't pry. She was a busy woman.

She went out into the lobby, mailed the cards. Good-by to New York. Good-by for the present to Juliet Marlebone. Julie Guille walked with certainty to the ticket office. She learned there that she couldn't take a train from here to Santa Fe. She had to go to the Dearborn Street Station.

A cab again, dodging through grimy streets under the pall of the elevated. The La Salle Street Station had been large and grim; this one was small and more grim, more soiled. She said, 'I'd like a compartment to Sante Fe on the next train.'

The wasted old clerk looked at her as if she were slumming. He said, 'I can give you an upper on the Grand Canyon Limited. Leaves at ten-thirty.'

She looked back at him as if he were deliberately subversive. She stated, 'But I said I'd like a compartment.' Julie Guille would have said it that way three years ago.

'War rulings.' His voice sounded like a wet twig. His eyes were faded behind the gold-rimmed spectacles. But they resented her; they would remember her. 'No compartment. You're lucky to get a berth at all.'

She didn't say, 'I had a compartment from New York.' New York was a turned page, forgotten. And it would make no difference; this mouse man ruled here.

He said, 'Do you want the upper or don't you?' as if there were a line of eager travelers behind her. There was no one in the gritty room but the two of them. 'It's the last one. You can get a lower by next Friday if a priority doesn't come up.'

She said, 'I want it.' There were only minutes to spare.

He did things to the slip of paper. 'Change at Belen for Albuquerque.'

She seemed exasperated but within she was wary. 'I don't want to go there. I want to go to Santa Fe.'

'Trains don't go to Santa Fe,' he said unpleasantly. 'Change at Belen for Albuquerque. Bus to Santa Fe.'

The minutes were moving. He wasn't a Gestapo agent hired to return her to Paul; she was in America. She paid, took the ticket, and, examining it, walked slowly into the station proper. It was like a depot at a neglected way station. The grayness, the grimness, belonged in a bad dream. The tracks ran to the gates; the trains, hideous dragons, pawed there. Their snuffings made speech a shout. The red cap who had met the taxi stood disinterestedly by her bags. She shouted, 'I'm leaving on the Grand Canyon Limited.' He started to the gate.

And she saw the gray man. In the uniform-crowded depot, she saw only the gray man. He was seated on a stool at the soda counter, right. She controlled flight. She was Julie Guille. He didn't know her. As long as she remained Julie Guille he couldn't know her. Julie Guille was a pampered, luxurious refugee from Paris. Not Paris. From a vague, large, overrun France. Julie Guille had always had everything material for which she wished; if it were sunshine in March, she would have sunshine. She went the few steps to the newsstand, bought magazines by size and shape, this large one, this medium, these small. Reading matter.

She paid for the magazines and her fingers with the change pushed the black covered notebook deeper into her bag. The stains didn't smell now; they weren't there any more. Popin's name was talisman: It brought Fran's actuality to her. Rapidly she followed the red cap through the gates. He found her seat for her, arranged her bags, left, still disinterested, with her tip.

Opposite her was a woman with frizzy, too-brown hair in some official-appearing uniform like that of a policewoman. The woman looked her over, didn't approve, returned her gaze to the ugly train yard. Julie sat there waiting for the man in gray. She didn't wait long. He passed her without a glance, took his place across and up two sections. He too had an upper. Had he not known where he was heading when he left for Chicago? Had he followed her from the La Salle Street Station? His destination must be the same as hers to be in the same car. Belen. A spot on a timetable. She wouldn't be there until ten-fifteen tomorrow night, another waste hour from there to Albuquerque. From Albuquerque someone would tell her how to reach Santa Fe.

She applied herself to her magazines. She read until lunch was called. She would have to pass the man in gray. She walked by without a glance, covered the three cars to the diner. It was already crowded, mostly with uniforms. She was seated at a table for four. Two oldish officers were opposite each other by the windows. That left an empty chair across from her. She was resigned to its occupancy. It was like a day when your fingers were buttered, one broken ornament followed another in succession. A private first class took the seat.

Impossible to kill time in a crowded diner. The waiters were adept at fast service. From under her eyelids she saw the seating of the gray man, the uniformed woman beside him. They were oblivious to each other. But when she swayed down the narrow aisle leaving the car, both of them raised their eyes and looked at her.

In her seat she read magazines until the print jumbled; she studied the timetable until she knew it by rote; she looked out of the window until small farms, small midwest towns, were an endless blur on her retinae. And always, no matter where her eyes faltered, they saw the back of the blond head, bisected with gray, two seats ahead and across the aisle. She closed her eyes. Arrive Kansas City nine P. M.,

33

leave eleven P. M. Two hours. She could disappear in two hours but to what avail? Waynola eight-thirty A. M. Could she sleep in an airless upper later than that? Canadian, eleven-twenty-five A. M. That would be lunch time. Amarillo, two-fifteen P. M., and still more than eight hours to Belen. How could she endure it? Clovis, four-forty-five P. M., leave Clovis four-fifteen P. M. A time change. Endless, endless hours. Without knowledge. She might be in a void. She wouldn't go to bed until after Kansas City, nine P. M. She could get the papers there, find out something.

She opened her eyes just as the gray man was passing toward the water cooler. His glance met hers alertly. She knew that look, the willing-to-make-conversation-with-a-pretty-girl look. She was familiar with it in Paris. After that, wanting more than conversation. The gray man wouldn't want what others had. He had passed by before she shivered.

The uniformed woman asked, 'Cold?'

Julie smiled automatically. 'A little.'

'That's the trouble with air conditioning. Either too cold or too hot.' The woman settled that by a brusque nod of her head, added patriotically but resentfully, 'It's the war. I'm willing to take a slow train but I don't see why the schedule is so long. And we're already late. The last time I went to Albuquerque it took me only from five one afternoon to the next. That was El Capstan, a fast train. I couldn't get a reservation this time. I have a daughter in Albuquerque. She's married to a professor at the University. I wouldn't be traveling if it weren't for my daughter. She's going to have a baby. Her first.' She broke off her confidences as the gray man brushed by again. Had a look been telegraphed between them? Julie didn't know. She had seen only the back of his head this time. The woman leaned across, lowered her voice. Her drawn brows were suspicious. 'Do you know that man?'

'No.'

'He looks at you as if he knows you.'

Julie gave a light laugh but her voice was quiet. 'He couldn't. I don't know him.'

The woman settled that with another brusque nod. 'A masher.' She boded him no good. 'He should be wearing a uniform.'

Julie said, 'He limps,' and wondered why she should offer the defense.

The woman ignored it. 'Every able-bodied man should be in uniform. They won't take my son-in-law. He's had T. B., has a scar on his lung.' She pointed to the *Reader's Digest* 'Could I have a look at that?'

'Certainly.' Julie passed it across. 'I think I'll go have a smoke.'

'No club car. It's the war.' Her teeth clicked. 'I say everything we give up is the least we can do for our boys.' But she resented it.

Julie swayed back to the washroom. It was empty. She sat on the plush wall couch, lighted a cigarette. She wondered if that woman and the gray man would communicate now that she was absent. Did they know each other? The woman's sudden entrance into conversation could have been at a signal from him.

It didn't matter as long as she remembered to be Julie Guille, unafraid, casual. She wouldn't forget. She hadn't once forgotten not to be Julie Guille when she fled France. If she had once forgotten, she would have been caught. Even if you were as young and witless as that Julie had been, you remembered when it was a question of your life or your death. No. If it had been choice of life or death, she might have forgotten. The alternative of failing to remember had been return to living death. She rubbed her hands together. She had never forgotten. Tanya had given her the name, Marguerite Duchesme; the part, a domestic. She had given the warning: If it is known you belong to the house of Guille, you are doomed.

It was Marguerite Duchesme who hid in ditches and under straw stacks during those endless crawling months. It was Marguerite Duchesme who had walked from Paris to Vichy, from Vichy to the Pyrenees. The sandals Tanya had supplied—how long had they lasted? A few weeks? Days? Barefoot over rock and stubble, bleeding foot over the bleeding roads of France. She had not whimpered, for that alone she was grateful. Julie Guille, who had never known what beat beneath the gabled roofs of Paris, who had never walked, whose eyes had never seen those who walked, the empty vessel of Julie Guille had been slowly filled on that long journey. The money Tanya had taken for her was gone too soon. There were so many more helpless than she. How many days before she was reduced to equality? She had never tallied. Her grief was that she had so little to give.

She learned to wrap straw, sacking, rags about her bleeding feet. She learned to scavenge for papers to pad under her blouse and skirt. When there were no papers there was dried grass, weeds. She gave her coat to a woman with a newborn child. An old, old woman whose black hair grew white at the roots divided with her a worn black shawl. She learned to share as well as to give. *Little children, help one another.* Those who did not learn fell by the wayside. Without the faith in brotherhood, the strength to go on faltered, diminished, and died. Only those of the spirit crept on blindly, stubbornly, across the Pyrenees, across the tortuous wasteland of Spain, across Portugal to hope, Lisbon.

During those aeons the Guille diamonds rubbed her flesh sore. They were without value. A loaf of bread, a sausage, a flagon of wine could have fetched over and again the treasure of India. In Lisbon, where every third man wore the fanatic mask of the law of the Reich, to produce the necklace would have meant her death. Only when she left reality behind and arrived again in a world to which once she had belonged, a fairyland, did they again assume value. One stone had opened barred gates to her, a second gave her a rooftree. When the time came a third would release Fran from bondage, would purchase their flight into safety. The other gems must sustain them until Fran was strong again after imprisonment, strong enough to return to the Free French, where both could do their part to conquer the ants.

Julie put out her cigarette in the small ash tray. Marguerite Duchesme was dead. She had been good, far better than that other Julie Guille, but her usefulness ended in Havana. Three years of flight had taught Julie the necessity of use. Juliet Marlebone had learned how to make a living in Havana, first in a laundry, later as an office worker because she spoke English as well as French. For that one whim of Aunt Lily's, Julie could be grateful to her. Both Fran and herself had been trained by English nursemaids, both spoke English as well as Aunt Lily herself. Some latent pride of her country had remained in Paul's exquisite, American-born wife. It was Juliet Marlebone who, after almost a year in Havana, learned the ways of illegal entry, who entered the port of New York as Señora Vigil y de Vaca. She had believed then that Julie Guille was left behind in Paris forever. She had believed it until Maxl lay dead on the pavement before her apartment house.

It was Julie Guille who must learn new ways of escape in Santa Fe. Because Juliet Marlebone would be halted for questioning. Escape would be a simple enough matter. She had been able to escape before, ragged, starving, impoverished. Now she had money; she was well-fed, comfortably clothed. There was nothing to worry about, merely a question of finding the right parties. Where was Tesuque? Could it be near Santa Fe? It was among those addresses. If she could find Popin before she fled the country— Her breath came quickly. Popin knew where Fran was. If he could buy Fran's release while she arranged flight ... Her eyes were calculating against the mirror. If she could reach him, he could. Bribery was an omnipotent key to prison camps.

Somewhere in Santa Fe was a connection with the airline to Mexico. The one by which Maxl had entered. The Blackbirder's route. Maxl wouldn't have gone to a small outlying place where no train ran unless there were a cogent reason. Maxl was urban. She shut from her mind the possibility that she couldn't find the necessary information. She had to locate it. It would be secret, yes. But she would uncover it. She had had experience in whisperings. She had had too much experience. All in three years. She closed her eyes wearily.

When she returned to her seat, Madame Uniform didn't resume conversation. Julie encouraged silence. She kept the magazine in her lap, turned unread pages. The endless hours must end. Dinner. More endlessness. The porter began making up berths at eight o'clock. She moved into unoccupied seats, then to the women's room. She sat quietly in the lighted room, not listening to the conversation other women were making to each other, bits of biography exchanged between chance fellows. Deliberately she shut her mind to the importance of the gray man. Either he was a danger to her or he was not. If he was she would move against him when the time was right. If he were not, there were too many other dangers that must be skirted, to weaken herself on imaginary ones.

It was well after ten o'clock when the plethora of lights against the night brought Kansas City. She put on her coat and hat, went into the corridor, slanted against the wall while the train moved into the yards. She was first in the line.

Two hours. Time. The fresh air was good to breathe. She climbed the steps into the vasty Union Station. This was smart, urbane, filled with bright shops. Chicago's grimness could be forgotten. This station was a smaller, less hurried edition of Grand Central. She didn't stand out as she had in the small and grimy Chicago depots. She was only one of a smartly dressed crowd.

She strolled to the news stand. The New York papers were the same ones she had bought in the city yesterday morning. She took the Sunday edition of the lone Kansas City paper and tentatively studied the book jackets. If she could engross herself in a book tomorrow perhaps the time would be less leaden. Julie Guille wouldn't hesitate over a few dollars.

The lunch room was large and bright, crowded with normal human beings, persons who could laugh and banter together, persons who were not hunted. There was a small, yellow-leathered cocktail lounge with subdued lights, beyond that a dining-room muraled in early Missouri Americana. She chose the yellow room, ordered Dubonnet. She sipped it, at ease here, in soft pleasant surroundings. She unfolded the paper, read the first page. War. Losses and gains. Defense work. Rationing. Alphabetical agencies. Roosevelt and Churchill. Nothing of a murder. She went carefully up and down each column, into the inner sheets. There was no mention of Maxl. This city was too far away to care about one little man's murder. She folded the paper and looked up into the eyes of the gray man.

He smiled a little. He said, 'Haven't I seen you before?' He said it with just the right humor.

She took time before answering. There was no inflection to further conversation. 'On the train from New York. My compartment.'

'I don't mean that.' He sat down unasked beside her. 'I felt it then, that I'd seen you somewhere. You're not a Hollywood actress?'

She couldn't help smiling but she clipped her answer. 'No. I'm not.'

'I thought that might be it.' The busboy brought him a Scotch and soda, set it on her table. 'On the screen, you know.'

She couldn't be led into volunteering information. She made a polite answering smile.

He was opening his wallet to pay the waiting boy. He asked, 'Won't you have a drink with me?'

She said, 'No, thank you,' set down her glass, gathered her purse, book, and newspaper. 'I believe I'll go to bed before the train starts up again. Good night.'

'Good night.' He rose with her, bowed pleasantly, and made no further attempt at pursuing acquaintance. She walked out as if his eyes weren't following her, strolled through the station. She was tempted by the doors to the street. The night air was gentle; spring had arrived in this midwestern town. The great grassy sward across with the tall lighted pyre was peaceful to look upon. A cenotaph for the dead doubtless; every town had its memento from the war to end wars. War seemed remote in this peaceful midland town. The men and women here wouldn't breed mad warriors; that could happen only in the old decadent slum of Europe.

If she could but have come into this country as her right. Her father and mother had both been American. But they had adopted France, expatriates; it was chic at one time, fashionable. And she was without a country. She had a right to be here in this cleanness, not hunted into exile. She walked in the mild night, there at the station square, until eleven-thirty. Regretfully she entered the station again.

She couldn't escape the man. He was crossing to the train entrance. His limp was slight. She felt impelled to explanation. 'I decided a walk before bed was a good idea. It's such a beautiful night.'

He didn't behave as if she had snubbed him earlier. His face accepted her words, mere conversation. 'It is. They've just called the train. Early. I was afraid you'd miss it.'

Had he been watching her while she thought herself unobserved save by taxi drivers there on the square?

He was continuing easily, 'It's too bad we must crouch on upper shelves instead of sleeping under the stars.' They descended the long flight of steps together. His smile was disarming and the way his eyes slanted with his lips. 'It won't be so bad for you. I'll have to fold up like an accordion.'

She laughed as if she were not wary of him. It echoed on the draughty stairs. 'C'est la guerre,' she murmured, and quickly, 'As the woman in my lower keeps reminding me.'

The eyebrows were amused. 'I'll wager she doesn't say it in perfect French.'

A chill encompassed her. They were at their car and he assisted her up the steps. He said, 'The man in my lower tells me about his glandular tour through the Mayo Clinic.'

The sleeping car was darkened, small blue lights showed the way. They said good night softly. Julie took her weekend bag in one direction while he headed to the other. The mirror startled her. Even in this poor light it was flattering. She didn't appear at all like the girl who had on Friday, only two nights ago, ridden the subway until dawn. Her cheeks had color, the dark hair curled away from her face, her blue eyes were alive. She didn't look as if there were something cold about her heart. She made a mouth at herself. She must take care. Because she'd had a moment's conversation with an attractive man, she mustn't forget what any stranger could stand for. She mustn't forget always to be alert. He was handsome and charming. And even now he could be congratulating himself that the fawn had sniffed at the pit. It had been so long since she'd had any pleasant occasions. For three years she had lived in silence, with books alone to keep away the Poulkes of memory. Perhaps that had been why, despite misgivings, she had gone with Maxl after the concert. She had been lonely, cramped into a fox hole for so long. She must remember. Until she and Fran were out of this country, the hole alone was safe.

3

A book discouraged conversation. A nap in the afternoon thwarted furthering acquaintance. She exchanged only a few vague nods with the gray man during the wasted day. She listened to a minimum of the uniformed woman's war remarks. The last hours were screamingly leaden. Belen didn't become a fact until past midnight; a small dark way station where a train waited, an unbelievably dirty, airless, and ancient train.

The uniformed lady sat beside her forestalling the gray man. The Mayo Clinic man and a covey of soldiers were the other passengers.

The woman said, 'This train is a relic. The good trains stop at Albuquerque. My daughter would have met me but for the war. Are you stopping in Albuquerque?'

'Yes.'

'With friends? My daughter's husband is at the University. Or did I tell you that? In the Philosophy Department. He's an assistant professor. Who are you stopping with?'

Julie said, 'I'm going to a hotel.'

The woman's eyes were suspicious.

She added, 'Just for tonight. Tomorrow I go to a ranch beyond Santa Fe.' She felt the need for some explanation to quell the suspicion. She didn't want the woman to wonder about her later. Obviously she was wondering now about a young girl stopping alone at a hotel.

The woman said, 'Santa Fe is a peculiar town. Full of religious cults and refugees. And remittance men. Rich people from the East. Their families get rid of them supporting them out here. And you're going to Santa Fe?'

Julie nodded.

The woman snapped open her gray fabric handbag. 'I'm going to give you my son-in-law's address.' She spoke almost shamefaced, not looking at Julie, rummaging for pencil and a scrap of paper. 'If you should want to look me up, I'll be there a month.' She pushed the scrap into Julie's glove. There was defiance in the shake of her head. 'I don't like Santa Fe. It's an unhealthy place.'

Julie made a sound. She was too tired for more than that. This last hour in the stuffy train with coal soot sifting everywhere was unbearable. The woman subsided. She too looked sooty, too tired for conversation. Only the soldiers exchanged words.

The conductor whined, 'Albuquerque.'

A Spanish hotel waiting, lying elongated in the bright moonlight below the brick courtyard where the train had stopped. The soldiers strode ahead. The Mayo man trotted. An evident daughter, big with child, a mild, unpressed son-in-law, greeted the woman. She had then been harmless all along. Julie lagged, waiting for the gray man to vanish. He was just entering the hotel as she turned the corner of the portal. When she reached the lobby he was not in sight. Evidently she'd been wrong about him. Fear made one suspicious of even the innocent.

She moved to the desk, registered in her own hand, 'Julie Guille, New York.' The room was up a flight, down a corridor. Relief came over her in a great gulp when she was alone, the door locked for the night. She heard the mournful bell of the little train going away, back to the dark way station. She quelled imagination that it mourned because it left her here alone; she wanted to be alone, and it wasn't ringing her knell. She wasn't afraid now. She had definite plans to carry out. She was safer than she had been for a long time.

She crossed to the window, opened it to the sharp cool night. Her eyes touched the scrap of paper there by her gloves. She stuffed it into her handbag and then she took it out again deliberately. The woman had meant it kindly. A scrap of paper was easily lost. She would never need the information but she copied it into Maxl's little black book. Prof. Otis Alberle, 417 N. Hermosa.

3

Julie slept late. Breakfast and lunch were one in the old Spanish kitchen which served as the Cantina. Afterwards she walked into the patio, dallied over a cigarette in the bright, hot sun. She didn't want to leave this pleasant town. She didn't want to go to Santa Fe. Something held her back, perhaps the grim woman's final remark. 'An unhealthy place.' But the woman had mentioned refugees. That held hope.

She packed, bought the local papers. The New York ones hadn't caught up with her yet. The locals didn't mention Maxl's death. New York was far away. She took the three o'clock bus. It pushed over the highway, past the same scenic barrenness of yesterday's long train ride, endless flat brown land spotted with scrub trees, barren, low-lying mountains on the far horizons. There was but one town, a half hour out, a Mexican village where some passengers left the bus. In the next hour there was nothing but the barren land, occasionally a small brown mud house, twice filling stations. The bus went on and on, climbed through a steep cut, and again there was wasteland. The sun was still high when the bus came into the town, past small tin buildings, past beautiful Spanish pueblo buildings, past the long sprawling barracks of an Army hospital. The wheels crawled through narrow, unattractive streets to the tiny bus station. She took a cab two blocks to La Fonda, the inn at the end of the trail. It had been recommended in Albuquerque. It was large and handsome, a dust-colored building in Spanish and Indian style with terraced roofs, a walled garden. The lobby was not as rich as that of the Alvarado but it was pleasant and spacious, beautifully decorated. It opened to a patio, on either side covered portals. She followed the boy down the right-hand portal to the lone elevator. Her room was on third; it was unlike a normal hotel room. The windows, opening to a tiny wooden balcony, were curtained with bright hangings. The furniture was painted in Spanish color and design. She had deliberately taken a higher-priced room; she must appear to be well-to-do, well able to pay, when she made inquiries about Mexico. If what Maxl had insinuated was true, blackbirding wasn't a political venture, it was for gain.

She unpacked. She must buy one or two dresses. The chambermaid might be inquisitive about an empty closet. She would have to get away quickly. She couldn't afford to be Julie Guille here for long. At this moment it wasn't fear driving her as much as economy. She had lost her imminent fear. The lack of news in the papers, the undisturbed sleep of the night before, her acceptance at face value at both hotels. Above all being released from what she had believed was the surveillance of the gray man. It had been foolish of her to be suspicious of him simply because he rode the same train west with her. That sort of coincidence was certainly a frequent one with a traveler leaving New York for the West. If he had been from the New York police, he wouldn't have wasted time on this trip; he would have taken her into custody before the Century departed. She had been silly. Fear created such distortions. Fear magnified curiosity into suspicion. She must remember to keep fear sublimated. Remember the lesson she had learned escaping from France. If you act unfraid, you are not suspected of being afraid.

What actually had she to fear? The agents of Paul Guille? They hadn't caught up with her in the cities where the representatives of the new order multiplied like rats. They would never have heard of this out-of-the-way village. The F. B. I.? They had not sought her in New York; only if she were brought to their attention would they learn she was an unauthorized visitor. The New York police? Yes. If the identity of the girl with Maxl became known. But she was certain she had covered her tracks leaving New York. Only by chance would she come into that again. If her name was given she would learn it from the newspapers in time to twist away on another covered trail. There was no imminent fear to face. There was time to breathe, time to make her arrangements with the Blackbirder. Ticklish business but she wasn't without resources as she had been three years ago. She had learned the tricks of evasion, of escape. She had learned to be sly and wise; she'd learned the animal importance of self-preservation without heed to the method. Only if some uncounted ill fortune touched her, need her plans be changed. If Dame Fortuna would but hold the wheel steady a few more days . . . She would gather information about Popin here, write to him to get in touch with Fran, before she departed. And if Popin did live in Mexico, she could see him personally after the blackbirding ship carried her across the border. Together they could work to effect Fran's release from prison, and his escape too on the Blackbirder's wings. Her heart beat more quickly. If the Dame were kind, she and Fran would be together so soon.

She was slightly apprehensive of carrying with her any

longer the diamonds and the large amount of money. Tickets for escape were seldom bartered for in savory surroundings. No need to add to her burden with fear of possible loss while the hotel safe was below. She removed her money belt, keeping out fifty dollars for current expenses. She rolled the belt neatly, thrust it into her handbag, went down again to the lobby. At the desk she signed a statement, the amount of money; personal jewelry, one necklace. The white-haired woman behind the desk sealed the belt into an envelope, placed it in the safe. She smiled at Julie. 'This is your first trip to Santa Fe?'

Julie nodded.

'It has an interesting heritage. There are many things you'll want to see.' She passed across a folder.

Julie walked out onto the sidewalk. She stood motionless there for a moment and then unaccountably she shivered. It could be the small wind that had crept into the golden afternoon, a warning of the falsity of early spring. It could be that the blueness of sky had become flawed by the faintest brush of cumulus white. She didn't know. She looked up the street to the right. The cold brown-gray Cathedral stood rampant on its terrace, its squat towers dwarfed by the mountains pressing behind them. She turned her head quickly to the left. Beyond the straggle of narrow street stood another mountain. Mountains. She shivered again. She didn't like mountains. The unyielding, unholy mass of inert matter dwarfed human mind and spirit. She turned swiftly, crossed cater-corner to the barren Plaza. It was deserted. The shabby old men huddled together on the soiled stone benches only added to its desolation. They spoke in Spanish to each other. They did not see her. Perhaps in the summer when blades of green might push against the flagstones, perhaps when the trees leafed again, there might be a remnant of the gay festivity here which the word Plaza connoted. Perhaps not. It would still face on three sides the motley shops in their old brick buildings. A few were covered over in copy of Indian architecture, the bank shone marble white, but the faded brick dominated. Julie walked slowly, past the ugly stone monument, to the far corner of the square. This was a grim little town. She hadn't known it would be so small. She hadn't known it would be a mountain town. She was familiar with others, in Germany, Switzerland, the Tyrol. Save for language, modifications of architecture, she might again be in one of them. Even in the winter-sports season, she had realized that gayety was not spontaneous in such villages, it was deliberately generated in defiance of the oppression of nature. The mountains only tolerated man.

She turned on her heel, started back to the hotel. She walked more rapidly now. Lingering in a sinister town was out of the question. She must find the Blackbirder without delay, make arrangements. Get out of this trap. Not only the encirclement of the merciless hills, but the very smallness of the village trapped her. If she were followed here, there would be no place where she might hide. Anonymity would be out of the question. If she could set the wheels in motion, it might be better to return to Albuquerque, wait for passage there. She would be safer in a city. She entered the hotel, grateful for its dim lobby, its room warmth. The white-haired woman was still behind the desk. Impulsively Julie moved to her. She asked, 'Have you ever heard of a place—Tesuque?'

The woman smiled. 'Tesuque.' Julie's pronunciation had not been accurate. 'It's about ten miles out. The Tesuque valley. There's the village and the pueblo.' There was a shade of regret. 'Before the war we conducted tours to all the pueblos and places of interest. Now we can't. But there's a bus.' She pointed to the folder. 'The information is there.'

Julie clutched the unopened pamphlet, was patient until the woman had finished. She said, 'Thank you so much.' She hadn't allowed her face to express the triumph that surged within her. Popin was that near at hand. Everything was simplified. Perhaps she wouldn't have to flee without Fran. She felt his actual nearness again as she hurried toward the carved wooden doors of the telephone booths. Everything, even her meeting with Maxl and his death which put into her hands the black notebook, was part of a magnificent cosmic plan. Dame Fortuna had twirled the wheel upward. It was meant that Julie find Popin. It was meant that she and Fran after these endless years should be reunited.

She closed herself in the booth, dropped her coin, read the number from Maxl's notebook. Tesuque 043J3. The operator repeated. Julie heard the three metallic rings. She waited, breathless. The call was answered.

The woman's voice at the other end of the wire was accented. 'Mr Popin, she ees not here now.'

Julie accepted the deferment. 'When will he return?'

'When I don't know.' The voice shrugged. 'He ees gone to Santa Fe for dinner. Maybe tonight later?'

Julie said, 'I will call him tomorrow.' She didn't leave her name. The lazy voice didn't ask it.

She came out of the booth, refusing to admit the keenness of her disappointment. It had been ridiculous to believe that because one sign had been favorable there would be no delay. She knew the maneuvering of escape better than that. The trouble was that the seven months of comparative safety in New York had left her responses rusty. But those months had had therapeutic value. She was rested, she was calmed, she had a reservoir of physical and mental strength on which she could draw to carry through her escape and now Fran's as well. She had no doubts that Fran would be at her side winging to a new and safer refuge; if not that, if she were impelled to sudden departure, that he could follow on the next blackbirding flight. Fran. She hadn't allowed herself the luxury of thinking about him for so long a time. She wouldn't now. There was too much to be accomplished.

Her watch marked past five-thirty. Too early for dinner. A cocktail bar was always the best place to observe those with more money than intelligence. It didn't matter if it were the Ritz, Paris, or La Fonda, Santa Fe; that verity remained unchanged. The Bible called them prodigal sons, the past knew them as remittance men, today they were playboys. The refugees would be there too, feeding nostalgia with the universal sameness of all bars. The Blackbirder would follow to offer his wares. If he were more elusive than that, a bar would brew loose talk, gossip. The refugees always gossiped. It was a way not to talk of the past. If she were a man and could browse at the bar with constancy, she would learn soon what she wanted to know. As it was she could enter upon occasion, sip and listen. She was confident she would hear the whisperings soon. Maxl had tied the Blackbirder to Santa Fe. If the refugees in New York whispered of him, those here would certainly hold the forbidden knowledge.

La Cantina was off the lobby at left, a small room, Spanish, gay. Great leather chairs were pulled to hand-carved tables, leather couches leaned against the walls. Waitresses swished in bright peasant skirts, embroidered blouses. There were Lantz green and scarlet murals on the walls and over the bar: cactus, cock fights, dancers, horse races.

Julie moved to a table for two against the wall, sat facing the entrance. A man and a woman, both in blue jeans, were at the table nearest the door. Behind her on the couch by the curtained front window there were two women in city black, modish hats. Another table held a khaki youth and a young girl. The bar was at her left across the room. Leaning against it was a tubby man in a cowboy hat, a lean empty-faced companion in a larger cowboy-hat.

It was all quiet, all pleasant. At the couch facing the bar, his back to her, was a man. The back of his head was pathed with gray. His shoulders were gray.

He hadn't followed her. This time she had followed him. She wasn't frightened of him. She ordered a Daiquiri. There was no reason why she should not be here. She would sip her iced drink. She wouldn't hurry. If he saw her, a vague nod. She had demonstrated to him on the train that she had no wish to further acquaintance. He had understood. He hadn't spoken to her after Kansas City. It was awkward that he had chosen the same town and the same hotel, but no more than that.

The swirling calico skirt brought her drink, placed it. Julie laid a bill on the tray. She kept the corner of one eye on the gray man. He was pushing up from the couch now but he didn't turn about. He was some four yards away. He moved to the right, still without turning. The pillar hid him. He emerged from it to cross the small clearance toward the door. She could see his profile. She held the cocktail glass to her lips, her eyes ready to lash if he glanced her way. The bright calico skirt bearing a tray crossed him, returning her change. He was halted and in that moment he sighted Julie. She wasn't prepared; her eyes drooped a fraction too late. He knew she had seen him and he would trespass again. She watched him limp toward her. He stood across the table, his hand on the back of the chair. His mouth wore that small smile, almost an amused smile.

'We meet again.'

Any answer must be provocation or snub. She was silent.

He said, 'D'you know, we have met before?'

She spoke without inflection. 'On the train.'

'I don't mean that.' The smile deepened. 'I've remembered. You're Julie Guille.'

She set the glass on the table without trembling the liquid. Her eyes were expressionless on his gray ones. 'Where did we meet?'

'In Paris.' He laughed. 'It must have been the Ritz Bar, of course. You were with your cousin, Fran Guille.'

She stated deliberately, 'I don't remember you.'

'You wouldn't.' Without asking he'd pulled out the opposite chair, dropped into it. It was done like sleight of hand and without seeming intrusion. 'You were surrounded by an admiring covey and I was one small visiting fireman. On leave. Even then, it was all of four years ago, I was in the R. A. F.'

She said rather than asked, 'You are English.'

'Yes.' He passed cigarettes, American, to her. 'You don't remember, do you? My name is Blaike, Roderick Blaike. My friends call me Blaike, however, never Rod.' He lighted the cigarettes. 'I'm again on leave.' His mouth had gone straight. 'Had a little crackup over the Channel—my leg . . .' He touched it. 'They tell me I'll have to relearn flying.'

She asked then, 'How do you happen to be in America?'

'I'm recuperating.' There was a moment before he remembered to slant the smile. 'How is Fran? With you?'

She answered, 'No.'

His brows pointed up. 'Not still in Paris?'

She took her time in reply. 'I don't know where he is. I haven't heard from him for a long time.' She raised her eyes then. 'We don't get much news from Paris now.'

He accepted that with a grave face. 'You're with your aunt and uncle here?'

'As far as I know, they are in France,' she answered brusquely. She didn't like this questioning. Maybe he was only a naïve young British flyer; maybe not. Gestapo agents, disguised above suspicion, had been instrumental in placing Fran in internment. There were Germans who could pass for British in Whitehall, much more easily in this remote New Mexican town. She could have been led here deliberately by Maxl, his death not part of the pattern. Reports of Paul's fury at her escape had reached her while she was still in the Paris underground. He had been determined to recover both her person and the de Guille diamonds. The Blackbirder could be Nazi. The whispers about him in New York had always started at the appearance of refugees who could not have entered the United States by legal methods. She rejected, definitely now, the coincidence of this man as a traveling companion. She finished her drink, scooped up part of the change. 'It so happens that I am an American. I do not hear from the Guilles.' She rose, slid her purse under her arm. 'There is no word from France since France's death.'

He apologized, following her toward the door. 'I'm so sorry. I didn't mean—I know how you must feel—'

She didn't answer; she didn't even hear him. Her eyes

disbelieved as she hurried forward. Beyond the man blurred in the doorway was another man. It was Jacques Michet.

2

Julie propelled herself forward, barely excusing herself as she brushed aside the man in the entry. 'Jacques!' She ran to him, caught his arms. 'Jacques! Jacques!' She could only repeat his name over and over in wonder, in faith.

He appeared thin but fit; his dark curly hair cut American; his tight denim levis and blue shirt, New Mexican; huaraches on his feet. His eyes lighted for a moment, his lips formed, 'Julie,' and then unaccountably both were shuttered. 'Pardon?'

She shook him slightly. 'Jacques, I haven't changed that much. It's Julie. I just can't believe you're here.' It was too good for belief. After the years of working alone, to have someone on whom she could depend, who would help. Jacques had been paid by Paul Guille but he had been Fran's man, Fran's friend. The Guille heir and the Guille handyman. The gap hadn't counted. Not with both of them so enamored of planes. That was before planes had become stamped as lethal weapons, when they were incredibly beautiful silver streaks in the sky. Fran had taught Jacques to fly his two-seater. It was the summer when she was fifteen. Fran from his six years of seniority had promised to teach her when she was older. Another summer.

Fran was in prison. But Jacques was free. He would help. 'I've so much to tell you, Jacques.' She didn't understand his restraint, then she realized. The gray man was standing there watching. The man she had brushed in the doorway was also watching. She hadn't looked on him until now. Slight, no taller than she, with a sad monkey face and a beautiful silken brown beard. It was the exact color of the corduroy jacket he wore. His eyes were brown, cinnamon brown. When she turned he peered and asked, 'You have a friend, Jacques?' His voice was gentle.

Jacques spoke formally to Julie. 'It has been good to see you, M'mselle. Give my regards to your family.' He took a step away, toward the beard.

She shook her head slightly. She was puzzled but she accepted it. There must be a reason. Her eyes suddenly lifted to the gray man, to that faint amused smile.

The bearded man was in front of Jacques. 'Your friend—'

Jacques' back was to her but she heard his words. 'We are late now, Popin.'

'Popin!' She echoed it aloud.

He had sidestepped Jacques. 'I am Popin.'

She was delighted. 'But amazing! I tried to reach you by phone only a little while ago. The—maid?—said you were in Santa Fe for dinner.'

'So I am.'

'For dinner with me,' the gray man said. 'Mr Popin, I am Roderick Blaike.'

Popin's laughter was unrepressed. His long fingers gestured to one and to the other. 'It couldn't happen.' He shook his beard 'No carnation in the buttonhole. No seeking a face for a name. We meet. We are all friends. That easy it is. We will dine together? Miss—'

Jacques spoke. His face was a graven thing. 'She is Julie Guille.'

'Yes?' If there was a flicker of surprise behind the silken beard it was swathed. 'And you are an old friend of my friend Jacques? How pleasant. A reunion. Mr Blaike, you do not object if the young lady joins us for dinner?'

Popin didn't know Blaike, the meeting was of strangers. He distrusted the gray man too, obviously; otherwise he would have mentioned Fran. She didn't want to dine with Blaike but possibly he could be eluded after dinner. If there could be granted just one moment alone with the bearded man, to speak Fran's name, to hear it spoken.

'I'd be delighted,' Blaike said. He might have been laughing at her. He looked from his height down into her face. 'You will join us, Miss Guille?'

'Certainly.'

Jacques stood apart.

Popin said, 'The New Mexican room is most pleasant. There are the delicate frescoes of Olive Rush. And in this— our new country—there is yet sufficient food.' His voice muted. 'We are the fortunate ones.' He raised his cinnamon eyes. 'I too am a refugee.' His head turned. 'Jacques—'

Jacques said unsmiling, 'I have the important errands, Popin. You remember. You will excuse me.'

'But dinner first. You must eat something.'

'Something I will eat. But first the list for Spike—and other more important things.' He did not wait for response. His huaraches clicked across the lobby.

Popin shrugged his hands. 'You knew him well before, Miss Guille?'

'He worked for my guardian, Paul Guille.' She made a little face. 'I've known him since I was a child—but not too well.' Evidently. She didn't understand. True, she had not known Jacques well but Tanya—Tanya was his wife. It was Tanya who had effected her escape out of France. Jacques knew; he must have known. And he knew her love for Fran.

A stringed orchestra in the velvet garb of Spanish grandees strummed outside the dining-room door. The room was pleasant, quiet, pastel on the walls and pillars: a delicate faun, a warm gray squirrel, white blossoming cactus. Popin led to a banco against the wall, placed her beside Blaike there. He took the chair across the narrow, painted table. His fingers touched the fat white of the candle. 'You have only just arrived, Miss Guille?'

'This afternoon.'

'Funny thing.' Blaike beckoned the wine boy. 'You'll have a drink before we order dinner?' Julie refused. Popin said, 'Bourbon, if you please.' Blaike gave the order. 'Funny. Miss Guille and I traveled from New York together.'

She scotched it quickly, her eyes warning the bearded man. 'On the same trains.'

Blaike laughed pleasantly. 'Yes. Funnier still, I'd met her in Paris years ago, with her cousin, Fran Guille.' Popin didn't move an eyelash. 'I didn't get it remembered until a while ago.' Blaike suggested from the menu. The starched white waitress wrote the order.

Popin laid his fingertips together. He spoke modestly. 'What I do not understand, Mr Blaike, is how you happen to hear of my painting back there in New York.' His accent was definite, not definable.

'I've always been interested in modem art. Cigarette?' He was playing the host, easily, practicedly. 'A fellow I knew there told me about your work. With great enthusiasm, I might add.' He hesitated. 'I'm on leave. R. A. F. Recuperation by travel, that sort of thing. I decided to drop off here and look you up.'

He was lying. She knew that. It was no sudden decision to drop off here; he had come deliberately as the crow would fly. Popin knew he was lying. He asked with incredible gentleness, 'Who was this fellow you know? Did he know me?'

Blaike finished lighting Julie's cigarette. He blew out the match, laid it in the diminutive brim of the clay sombrero. He said, 'His name was Maximilian Adlebrecht.'

She was as quiet as the small painted burro on the wall. She made no waste gesture with her cigarette nor with an eyelash. He knew. He had known all the time. He was waiting, the way the mountains were waiting, for something, and she did not know for what. She could only wait too. She could not ask.

Popin was turning the name unfamiliarly on his tongue. 'Adlebrecht. Maximilian Adlebrecht.' He was apologetic. 'One meets so many.'

'Young fellow,' Blaike said. 'Good broth, what?' He tested again. 'He was here last autumn, I believe.'

'A German?' There was a faint suspicion in the question. 'Refugee,' Blaike said.

'I do not know,' Popin decided promptly. He began to eat as if he were very hungry. He repeated, 'One meets so many. He told you of my work?'

'Yes. He was well pleased with it. I was hoping you'd be good enough to allow me a look at it.'

'Perhaps it can be arranged,' Popin murmured. He put his napkin to his beard. His head tilted at Julie. 'You too are interested in my work?'

She wasn't certain what the answer should be. He was trying to convey to her something beyond the words but she knew too little to decipher the message. It was necessary to fence, neither rejecting nor accepting until she became wiser. 'I'm afraid I don't know much about modern art. I was toured through quantities of galleries in Paris, of course, but no one bothered to explain to me what were the requirements of quality. As far as I could judge it was all based on fashion, and as tenuous as that.'

Popin was smiling under his beard. 'You do not know much, do you?'

She shook her head. 'I'm the blank page.' Her eyes held his a moment. 'Really a find for an artist. And certainly I'd like to see your work, Mr Popin. But I warn you in advance my personal taste is Rembrandt.'

'You could not go wrong.' He attacked his plate again.

Blaike emerged from his. His eyebrows were puzzled. 'You must have known Maxl in Paris, Julie.'

'Paris is a large city.' She raised soft blue eyes at him, deliberately innocent eyes. 'My circle was limited.' She was casual as a breath. 'This—the fellow was Ritz Bar?'

He wasn't. He'd been poor. Studio parties, free lectures, music—how had she happened to know him? The Russian choreographer? The Spanish guitarist? Some toast of the town who had crept from the fringes.

'You should remember him,' Blaike insisted. 'Young fellow. Rather good-looking in a dark way. Neat dresser.' He was describing the New York Maxl. She listened without expression. He stated deliberately, 'He was a friend of Fran's.'

He wasn't. Fran's friends were not poor students. The corners of her mouth taunted but her voice was milk-mild. 'Fran is quite a bit older than I, almost six years. I didn't know many of his friends.' She asked a question lightly. 'You knew this'—she forced her lips to form the name—'this Maxl in Paris?'

He answered slowly, 'No, I didn't. I ran into him in New York.' His gray eyes were cold as granite. 'It was he who told me he was a friend of Fran Guille's.'

She dismissed the subject. 'Fran had too many friends.'

She saw him suddenly, tall, dark, gallant, always gay. Her heart wrenched. Fran in prison. A falcon caged.

Something must have flickered in her face. Blaike said, 'Sorry. I forgot.' He turned to Popin. 'Miss Julie hasn't heard from her cousin. She believes he is still in France.' There was something ironical in the intonation.

She touched the cold of her dessert. Could it be he was looking for Fran? Had he too learned that the bearded man was Fran's friend? Was that, not an interest in art, what brought him here? She couldn't warn Popin to say nothing. She could only pray that intuitive sensitivity would allow him to realize the danger of discussing Fran with an inquisitive stranger. If the gray man were after Fran, from what source did he stem? Not the British secret service no matter the accent, the pretense of R. A. F. affiliation. Not the F. B. I. That organization would know that Fran was already in custody. She faced it with cold terror. It could only be the Gestapo. Had word somehow failed to reach headquarters that their American agents had put Fran in prison camp? Their men, masked as loyal Americans, bearing false witness against Fran, linking him with Paul's sedition. It was possible. How long had he been locked up? At least a year. But if those agents had been unmasked, also put away? This was credible. But why would they seek Fran, why wish to harm him? Why? Paul Guille was a collaborationist. Why would the Nazis believe his son a danger to them? Fran had been in the United States before the war began. He hadn't been in Paris to bore against the reign of horror. Why? Unless the Gestapo had ferreted the secret which she and Fran alone shared. If they had learned, he was in danger because of her. But she was in graver danger.

She faced that, meticulously spooning the faint mauve ice. Why hadn't the gray man moved against her before now? The answer came with shocking certainty. Because he didn't know where Fran was. He believed that she knew. He was waiting for her to lead him to Fran. The gray man was not coincidentally on the train west. But how could he have known she would take that train—*she hadn't known herself!* Unless she had been followed from the apartment that night, followed all the next day. Her spoon clicked against her teeth. She couldn't have been. She would have known. But she realized with sinking heart that she wouldn't have known. The months of inaction had dulled her perceptions. She put down the spoon. It made a definite sound against the china plate. She bent toward the gray man. 'Maximilian Adlebrecht? Is that correct?'

His eyebrows pointed in mild surprise. He nodded.

'You saw him shortly before you left New York?'

Again he nodded.

Her eyes narrowed. She held a cigarette carelessly between her fingers. 'It's rather an unusual name in this country. I wonder. I read in the New York papers of the death of a man of that name.' She opened her eyes wide now on Blaike's face. It expressed nothing.

It was Popin who asked huskily, 'Maximilian Adlebrecht is dead?'

Blaike's statement was sharp. 'Yes, he is dead. He died the night before I left New York.'

Julie said, 'I'm sorry.'

'You needn't be,' Blaike said.

It was Popin who pressed on, his beard sagging down on the soft brown coat. 'How did he come to die?'

Blaike looked at her. Her eyes did not falter. It was he

who turned his head, explained, 'I know little about it. A friend told me over the phone. I was packing then to leave. We were only chance acquaintances. He was found dead.'

Julie said cruelly, 'He was shot in the back. At close range, the story said.'

Popin's soft eyes closed for a moment.

Blaike asked, 'You remember him now?'

The brown head nodded. 'Yes. I remember him sooner. A young man who would not wish to die.' His voice was metallic. 'He had escaped from France.'

Sorrow for the bearded little man, sorrow even for Maxl, hatred for the gray man and for what he stood, emerged from her. She said, 'None of us wish to die. No one wishes to die. But there are those who have been bred to kill, who—' She broke off. 'I'm sorry. I too escaped from France.'

Popin touched his beard. He didn't speak. He looked old. He pushed back from the table. 'I must not miss the return ride that waits for me.'

'I was about to suggest a liqueur.' Blaike was bland.

The head shook. 'If I miss the ride, it is a long walk to Tesuque. There are not many rides these days.'

'What about seeing your work? Soon.'

'Yes. My work. Soon.' He was being put together again. The three moved from the table, crossed to the portal. 'Tomorrow night? That is soon enough? You dine with me?'

'Good enough. How do I get there?'

'You catch the Tesuque bus outside the hotel. Someone will show you where. Jacques will meet you at the filling station, bring you to my house. And you, Miss Julie? You too wish to come see my work tomorrow?'

'Yes.'

'For dinner then. I will expect you.'

She could phone Popin in the morning, make wiser arrangements. The less said before the gray man the better. They spoke good night in the lobby, watched the stooped brown figure vanish down the steps to the side entrance. She held out her hand to Blaike. 'Thank you for dinner, and good night.'

He held her withdrawing fingers. 'You've no ride to catch. A liqueur?'

'No thank you. I'm tired.' Her hand was free.

'As a matter of fact, so am I. The westward journey wasn't exactly luxury travel.' He walked beside her as if without deliberate thought. She crossed to the news stand. The bread-and-butter local sheet. The New York papers. Sunday's editions on Tuesday.

Blaike said, 'You're quite a reader, aren't you?'

She didn't answer that. He was beside her in the portal. It seemed casual. At the elevator she would extend her hand, speak definite good night.

He gestured to the papers. 'Typical New Yorker. Were you there long?'

'Not very.' She had no information to offer him. 'But I don't find much world-news coverage in the local products. And, of course, the Sunday papers are more than just newspapers; they're a well-stocked library.'

'Rather.'

The pretty, dark-haired girl, Spanish blouse, wide peasant skirt, opened the elevator door. Julie's hand was ready. Blaike said, 'I'm on third. You?'

She didn't appear disturbed. 'Third, too.'

They rode up in silence, in silence left the elevator. Julie half turned to the Spanish girl, wanting to clutch the red skirt, to cling. The elevator door closed in her face.

She turned left. He walked beside her. Her hands knotted over the papers.

Halfway down the corridor he said, 'I stop off here. I can't tempt you with a nightcap?'

'Not tonight, thank you.' She was alert, waiting a move.

But his key turned in the lock of 346. He opened his door. 'Good night then. See you tomorrow.' He went inside, his smile closed the door.

That was the end of today. She was actually weakened from relief as she proceeded down the corridor across to the right, 351. Her key was in her handbag, she hadn't turned it in to the desk earlier. She fumbled for it, her elbow holding the heavy Sunday papers awkwardly.

'Julie!'

It was a whisper. She started, then tautness held her. She felt someone moving in behind. She stepped away from the door as she swerved. It was Jacques, his face hunted.

'Julie, quick. Open the door.'

Her fingers had found the key. She passed it to him. He went inside swiftly. She followed, flicking the switch just inside. He closed the door with a thud. Even in room light his face was green as it had been in the dim corridor. He pointed across the room. 'Pull the curtains, Julie. Close the windows.'

She didn't question. She knew livid fear; she had experienced it herself. She dropped the papers on the bed as she crossed. She fastened the windows leading to the small balcony, automatically her eyes looked down into the street. It was empty. She pulled the draperies across the panes. She turned then. 'No one in sight. What is it, Jacques?'

He wiped the back of his hand across his forehead. He looked young and rugged but he wasn't. Someone must have broken him before he reached refuge.

She urged, 'Sit down.' His knees were wavering.

He spoke mechanically in his own tongue. 'I do not believe I was observed coming here. I do not believe I was followed. I went most carefully.' He seemed to see her now. 'Julie.' His muted voice was sharp. 'You must go. Go quickly. You must not remain here. You are in danger. Terrible danger, Julie.' His eyes were impassioned.

'I know.' She sat down on the edge of the bed, flung off her hat. 'I know,' she repeated. She didn't know how he knew. He must have recognized the gray man.

'Why then did you come here?'

She hesitated. 'I had to come here.' She said steadily, 'It is important that I find the Blackbirder.'

He seemed to shrivel before her. His head turned, hunted over his shoulder. He edged the chair in order that his back was not to the door.

'You've heard of the Blackbirder? Certainly you have. All refugees have. Even in the East.' She chose words carefully. 'I do not want to involve you, Jacques. It is better you do not know why I am running away. Only that I must.'

He swallowed with difficulty. 'That only is why you came? To find the Blackbirder and to go away?'

He knew the Blackbirder. It was in his inflection. She said, 'If he will take me across the border into Mexico—I have the money to pay—that is all I want, Jacques.' She lowered her voice eagerly. 'It can be arranged?'

'I do not know. Why do you think I know?' His words trembled and he wet his lips. 'What makes you think I might know?'

'Don't you know, Jacques?' She laughed a little. She felt so certain, so free from fear in the face of his. 'How long have you been here in Santa Fe that you do not know? His headquarters are here. I learned that in New York. He does not ask questions. If I have the fare I can leave without questioning. You must have heard of him, if you have been here—'

'Almost two years now,' he said dully.

'Then certainly you know. You have heard of him.' Her glance was oblique. 'Perhaps you can tell me how I can be put in touch with him?'

He didn't look at her.

'His name?'

He said doggedly, 'That is why you came. Only for that? You do not intend to stay here? You wish only to go away quickly? That is all?'

'That is all. Don't you see, Jacques, I must go quickly? You said it yourself. I'm not safe here. There is one small thing I must attend to. That I will do tomorrow. Then as soon as I find the Blackbirder, I must go.'

His voice scratched. 'What is this one small thing?'

'It's Fran.'

'Fran?' Terror shrouded him again.

'He's in prison, Jacques,' she said quickly. 'An internment prison for dangerous aliens. The Gestapo put him there. Some who were disguised, above suspicion. They—they framed him. That's the American word, you understand it? Somehow they did it. False accusations, false information.' Her voice beat against the gray masque Jacques had laid across his face. 'I can't leave him there to suffer. I don't care how decently he's treated, it's indecent to be locked up. Like an animal. Caged. Helpless. I know.' Her voice whispered the horror. 'I was locked up once in Paris.'

She steeled the words. 'Did you know that? I was locked

68

up. Paul did it. So I couldn't get away.' She wasn't looking at him, not speaking to him now. 'I was always afraid of Paul. I didn't know it but I was. There was something cruel in him, the way a beast would be cruel, not for any reason, just because he is. He came to my room in the night. It was the night of Monday, June tenth. Do you remember that night, Jacques? The night Italy marched. Where were you? Somewhere on the front fighting. No, not fighting. The generals wouldn't let you fight, would they? They made you lay down your weapons. The Maginot Line had been broken. We knew it was the end. I told them at dinner, Uncle Paul and Aunt Lily, that I was going to leave Paris before it was too late. I wasn't going to stay to be bestialized by the Nazis. If Paul and Lily wouldn't go with me, I'd leave alone.'

After trying to erase it for three years, the memory was still brutally livid. 'Paul came to me in the night. I didn't know what he was going to do. I was afraid to go with him. But if I hadn't he would have laid hands on me. I was more afraid of his hands. I went—up—up—he was behind me on the stairs. I don't know where Aunt Lily was. I don't know if she knew.' She pushed the damp hair away from her forehead. 'In the very top attic there was a slant room with a tiny dormer window. I'd never been in it. You could just see the Boulevard far below. He told me the Nazis would march there on Thursday afternoon.' Her eyes closed. 'He knew the day. The very hour.'

Jacques' face was empty.

'He locked me in there.' She pressed back the nausea. 'He came at night and brought food. Once I tried to break past him. He struck me.' She let out her breath slowly. 'The third day—I heard the planes first, then the machines, and then—the feet of marching men, thousands of them, little gray things far below—like ants.' She steadied her voice. 'I thought Paul had left me there. For the ants.'

She had to touch the bedstead now, to know the reality of solid form. She had to wait before she could continue.

'That night Tanya came for me. The house was full of Nazi officers. They were having a Victory dinner.' Her voice was dust. 'Paul and Aunt Lily were with them, drinking toasts, laughing. I saw them. Tanya got me out of that house, through the streets, into an underground. She started me on my way to freedom. She wouldn't come with me. She said her work was there.'

He spoke now. His voice was empty. 'Tanya is dead.'

It was a moment before the import of it smote her. 'Dead?' He said it again. 'She is dead.'

'They killed her.' She spoke with tight throat. 'Didn't they? They killed her because of me. That was it, Jacques?'

'She helped many.'

'It was because of me. Wasn't it?' Her voice sharpened to pierce through his lethargy. *'Wasn't it?'*

He saw her again. His eyes turned on her. 'Yes. The Duc was angry. Because you escaped. Because you took the money, and the necklace, the de Guille diamonds.'

'She—' She couldn't speak Tanya's name, not without her voice trembling. 'She took the money for me. Paul was wise. He had filled his house with francs while the banks were operating. We didn't take much. It was all mine.' Her voice rose. 'My money supported all the Guilles for years, since I was a child. That's why Paul had himself declared my legal guardian, so he could have my income without report, for his own purposes.' Even the diamonds were hers. She had bought them over and again. They hadn't been

70

out of pawn for fifty years before the Guilles found her. She hadn't taken them for that reason. It had been in order that the pride, the ancestral treasure, of the Guilles, wouldn't fall into the desecrating hands of the Nazis. Frozen with fear, trembling through the darkened upper stories of the house, she had halted Tanya while she slipped into Aunt Lily's room, filched the necklace from the familiar blue velvet box. Paul had brought it home from the vaults the day war was declared. Stealing? Not then. She who was escaping would act as their custodian. That was before, peering through the banisters, she saw that scene she could never forget. Emeralds in the gilt of Aunt Lily's hair, the gold green of her Patou model. Paul's waxen toupee, waxen mustache, above his white tie. Nazis in dress uniform and grating medals. The acrid scent of champagne. The shame of laughter.

She turned on Jacques fiercely, as if he had spoken. 'Certainly they supported me. They kept me. I was their kept child. I thought I had everything. I had. Everything but freedom. I could say and do and go any place and anything I wanted as long as it was what they wanted. I didn't know it then. They kept me stupid, ignorant, so that I wouldn't know. I've learned in three years.' She halted her words. This personal problem couldn't interest him, more important things had laid their weight. She demanded, 'Paul gave Tanya over to them?'

'I didn't know,' Jacques said. 'I came back to Paris. I went to the Duc again. For work. I didn't know he was searching for Tanya.' His voice was iron. 'I killed her. I led them to her.' He didn't ask sympathy; he told Julie, 'I killed her.'

'No.'

'They put her in a concentration camp. They tried to

find out where you were. She didn't know. They didn't kill her right away. They didn't kill her until—until she was dying.'

She whimpered, 'Jacques. How do you know these things?'

His mouth was vicious. 'The Duc told me. When he was trying to convince me I should do a task for him.'

'That is why you are here. To find me.'

He said simply, 'You were Tanya's friend. I would not hurt a hair of your head, Julie. You were kind to her.'

'I?'

'Don't you remember? You protected her from the Duc's anger?'

She hadn't remembered. It wasn't kindness; it was what anyone would have done. When Tanya first came to work for the Guilles. Julie had stepped between Paul's cane and the girl. Julie hadn't been more than fourteen years at the time. She hadn't thought of it in years. The cane had left a red wedge on her face for days. Her fear of him must have come after that scene; there was none in her when she threatened she would leave his house forever, go to the trustees in America, if he dared touch Tanya again. Julie had won. He wasn't going to let her money escape him. But he had held hatred since that day for a child's defiance of him. There had been residue of that hate when he gave Tanya to torture. She said now, 'It was I who killed Tanya.' And she knew with certainty one thing; she herself would see that he answered for Tanya's death.

Jacques shook his head. 'She helped many to escape. She knew the risk. That was her work, what she remained in France to do. They called her a Communist. They said that was why she was arrested. She wasn't. She'd never even been to a Popular Front meeting. She was a Frenchwoman.'

72

Jacques and Tanya had been married just before he went away to war. They hadn't known the war would be so short. They hadn't dreamed he would be the one left to mourn.

Julie was deliberately matter-of-fact. 'Paul sent you to find me.'

'No. He sent me to help Fran.'

'He knew that Fran was in prison?' But of course he would. Fran would write his father for help. Fran didn't know that Paul's allegiance was to the Axis. Fran should have known as she should have known. The Croix de Feu meetings in the Guille ballroom. Later the Francistes. The dark oily little man with blubber lips. But his name hadn't been synonymous with traitor then. And she and Fran were young.

No, Paul wouldn't allow Fran, the beloved son, to waste in prison. Even the Nazis wouldn't be as important as his son. Paul was sly. He would attempt to play this hand along with the other hand.

'Have you found him? Do you know where he is, Jacques?' She wouldn't let Paul help Fran; she would do this alone. Paul mustn't put his smear on Fran. He was tarred with Fascistic France. 'We will arrange his escape. Guards always can be bribed. I have the diamonds—'

'Julie.' He interrupted, half out of his chair. 'What is that?'

She lifted her head. She had heard nothing. He gestured to the door, slipped behind the chair, against the wall. There was a rap. He gestured again. She saw that in his hand was a gun.

She walked steadily but slowly toward the door. There must be no trouble here, nothing to call attention to her. Whoever was there must be handled without violence. She

73

opened the door a little, closing her hand tightly over the knob. She hadn't force to hold it against the gray man.

He pushed into the room. 'I wondered if you were through reading your *Trib*—' He broke off, raised his eyebrows. 'I'm sorry. I didn't know you had company. Particularly a gunman.'

'Put it away, Jacques. It disturbs Mr Blaike.' Her lips curved without smiling. 'You remember Mr Blaike, of course.' She looked up at him. 'Jacques was showing me how to handle a revolver in case—in case the need for such information should arise. One never knows.'

Jacques thrust the gun into his hip pocket but he didn't remove his eyes from the gray man. Not while he was saying to Julie, in English now, 'I will go. Tomorrow I will see you. Yes, tomorrow. Tomorrow we will conclude this conversation. Tomorrow.' He didn't walk to the door. He edged, never once moving the black of his pupils from the intruder. There was moisture on his temples. It shone under the light. The door closed on him.

The gray man's eyebrows quizzed her. 'Your friend doesn't like me.'

She said slowly, 'Why did you come here?'

'Isn't it a bit dangerous to entertain a man with a gun at this hour in a strange hotel?'

'I have known Jacques for years. He wouldn't harm me. He was a retainer of my uncle's in Paris.'

'Do servants usually address the young lady of the house by her first name?'

'I was a little girl when I first knew Jacques. I hated being Missed. It was stuffy. Un-American.'

'You are an American?'

'Surely your good friend, Fran, told you that?' She turned

her back on him, walked to the windows, pushed aside the curtains, and opened them wide. The street below was a black, flickering side way, deserted.

'I wasn't interested in your nationality.' Blaike made it provocative.

She ignored that, taking a cigarette from the table. 'My father and mother were both American. They died when I was young. Lily Guille, my mother's sister, raised me.'

He seemed dubious. Mention of her father, Prentiss Marlebone, would dissipate that. She must forget the name Marlebone. She lit the cigarette, blew out the match. 'May I say good night now? I have not read the news, as you can see. Tomorrow I shall be happy to lend you the *Herald Tribune.* Meanwhile you have satisfied your curiosity about my visitor.'

Blaike didn't move. He didn't wipe the amusement from his face. 'You win,' he announced. 'You won't have it according to Queensberry rules. You want it straight. Very well. I didn't come to borrow the paper. I didn't even come to see who was your visitor. I thought he would have departed long ago. Oh yes, I knew you had one, although the light was too poor and my door open too slightly to get a good look. I came here to ask you an important question. Who steered you on to Popin?'

'I beg your pardon?'

She took the cigarette away from her lips. 'I could say that that is not any of your affair. It isn't, you know. However'—she took her time—'I see no reason why your curiosity shouldn't be satisfied. I heard of Popin through a friend of mine many months ago. In a letter. Popin was also a friend of this person's. When I came to Santa Fe, knowing no one, I decided to look him up. I didn't realize he was supposed to be a secret.' If you mixed truth with lies and added a touch of arrogance, the lies would hold.

He was digesting it. She thought that he was satisfied. But his gray eyes were sharp when he asked, 'And why did you come to Santa Fe?'

She had that ready. 'I was tired of New York. Cold. Damp. I wanted some sunshine.' She lifted the cigarette. 'That also is none of your business, Mr Blaike.'

'It takes money to traipse around the country.'

She was quick with anger. 'Just what right have you to question me?'

'The right of self-protection.' He took a stride into the room. She made a backward move closer to the windows. 'I came here to see Popin on business. I'm not having any queering of that game'

She didn't understand. If he were a Gestapo agent meaning harm to Fran, he wouldn't warn her, not and leave her to report to the authorities. What more could he do here? They were both strangers; they had been seen together at dinner. Jacques could tell of Blaike's presence in this room. She tried to make her laughter a reassurance. 'I merely wanted to make a friend. Truly it's not business with me. I don't want to buy any of Popin's paintings. I'm not in the least intrigued with modem art.'

He said brusquely, 'Nor am I.' His face held suspicion. 'You don't know Popin's real stock in trade?'

'You mean he isn't a painter?'

'He is a painter. He is also a station master. I suppose you've never heard of the Blackbirder.'

She sublimated her triumph. If Popin was the Blackbirder, it would be so simple. The Blackbirder and Fran's friend in one. Too simple. Her original suspicions of the gray man flooded back upon her. She knew he wasn't an Englishman; she had known that all evening. She had had too many British friends. The accent and intonation were true enough. Those qualities were easily acquired by anyone with an ear. Roderick Blaike's idiom was American. He could be a German-American, loyal to Hitler. He could be a member of the F.B.I. The bureau which had unjustly interned Fran would be suspicious of any Guille. Even if it didn't know that Julie Guille was Juliet Marlebone who had been with Maximilian Adlebrecht five minutes before he was shot down. Worse, this man had known Maxl.

She flaunted her lies. 'Blackbirder? Who or what is a blackbirder? And why should I know about it?'

He believed her anger, her ignorance. He held a vestige of suspicion but he believed. He was easier now. 'You don't know your country very well, do you? The blackbirders flourished in certain dark pages of history. They smuggled men out of one country and into another. Strictly speaking they were slavers. They shipped blacks out of Africa and into America. Not a very savory business.'

'You mean to tell me that sort of thing goes on again today?'

He said, 'No, my dear. The modem Blackbirder doesn't deal in slaves. He deals in refugees. Men without a country and in need of one, or the quite accurate facsimiles thereof. Now do you understand?'

She put out the cigarette. 'I'm afraid I don't. And I don't see what you have to do with it.'

'Don't you? It's the one way of getting into Mexico without fanfare. I've always wanted to see Mexico.'

She shrugged. 'It seems the hard way to go about it. And really I'm not interested in your travels.'

His smile widened his face. 'And as you told me hours ago, you're tired. You doubtless are by now.' He turned to the door. 'You still intend to go to Popin's for dinner tomorrow night?'

It could have been a warning. She ignored it. Her eyes were placid. 'Certainly I do. If it makes any difference to you, I promise I won't interfere with your business discussion. I shall study the paintings while you are in conference.' She let one small arrow fly. 'And I don't listen outside of doors.' She didn't know if it struck target. She didn't know if he had heard her conversation with Jacques. They had spoken in French. Doubtless French was one of Blaike's linguistic accomplishments, along with English and American. Whether he was Gestapo or F.B.I., he wouldn't be put on the Guille trail unless he was versed in that language.

He said, 'Good night.' After he had closed the door, she moved from the windows. The papers she had hungered these hours to open were disappointing. The story had moved far inside. The police were still waiting for the cab driver to appear. There was no mention of the Yorkville rathskeller or of a girl who had been there with Maxl only four nights ago.

4

Julie woke with a tremor. She'd been riding the subway again, on and on, faster and ever faster. For a moment her eyes were bewildered. This quiet Spanish room. Sun breaking through the bright draperies at the window. Then she knew. La Fonda in Santa Fe. But she alone hadn't sought this out-of-the-way mountain town. There was a man in gray, who called himself Roderick Blaike and who said he had come to find the Blackbirder.

She sat up in bed. She must see Jacques. Alone. He hadn't said it but she knew it must be alone. He was afraid of someone; he hadn't given that someone a name. But the death fear had been on him when he saw the gray man last night. He knew for what the gray man stood. She must learn that. She mustn't fight longer in the dark. For whatever the gray man stood for, he was inimical to her. If he were Nazi, if she were to be taken like Tanya—Julie clutched the bed linen. Deliberately and at once she forced her fingers to open. Terror was a luxury. She couldn't afford it now. If Blaike were Gestapo—she had outwitted them before. He was waiting for something before he moved. She would be ready for him when he did move.

If he represented the American government, there was more immediate danger. He could be making inquiries about her even now. He could have discovered there was no record of Julie Guille's entry into the United States. If she were detained for passport questioning, Maxl's murder would come into it. She would be locked up again. In New York, it had been the other way around. Question about the murder, knowledge of illegal entry. Whichever way it went, circumstantially she stood against the right. Either way she'd be imprisoned. She mustn't be. She mustn't ever endure that again. She must escape into Mexico, escape before this man closed the way of escape, before he apprehended the Blackbirder. It didn't matter how much good the Blackbirder was doing for the poor and hunted, he was illegal.

First Jacques. She didn't know where to reach him. Popin would know. Perhaps she should wait for Jacques to communicate with her. Surely he would. If he could. She was tired of coming up always against the stones of if, maybe, perhaps. She would call now. Her watch said after ten o'clock. She gave the Tesuque number.

She recognized the same lazy voice. 'Mr Popin, she ees not here now.'

Julie asked, 'Do you know where I could reach Jacques Michet?'

The voice repeated the formula. 'Jacques, she ees not here now too.'

Julie left no message. Evidently Jacques lived with Popin. She would see him this evening if he did not get in touch with her before then. She arose, showered, dressed: the tailored blouse today. She combed out her short curly hair, put on lipstick. She must buy another outfit. Maybe a sweater and skirt like the soldier's girl in the Cantina last night. It would be nice to look young and happy, an outward manifestation of the hope that some day again you could be that. Facing herself in the mirror, Julie also faced fact. She would never again be what that girl was, what Julie Guille once had been. Three years ago. It could as well have been three hundred years. She had been aged in sorrow and pity and despair. You couldn't rebuild to careless happiness over the murdered bodies of your friends.

She turned away from remembrance. She was hungry. Hunger was one essential which could never be beaten. She put on her hat, took gloves, bag, her room key in her purse. She wouldn't need her coat if she decided to walk out. Yesterday's cloud web had been a false alarm. Sunshine beat down from the dark blue sky.

She passed the door of 346 quickly. It did not open. She didn't want conversation with the gray man, not until she learned more about him. She mustn't jeopardize Fran's chances. She might inadvertently give something away. Blaike wasn't in the lobby. No familiar face there, no curious one. There was no coffee shop; the dining rooms were closed at this hour. She bought the Monday papers, left the hotel. She crossed the street, continued on down to a restaurant. It wasn't prepossessing but there was coffee, toast, and fruit. She didn't open the papers. Delay the news whether bad or yet inconclusive. When she finished eating she crossed into the barren Plaza. The same somber scarecrow men sat on the same stone benches, spoke the same Spanish heedless of the mountains pressing down upon the little village. Julie walked to the opposite side, to an unoccupied bench facing the old Palace, a long adobe building, comfortable with age. Under its open portal was a group of Indian women in shapeless calico Mother Hubbards and blanket shawls. A few beads of corn and some black pottery were in front of them.

Julie opened the *Times,* began her systematic search. The

story had moved farther inside. But it had come at last, the hunt for a girl. The police had been informed that Maximilian Adlebrecht had been seen with a dark-haired young woman in a Yorkville rathskeller shortly before the killing. No clues to her identity. The *Herald Tribune* offered little more. It did mention the brown coat she had worn that night.

She folded the papers slowly. The name would come later. The police would find out that Juliet Marlebone had disappeared from her West 78th Street apartment on that same night. If Mr Tolfre would only believe that postal card from Chicago. He wouldn't. Not on West 78th Street where a murdered man had lain. Even if he did, that janitor with the unpronounceable name, released from questioning, would understand from the card. She laid the papers neatly on the bench. The police might have her name already. This news was three days old. Before she could know if they had learned of her identity they could be here, arresting her. She had no guilt of the crime. But she had run away.

The sun wasn't as hot as it had seemed earlier. Cumulus clouds were again beginning to drift across the turquoise sky. She shivered there in the small emptyish plaza, open to all attack. The gray man wasn't the only enemy to outwit; the New York police would close in soon.

She must move quickly. See Jacques. Not wait for tonight. Get the information he must have been about to impart when Blaike interrupted. See Popin alone, ask him to arrange quickly her escape from this country. She dare not wait for Fran now; she must ask Popin to take care of that for her. She must get out before it was too late. Even now, every train into New Mexico, every bus into Santa Fe, carried presumptive danger.

Her jacket was too thin. The wind was blowing a few

torn brown leaves across the flagstones. The sound of them was of someone running in fright. She was chilled through. She rose, walked swiftly down the path to the memorial shaft, rounded it. There was something more sinister today in the mountains walling this town. They were great beasts lying there behind the Cathedral waiting, their paws quiet, but waiting to pounce, and pouncing, crush. She didn't like the feel of the village. She must get away before it was smitten by its crushing destiny, before she was crushed with it. The wind was following her as she crossed one lane to the Botica, crossed another to the hotel corner, past the two black-banged Indians, turquoise-decked, blanket-wrapped, who squatted by the walls.

She slowed her steps in front of the hotel. It was ridiculous to flee from your own thoughts. Keep them steady, objective. She couldn't be traced to Santa Fe. That was an impossibility. Unless someone from this town sent word to New York that she was here. Someone who knew her true name was Juliet Marlebone. There was only Jacques, possibly Popin had learned from Fran; both were her friends. Blaike couldn't be connected with the Manhattan police; had that been true he would have arrested her at Grand Central. He was perhaps F.B.I. but he wasn't the police. He didn't know the New York police were looking for her; he wouldn't until he read it in the papers; therefore, she would know as quickly as he. She mustn't appear frightened. She must be Julie Guille. She would get her coat and stroll the town. There might be more shops on the two side arms away from the Plaza.

She went up the walk and into the hotel lobby. She hoped Blaike wouldn't be lying in wait for her; she wasn't up to an encounter at this moment. Her eyes rounded the room quickly. They froze with her faltering steps.

There was someone on the deep leathern couch in the shadows across the room. A beefy man in a dark, ill-fitting suit, a bowler covering his head. She knew those hands folded against the tight waistcoat. She saw the square red ears. She knew the black eyebrows. She knew the eyes that were turned on her.

They weren't watching her. No. The man was waiting for someone. He hadn't noticed her. She moved, easily, carefully toward the right portal and the elevator. She said, 'Three,' mechanically to the Spanish girl. On the floor, she walked the corridor softly. She went on unconscious tiptoe past Blaike's room. When she was safe behind her own locked door, she realized how she was quivering.

She stumbled to the bed, sank down on it. Why was the waiter here? How had he learned her whereabouts? How didn't matter. He was here. He couldn't have recognized her in the poor light of the lobby. There was the chance that he wouldn't recognize her even if he did see her.

He would. Change of hairdress and attire wouldn't distract him. He hadn't watched unessentials, only her face.

Before he knew she was here, she must get away. That meant going again into the lobby. Even if she slipped out, paying her bill by mail, her money was in the safe at the desk. She couldn't travel far on what was in her purse. She could go to Jacques and Popin. She could, if it were necessary, tell them what had happened in New York, involve them. She put her hand on the phone and then removed it. She couldn't inform Jacques over the phone, not with anyone able to listen in. Nor could she go to Tesuque now. Not when the path lay through the lobby.

She must wait until evening. The dubious escort of Blaike would see her through the hotel to the bus. The waiter wouldn't make a move if she were with a stranger. He would bide his time. By evening she could be safe in Popin's house. She would stay there until arrangements for her departure could be arranged. She wouldn't return to the hotel. Her money, the necklace. She would have to return for them. Jacques could bodyguard her when she did, at the last moment, just before the Blackbirder was ready to fly.

Her door was locked. It was foolish but she put a chair under the round of the knob. She would barricade herself here until evening. She wasn't hungry. She could wait until dinner to eat again. If she couldn't there was still the chocolate box she had bought in New York, barely touched. She wouldn't open the door to anyone until time to leave for the bus. She made herself comfortable in pajamas. The suit would have to serve again tonight. She hung it carefully, stretched herself with the book on her bed.

She didn't know she had slept until the ringing of the phone awakened her. She fumbled for it, was surprised to hear Blaike's so British voice. 'You weren't sleeping? I'm sorry. I was afraid you were out. You're still going to Popin's?'

'Yes.' She wasn't short with him now. She wanted his help. She must have it. 'What time is it—wait—' Her watch read four. 'What about the bus?'

'Leaves at five. If you'll hurry like a good child we'll have a drink before we start out.'

She agreed. She was sweet femininity. 'I'll throw myself together, Blaike. Come over for me in about half an hour?'

If her friendliness was unusual he didn't mention it. 'Right.'

She was still gay. 'Three knocks will admit you.'

He couldn't know it was deliberate. Not unless he knew the waiter, knew the man was here in Santa Fe. The waiter. Maxl. Blaike. She put her hand to her throat.

The window was leaden. The sound of wind flung light handfuls of white against the pane. This had happened while she slept. Spring had fled, winter returned. It was an ill omen. She scoffed at her superstition. Once she reached Popin's she would be protected from attack. She must chance Blaike's company until then.

She wore the blue sweater. This cold might continue. She tucked her toothbrush and powder deep into her purse. Her hairbrush was too bulky, the comb must suffice. She was ready when the three knocks sounded. She flung the door wide.

He touched his knuckles. 'Why the code?'

'You frightened me with your talk of strange men with guns.' Her hand lay on the phone. 'Are you certain of that bus time? I thought it was five-thirty.' As she spoke she lifted it from the cradle. 'There's no reason to wait in a stuffy bus station.'

He grimaced. 'There's no bus station. We wait on a blizzardy street corner.'

She spoke to the switchboard. 'Is the Tesuque bus five or five-thirty? Mr Blaike and I aren't in accord.'

The girl said, 'Five.'

Julie smiled apology at him. 'You were right.' But someone downstairs knew now that she and Blaike should be in the lobby soon. If anything happened to her before reaching it, there would be suspicion.

He consulted his watch. 'We still might manage a quick one. We'll need it. Before we brave the street corner.'

'Yes.' She had bag, gloves, coat. If she did not return, nothing was left here by which to trace her. A few clothes, a few articles of toilette, a suitcase and a weekend bag. Nothing that could not be replaced in Mexico.

She walked rapidly to the elevator. It was her finger which pushed against the summoning button. She kept words moving in the semi-gloom. 'It looks bad out, doesn't it? Unusual I presume.'

'Usual they tell me. March is a bad month here. They've been expecting it. Denver's just had one of the worst blizzards in years which generally means trouble in Santa Fe.'

They entered the elevator, empty save for the Spanish girl, were lowered to the main floor. Now came the test. If she could get out of the hotel without being seen by hostile eyes. She slowed her heels to his limp, turned her face up to his, chattered brightly, emptily, any girl to her evening's escort. Her eyes scuttled the lobby as they entered. The waiter wasn't in sight.

Blaike turned toward La Cantina. Her fingers touched his sleeve. 'Have we time? It's quarter to.'

He laughed. 'We don't want fifteen minutes on a street corner. We'd be living snowmen. We have only to walk to the end of the block.'

She couldn't run for the doorway, not without explanation. She pushed her toes forward. Her chat broke forth with renewed frenzy. The waiter wouldn't be expecting a light-headed girl with boy. She didn't seem to look at anyone when she entered the Cantina. She saw every face. His wasn't there.

She drank a sherry standing at the bar while Blaike swallowed Scotch. It was five minutes to five when they left the room. She didn't examine the lobby.

The wind caught her roughly as she stepped out on the sidewalk. The wind was addled with white. She anchored the Breton with the hand holding her purse, with the other buttoned her coat at the neck. Blaike took her arm. His voice was a shout. 'This is a debacle. Maybe we should turn back, phone Popin to make it tomorrow.'

The idea was appealing but turning back was impossible for her. With her mouth she laughed at it. 'I think it's a lark. You go back if you're nervous.' She wished that he would now that she was safely out of the hotel. He wouldn't.

'I'm never nervous,' he scorned. 'A flyer daren't be. I thought perhaps you were.'

Had he noticed the tension under her false gayety at the hotel? It didn't matter now. The small bus throbbed there across the street by the garage. She and Blaike waited for a truck and two slow cars to round the corner. The bus driver was hoisting himself into the interior as they plunged toward him.

'We made it.' Blaike exhaled. He helped her up the high step.

The driver was a pointed-nosed old fellow. He said cheerfully, 'Almost didn't.' He did something that made the engine more raucous. To Julie's purse he shouted, 'Better pay me at the end of the run. Got to get off. This isn't no day for fiddle faddle.'

Julie turned to the interior. Blaike was at her shoulder waiting for her to move. She didn't. She looked up the short aisle at a man with a black bowler potted on his round head. He was wedged into the exact center of the long back seat. He appeared hot and cramped yet stolidly unconscious of discomfort. His thick fingers were interlaced on his knees. The lusterless black eyes didn't move nor did they light. But he saw her. He couldn't help but see her.

It took her a moment to concede this setback. She spoke then, over her shoulder to Blaike, turning as she did. 'Let's sit here in front. The air's better.'

The bus was already buffeting the Plaza. She half thrust Blaike into the right-hand aisle seat. She herself dropped into the one on the left, behind the driver. At the window was a man who looked as if he might be on the five o'clock to White Plains. His brief case lay on his knees, his evening paper atop it. Blaike's seatmate was an Indian woman.

There was no opportunity for conversation above the chug of the motor. Julie was grateful for the temporary silence. By pushing with her toes against the floor board, she raised herself enough to glimpse the rear-view mirror. The waiter was there, a dark lump amid other dark lumps. The bus plodded slowly into the dervish storm, heading into open country now. There was nothing Julie could do at this moment. When she reached Tesuque, Jacques would be waiting. She could be safe at Popin's long before the waiter could find a conveyance to follow her. Tesuque wasn't even a small town, it was a hamlet. There wouldn't be cabs lined up waiting.

If the waiter did accost her before she could enter Jacques' car, the dubious protection of Blaike would again be her refuge. There had been no recognition of the gray man in the burly waiter's eye. Nor of her. He might have been a dead man there in the back of the bus but for the thin stream of perspiration on either side of his jowls.

She hadn't realized how short the ride would be. They left Santa Fe, traveled slowly along the empty road, through a cut, down a hill, rolled to a stop in front of a diminutive filling station. Nor had she realized how much less than a hamlet Tesuque would be. Two small filling stations, a few small adobe buildings huddled together in the snow. The storm had turned twilight into darkening dusk during the ride. The shadow of several cars waited by this filling station.

She sat tensed, ready to spring, while the driver pulled on his heavy brakes, muttered, 'T'sukee,' and spent interminable time with old leather folders, papers, and a small jangling sack. In the mirror she could see the passengers beginning to wedge into the aisle. The man was thrust behind them. She moved to block the way, to be certain she wouldn't be left in proximity with his bulk. She could feel how his thick fingers would clutch her arm. If the driver would stop his puttering, she and Blaike would be out of the bus and with Jacques in Popin's car before the man could make his way through the passengers.

She let her lips smile down at the gray man. His gray hat was tipped over one eye, his overcoat collar turned up against the menace of the storm outside. He raised one eyebrow. 'Why the rush? You can't get out of a closed door.'

She wrinkled her nose. 'Fresh air.'

The driver eventually released them, clambered wirily out. She was on his heels. Blaike wasn't behind her. The commuter was. He went on to one of the parked cars. The lights went on and it began a turn. That left three cars but no Jacques called a welcome. She almost started at Blaike's touch on her elbow. He muttered, 'Wonder where mine host is.' The snow was falling more steadily now. They stood there together, peering into the gloom, seeing no face, hearing no voice at all. The other passengers were filing out, one by one, turning to right and to left, following the lane ahead. A group of women went to another parked car. She shielded herself as best she could near Blaike's shoulder, she saw from slanted eyes the waiter emerge. He stood indecisively for a moment then made heavy tracks to the two remaining cars. One drove away as he approached. He seemed to be speaking to the driver of the other. But he didn't get in; he turned, entered the filling station.

It was like a way station to hell. The snow, the cold, the darkness. Mountain horizon pushing blackly down into the small hollow of the valley. Within the one haven of light and warmth, solidified danger was waiting. She put her arm through Blaike's, edged closer to him. 'You don't think he forgot, do you?' She remembered. 'Our fares!'

'I paid. Most likely Popin couldn't get through. We'll have to return to town.'

She wouldn't go into the filling station, she would climb back into the bus. The starter sounded on the lone car, it maneuvered, its headlights seemed bearing down on them. She clung suddenly to the man by her side. Was this death, hired death? The car halted beside them. She could only just distinguish the square, dark Indian face above the wheel. The driver opened the window a narrow wedge. 'You the ones? Go to Popin?'

Her hand clutched more tightly Blaike's arm. In reprieve. 'We are.' They spoke in unison. The driver should have known without asking. They'd stood forsaken long enough. She and Blaike climbed quickly into the back seat. There was an Indian rug on the floor. He took it, covered her knees and his own. The weight was good.

The driver nosed the car back to the highway, pointed it beyond Tesuque.

Blaike passed her a cigarette, took one himself, lighted them. He spoke to the driver, 'Shall I light one for you? Where's Popin?'

The Indian took one hand off the wheel, held it back for the cigarette. The car swerved in the snow and he righted it while he took the cigarette, put it between his lips. 'He send me. He do not like snow.'

'Who does?' Julie echoed faintly. Evidently neither did Jacques.

'Good for ranges,' the driver stated. He puffed on the cigarette. The car rattled and clanked and crawled along the snow-wet road. They had covered about three miles before the headlights of another car flashed into the mirror. Stolidly the Indian tipped it. She could not resist looking out behind. Her gloved fingers rubbed a circle clear on the back window. The car must be at least a half mile back. It could overtake this turtle driver with effortless ease. She turned to the front again. The following car couldn't if it obeyed wartime regulations. The speedometer here was holding thirty-five. No hired driver would risk losing a ration card, not for any amount of money. Money wasn't today's most formidable means of exchange. It couldn't restore lost privilege and power.

She was suddenly brutally conscious of the interchange between this driver and the waiter, back there at the intersection. There were no penalties for a staged breakdown, for losing the way. She bent toward the front seat. Her voice was careless. Even Blaike, leaning back against the worn upholstery, his hat pulled over his eyes, couldn't know her teeth were set. She began, 'We thought we'd been deserted. Particularly when that man went over to your car. What did he want?'

She had to wait for answer. The driver was turning now off the highway to a right-hand side road. The wheels slipped, quivered, righted again. This road was leading directly into a mountain. There was no sign of habitation. Her voice shrilled slightly, 'Is this the way to Popin's?'

'Maybe a mile now,' the Indian said.

She repeated with careless curiosity, holding her fear in tight check, 'What did that man want?'

'He ask am I a taxi.' There was a grunt of disgust. 'I am not a taxi.'

She sat back, looked again out the rear window. No headlights showed. The road was winding upward toward the mountainous mass. Blaike hadn't said a word. She glanced at him. He seemed to be asleep. If unruffled breathing were indication, he was asleep. Her eyebrows drew together. Why? What had he found in that definitely nine o'clock town to so tire him that he could sleep peacefully now in the midst of storm, uncharted roads, a strange driver? For a moment she believed his story, invalided from the R.A.F. But he was too American. Yet—there had been, were Americans, in the Royal Air Force. He hadn't stated he was English. There were American dialects which were scarcely discernible from British. He did not stir under her scrutiny. She took another peer backward. No car was following. Their own, piloted by the silent young Indian, moved on and on into the night and the storm. Again she felt that frightening isolation from all of remembered reality. Actually where was she? Where was she going? The relief was painful when she could see the dark blur at which the car was slowing, in the headlights, the outline of a low-lying adobe house. Her hand flew out to her companion. She must have touched the bad knee for Blaike started and his hand went automatically to protect it before he pushed the hat back from his sleep-blinded eyes.

She said, 'I think we're here.'

The car had stopped. No light showed from the small house. Unaccountably she edged back into the corner of the car. She was reluctant to step out into the cold darkness, to invade this unwelcoming place.

The Indian said, 'This Popin's house.' From him it was impatience.

'I hope he's at home.' Her laughter was shaky.

Blaike put away the robe. 'If he isn't, he's having visitors just the same. Even if I have to break a window. I'm hungry enough to eat a tin can.' He opened the door, helped her out.

The few paces to the dark walls were through deepening snow. She jerked back as the door opened before either she or Blaike could touch it. And then a second wave of relief in the short space of time overwhelmed her. For there was warmth and golden light to be seen beyond the door. Popin's gentle eyes and voice offered welcome to them.

2

Popin shut out the cold, the blackness. He shook his head. 'I did not know you would come in this storm. It is a bad one. I should have called you but my telephone has been out since early.' He held out his hands for her coat and hat. 'The snow came more soon here.' He hung her wraps in the hall closet, took Blaike's as well, then led down one step into the living-room. It was a good room, small enough for friendliness, comfortable with brown leather, warm with dark red and brown of Navajo weaving, with blue of Chimayo. A sweet piñon log fire burned bright in the Indian fireplace. On the mantel were two five-branched candelabra of black Indian pottery holding shimmering waxen candlelight.

'I did not know you would get through. The radio says the roads are being closed.' He passed a cup of warm spiced wine to Julie. 'Do not be distressed. I can give you lodging this night if this is true. There is the guest room above. You, sir, I should be happy for you to use my humble room.'

'And you sleep in the barn?' Blaike took his goblet, tasted. 'Good this.'

Popin twinkled. 'I sleep in the studio. On the couch, yes. A most comfortable couch. A studio couch.' He laughed once. 'I have slept there before. We westerners are hospitable.' He tinkled and twinkled, sliding his hands into the pockets of his worn brown corduroy jacket.

Julie was relaxed. That easily it had been arranged. She would not find it necessary to ask refuge here. It had been offered. Even Blaike's statement didn't disturb her. 'Good of you, Mr Popin, if we can't make it back to the bus.' He had slept; he didn't know how bad the roads were, the progress of the storm. She had faith in worsening snow. Her eyes lifted as the young Indian driver, in overalls and moccasins, entered through the far door. He said without expression, 'I put the car in, Popin. Too much snow. Reyes says come to dinner.'

'Thank you, Quincy.' The Indian went out. Popin said, 'Finish the cups before we dine. I trust Quincy—it is actually Qi'in Tse—I say it better like Quincy in the Massachusetts—I trust he brought you in comparative safety. I sent for you against his judgment. He said no one would come in this storm. No one wise.' He took Julie's goblet. Blaike set his on the table. Popin led the way to the arch at the far end of the right wall. Two steps up into the dining-room. Another Indian fireplace, another candlelit room. 'Nonetheless, I plan the dinner. If you do not come, tomorrow there is hash.' He sat at the head of the table. 'But happily you come.' He raised his voice. 'Reyes, bring the feast.'

The woman's face was an Aztec carven mask, not young, not old, not unpleasant, but unsmiling. She wore a print housedress, dull black oxfords. Only her face was Indian and the quietness of her hands.

'Chicken from my own chicken yard,' Popin boasted. 'Carrots, garlic, onions, herbs, squash—all from my own small garden plot. I do not art all of the time. When war makes want, it is well to eat one's own soil, yes?'

He too was a refugee. He had known want, hunger, fear. That was why he helped the helpless. If Blaike were not present she could speak now of Fran. But she didn't know Blaike's true purpose yet.

Popin brushed the shadow aside. 'After dinner I take you to my studio, through that door behind Julie. You will see my paintings for which you inquire.'

Incredible but only then she remembered Jacques. 'Where is Jacques? He was to meet us, you said.'

Popin raised soft eyebrows. 'Where is Jacques? Absorbed in his work doubtless. An earnest young man. Often he forgets the dinner bell.' He smiled at her. 'He does not starve. Reyes remembers him.'

'He does live with you.'

'He does and he does not. There is a guest house there. Always on the rancheritos there are small guest houses, here, there, everywhere.' His gesture over his shoulder was in a vague direction toward the kitchen. 'Jacques occupies my guest house.'

'What is his work?' Blaike was too carefully casual.

Popin shook his head. 'I do not understand much. He is mechanical. I artistic. Here the minds do not meet. I cannot be mechanical.' Popin had been deliberately indefinite. Mistrust of Blaike.

Julie forestalled further questioning. 'Jacques was always that way. Fran—my cousin, Fran Guille'— she explained

96

carefully to Popin—'often said that Jacques was better than half a dozen trained mechanics. He always serviced Fran's plane before the war.'

Blaike asked lazily, 'Didn't he ever want to fly himself?'

'He could. Fran taught him.' She wasn't certain after she had spoken. The Blackbirder could be Jacques. He held a pilot's license. She filibustered into Fran's air accomplishments. She held the conversation as long as it was possible.

Blaike had waited for her pause. 'Why wasn't Fran in the French Air Corps?'

She said slowly, 'France wanted peace. There was no Air Corps to speak of before the war.'

'Or even then,' Popin said softly.

She agreed. 'Fran was in the United States on business when war broke. It was impossible for him to return. Events moved too quickly to the fall.'

'Perhaps he is now fighting with the Free French,' Blaike suggested.

'Perhaps,' she said. It was where he would be if he were not imprisoned. Grounded. 'I do not know where he is.'

Popin changed the subject eagerly. 'This is Mexican chocolate. Perhaps it will please you as it does me. You will notice a strong cinnamon flavor. It makes a good pudding as well, I find. Tonight however I give you baba au rhum. In honor of a new friendship.' Again his face shaded. 'Although the new is out of one broken forever. I have thought much of that poor young man, Maxl. It is true. He is dead. I have heard this from friends in New York. A lively young man. So pleased to be in these United States, so eager to begin a new and useful life.' He concluded, 'Too bad.'

Blaike asked, again with that studied casualness, 'Your

friends didn't send you any information as to why he was killed?'

Popin's eyes looked beyond the candles. 'The police do not know this. Only they know it was violence which killed him.' Blaike asked with awful quietness, 'Or about the girl who had been with him that evening?'

'Girl?' Popin shook his head slowly, back and forth. 'They mentioned no girl.'

Blaike was brusque. 'The police are looking for a girl. That was in the papers.' He gazed directly across at Julie now. Her head remained poised, her eyes held no information. 'Did you read that story?'

She answered, 'Yes. It was in the morning's—I should say Monday morning's—New York papers.'

There was a pause. Blaike passed his cigarette package. 'You say you never met him?'

'Not that I recall.' The candle she lifted to her cigarette illumined her face. She knew that nothing was revealed in it. 'I may have. One met so many. Teas. Dancing. The races. I may have.'

Blaike shook his head. 'He wasn't the Ritz Bar.'

She rose. It was better to end this. 'Might I powder my nose, Mr Popin, before we view the paintings?'

'Certainly.' He was apologetic. 'I am not accustomed to young lady guests. I forgot. I will call Reyes. She is Indian, the Tesuque pueblo. However, she speaks English as well as Tewa. Ask what you wish. Reyes!' The Indian woman came softly. 'Will you show Miss Guille upstairs to the guest room? Light the fire. The room must be warmed for her if she is to stay the night. Tell Quincy to see that the wood box is filled.'

The woman said, 'He did, Popin.' She led the way back

through the living-room, into the hall, and up the stairs. There was in this half story only the guest bedroom and adjoining bath. Reyes lit the table lamp, stooped to the fire. Without words she descended the staircase again. Julie closed the door after her. The room was comfortable, Spanish. There were windows, heavily curtained at the front and the rear. Stepping between curtains and window, shutting out the lamp, she could see the square buildings beyond the house. The one at the right must be garage. At the left the faint outline in the snow of a smaller place. That must be where Jacques lives. No light shone. Doubtless it was as well equipped for blackout as the main house. She stepped again into the room. The wind was blasting this turret. The fire had caught now. Perhaps Jacques would join them later. Perhaps he had believed, as Popin and the Indians had, guests would not dare this storm. He wanted to see her. Today. He had stressed it. She might send word out to him that she was here. She rearranged her hair, freshened her lipstick. If she didn't get in touch with Jacques tonight, she could see him in the morning. Before morning, before the roads were reopened, she must think of some reason for remaining here. Some reason Blaike would accept, if not believe. If she could go to bed now, not face him again. He was suspicious of her, he thought she was the police-wanted girl. He didn't know it; he hadn't accused.

She couldn't shut herself away, not this early. The courteous little host would be hurt if she didn't look at his paintings. She must face at least another hour of the gray man before she dared suggest bed. She could endure it. She had faced suspicion more definite than his and dissipated it. She wasn't afraid of him. Not at Popin's. She took a last glimpse in the mirror. Her face was without visible care. She put out the bedroom light, went into the hall. Below it was lightless, she left the night light burning here to guide her steps. She moved slowly, gathering wit and courage in these last moments alone. Halfway down she could see into the lighted living-room.

On the couch was a bowler on a round head, thick fingers intertwined across coated knees.

Her hand froze to the banister. Her foot, poised between steps, didn't move. Somehow he had traced her from Tesuque. He was waiting for her now, stolid and menacing as a mountain. If she could only reach the studio where Popin was, but to do so she must pass through the room where the man waited. It might be possible to steal down to the front door, make a dash to open it and reach the guest house. There was too much risk. Not only in reaching the door but, having opened it, in outdistancing the man around the house, up the path, to that blacked-out shape in the snow. And no reassurance that Jacques was within. Popin had believed he was working; he hadn't even implied that the work was on the premises. Jacques wouldn't have machines in his bedroom. If he were in his house, he would have heard the car arrive, would have known of her presence here. She only now recalled. Jacques didn't know she was coming here tonight. He hadn't been present when Popin offered the invitation. In the rapid crossfire of more important talk, she hadn't mentioned it during their interrupted interview last night.

She could turn tail, repair to the upstairs room. It wouldn't be possible to stay there forever. But she could remain until she was missed below, until someone came for her. She wouldn't have to walk alone into the firing range of this man's pig eyes. The stair cracked sharply as she shifted her weight. He must have heard even if he couldn't see her on the darkly lit stairs. He didn't move.

She decided. She would back softly up, up, out of sight, to her room. It was the wiser way. She took one step. She hadn't noticed the sound of the stairs coming down them, each one was a drum now. She looked into the parlor again. The Indian girl, Reyes, was coming through the arch from the dining-room. The waiter hadn't heard her steps. He hadn't stirred. Julie watched Reyes; she moved then swiftly, softly, careless of sound. She reached the foot of the stairs, entered the room as Reyes came behind him.

He saw Julie. He stood on his ugly, box-toed black shoes, high-laced. His big mouth didn't smile but his dull little eyes held glittering recognition.

Julie looked at him the way she would look at someone in a waiting-room. She asked of Reyes, 'The men are still in the studio?'

'They are.'

Julie passed without another glance at the man. She heard Reyes' lazy voice, 'Popin says you wait a minute. He ees coming.'

Julie didn't turn back. She went up into the dining-room, chilled now, lightless but for the red flicker of the dying fire. She opened the wrong door. Quincy was at a white table, dipping bread on a gravy-pooled plate. He raised his eyes to her, returned them to his meal. For no reason she said, 'I'm sorry.' He ignored her. She shut the door on the warmth and light. The studio door had been in back of her at dinner. She moved toward it. Reyes passed her now, ignored her. She hurried to reach the studio before the Indian woman could vanish. She wasn't quick enough. Her hand was on the latch but there was compulsion to look toward the arch. She stifled a scream. She knew better than to scream in face of danger. He stood there peering at her. The latch clicked under her hand but it didn't give.

He said, 'You were with Maxl.'

She must get the door open before he came nearer. His box-like shoes clodded on the rough brick floor. Desperately she took her eyes from him long enough to press her hand down on the latch. The door opened toward her, she had to step back, nearer to him, to widen it. Two steps below was the studio, lighted, warm, faintly tuned with music. At this end narrow, a mere aisle, beyond a wide room where Blaike and Popin stood near a great fire, one head bent, one lifted, earnest in conversation.

Out of her constricted throat her voice came, a rasp. 'You have company, Popin.' She managed the steps without tripping, feeling the weight of his shadow behind her. She almost ran to the men, the clod of his shoes inexorable behind her. Not until she stood clutching Blaike's sleeve did her breath come again.

Popin, head sparrow-tipped, hands in his soft brown pockets, sauntered toward the waiter. 'I sent word I would see you in a moment.' The voice was gentle as ever, gentle with rebuke.

'I followed the girl.' There was no accent but the tongue was guttural. 'I'm tired of waiting. I have waited all day.'

'You must be tired.' Blaike moved away from Julie. He was hearty. 'And cold as well. Lay off your coat—your hat. Popin and I have been hatching a hot rum punch.'

The man didn't move, didn't speak. Julie was very still. He was looking at Blaike, at her, now at Popin.

The artist said, 'Yes, Mr—?'

'Albert Schein.'

'Mr Schein, Mr Blaike. My dear Miss Julie, I forget you have rejoined us. Miss Guille, Mr Schein.'

She didn't have to speak. Blaike continued, 'Another art fancier?' He had the coat, the bowler. The man's head wasn't all stubble now. There was a neat, red-brown, center-part toupee pasted atop it. It didn't fit very well. There was black stubble beyond the fringe. 'However did you get here?' Blaike asked. 'Popin and I just heard by radio that the state police closed all the roads a bit after six o'clock.'

Schein stated, 'I came by the bus. I have waited and waited for a car to come this way. At last one brought me to the turn.'

Popin said to the man's feet, 'You walked it from there?'

Schein said heavily, 'Yes, I walked.'

'For God's sake—in the snow?' Blaike drew Schein to a chair close by the fire. 'Here. You do need attention.' Julie moved away from the hearth. 'Let's get that punch moving, Popin. How about a shot of straight while you're waiting?'

'I am not a drinking man,' Schein stated. 'I will smoke.' He took a thick brown cigar from his pocket, bit the end, spat toward the fireplace. He put a match to the tip.

He too would remain overnight. Popin would invite him. The studio was rich in couches. There were two against the back wall, another in the narrow aisle, one against the right, the one here facing the fireplace. Popin could put up many guests. Nor was there chance that she could get away tonight. And her bedroom was far and away at the opposite pole of the house, unprotected against danger in the dark. While the others were in wine sleep, one who was not a drinking man could move.

Popin said, 'I will see to the ingredients at once.'

She wandered to the plastered walls, hung with bright

blurry landscapes. The queer shape of the room was because of another room jutting into it. No doubt Popin's own bedroom. It looked as if it had been a late addition to the old adobe house. Its walls were of plywood. Heavy brown curtains from their size covered two great windows, north light at the rear, east from the side.

Blaike was on the couch, conversational with Schein. 'Where you from?'

'I am Alsatian.' Were the black eyes boring into her back? 'Seems to me I've seen you before. In New York.'

'For twenty years I have worked in New York. You saw me there.'

'Possibly. I was in the city a couple of weeks before starting west. You are here on business?'

Schein said, 'No.' A final, unelaborated no. 'Are you?'

'I'm trying to do a little business along with pleasure. I was invalided out of the R.A.F.—crackup over the Channel—but I helped drop tons on Cologne before the bastards stopped me. The experts say a man can't fly with a silver plate in his knee. I could show them.'

He was playing a part. Of that she was certain. He wasn't normally chatty, informative. The part might be for the waiter; it might be they played the game of strangers for her. Popin was returning bearing a bowl of Mexican silver. The Indians followed with trays of glasses and bottles. The artist's elbow cleared a space on the crudely carved refectory table.

Quincy and Reyes set down their loads. Quincy said, 'We go home now.'

'Good night.' Popin was busy with the punch bowl.

Blaike said, 'Let me do it.'

Schein put down his cigar. 'I know better. I am a restaurateur.'

'That's it.' Blaike had quiet triumph. 'I knew I'd seen you.'

Julie's hands pressed tightly to her side. He mustn't say it. He did.

'Yorkville. The bierstube. Yorkville.'

Schein said, 'Yes.' He turned to Julie. And he looked away. She was cold. She returned to the hearth, stood backed to it, waiting to see where the man would be placed before she sat down. She would drink a mug of punch, make early excuse for bed. Before the conviviality of the men was diminished, while they remained by the fire with the overflowing bowl, she would steal out, the front way, get to Jacques. He would surely be in his little house by now. He would allow her to stay there. This night, he would guard her. Popin couldn't be offended. He wouldn't have to know.

The men were coming to the hearth. Blaike carried her mug. Schein took his same chair, Blaike motioned her to the couch. She sat in the far corner, he beside her. Popin was cross-legged like a gnome on the rug. It was he who said, 'A night like this. It is good. Without, the storm. Within, good companions gathered round the fire.'

Blaike stretched out his long legs. 'What brought you to these parts, Mr Schein?'

Again her hands tightened. If he'd only stop talking, let Popin speak of simpler things, kindlier things. He wouldn't. He was playing a part and its purpose was to entrap her. He too had seen her with Maxl. He had long ago recognized her. He had sent for Schein. They were working together against her. All this was angling before the waiter accused her openly.

'I come to see someone.' Schein eyed Popin again, coldly. 'All day I have tried to reach you. You do not answer the telephone.'

'Mornings I work in the open, under the sky.' The artist was mild. 'This afternoon the storm broke down the wires. I am regretful. Had I known I could have sent the car for you as for my other guests.'

Good that he hadn't known, that Schein had been forced to walk that cold upward mile. His Germanic arrogance had been his undoing. Quincy was not a taxi. Schein was a Nazi; the smell of it exuded from his pores. Alsace? Perhaps. That country had changed hands so often. Or he implied French heritage for his protection in these times.

She had her cup to her lips when Blaike cut in, still pursuing, more determined. 'How did you happen to know of Popin?'

Popin perked his head. 'Yes. Who was it told you of my work? That you should come so far to examine it. That is good. You are a dealer perhaps, Mr Schein.'

Schein said, 'Your work is well known among the refugees, Mr Popin.' He rolled his cigar across his face. 'Many refugees come to the rathskeller. Where their language is spoken. They are sick for the homeland, even if they have been driven from it by war. I have heard some of them speaking of your work, Mr Popin.' He said it as if it were a memorized piece.

Popin smiled happily. 'It is good when men like your work, speak of this to their friends. Yes, there is satisfaction in it then.' His hand fluttered to the paintings. 'You see I am trying something new. The New Mexican scene. That means my homesickness is over. No longer I paint out of the past.' He was enthusiastic speaking of painting. This was his true work. He had taken a small painting from the wall, was explaining technique, brush work, mixing of colors to the disinterest of the other men, to Julie's half mind. It wasn't blackbirding he cared about. That was doubtless a self-imposed task, to help refugees. There was always a gauze of wariness over him when Blaike forced the conversation from painting to the generalization work.

The gentle brown-bearded man was afraid, that was it. Julie had seen fear in too many of its guises not to know it. Popin feared. Rightfully so. He wasn't a man of violence but he was involved in a violent movement, fraught with ever attendant danger. Danger from within and without. She realized now that he couldn't be a lone wolf. There must be someone to fly the black plane; there must be agents outside the states; there must be some way to make contact with them, possibly short-wave radio; and there must be more agents in this country to handle the dissemination of the refugees upon arrival. A nucleus of strangers in this poorly populated countryside would attract attention, investigation. She recalled Blaike's words, a depot, the station master. That explained the ability to put up any number of guests. Refugees were landed here by the blackbirding ship, kept out of sight until they could be shipped compass-wise into other states. The Indian servants? What did they understand about the presence of strange guests at any hour? They didn't need to understand; they weren't interested. No. Popin wasn't a lone blackbirder. There must be an organization. Jacques to fly the plane? Other men in other cities. Maxl in New York? Was that what he had been hinting? Why had Maxl been murdered? Always the imminence of danger. Blackbirding was illegal. The F.B.I. must even now be seeking its source. Not the U.S. government alone. The Gestapo didn't remain dormant when prey escaped its bloody fists. It too would be hunting this American underground. It wasn't an underground. It wasn't moles burrowing through degradation for the promise of escape. It was clean and sharp, a bird's talons snatching the harassed, the hopeless, cutting escape through infinity. Smuggling in the sky.

And poor little Popin, knowing all the dangers, feared. He wasn't meant for reckless uncertainties. He was born for painting, for puttering in his garden, keeping his neat little house. Even now he didn't know whether he could trust these men who came knowing of his work. He kept on deliberately confusing work with painting. Neither Schein nor Blaike had as yet forced him to open discussion. He feared. Because Maxl had died. He might be next. An organization such as this couldn't be carried on without conscienceless men involved, men unafraid of violence. Men who would kill if need be, men who didn't flinch at meeting death. They would be selected for this quality. If someone within the organization wished Popin out of the way, he wouldn't be safe. And he didn't know who killed Maxl. He hadn't known that Maxl was dead. He had cringed at the knowledge.

She had been listening only faintly to the conversation. She yawned now. She was surprised at the lateness, already by her watch it was eleven o'clock. ''Would you mind if I excuse myself, Mr Popin? I'm frightfully tired. The punch has been my stirrup cup.' She was on her feet.

So was Schein, even before the other men. He pointed a pudgy finger. 'Where is she going?'

She herself answered, smiling, seemingly at ease. 'Well, really, Mr Schein.' She saw something else then. He was afraid of her. It didn't dissipate her fear of him. For he wasn't one to scurry from fear; his answer would be brutal liquidation of its source. He had been the driver of the taxi. He was afraid she had witnessed Maxl's death. He was the murderer.

He said now, heavy, ugly. 'She was with Maxl.' He looked with import at Popin. 'The night he died.'

3

No one said anything. All were watching her, Schein with stones for eyes, Blaike with suspicion alert on his face, Popin just a little timidly.

And she laughed, brightly, without care. 'I haven't the least idea why you're saying that.' Her face lifted to the others, shone with quiet truth. She knew it did. She'd practiced it often. 'I didn't know this Maxl. I was never with him.' She turned her shoulder on Schein. 'You will excuse me, Mr Popin?'

'I will show you the way.'

'You needn't. I've already been up, you know.'

Blaike stated, 'I'll go up with Julie, Popin. See that her fire's shipshape, all that.'

Her hands were icy. If anyone was to go it should be Popin. She needed a moment alone with him. She had refused only to keep the men together. They mustn't break up their bibbing this early; they must give her a chance to reach Jacques. She began, 'Really, you needn't—'

'But I will.' He smiled and his smile was cold as her hands. He wouldn't be disputed. Popin settled uncertainly back on the rug.

She said, 'Good night. I'll see you in the morning, Mr Popin.' She didn't speak to Schein. She led through the cold dining-room. She was wordless through the living-room, the hall, the stairs. At her door she turned to the gray man, 'Good night.'

The smile remained on his lips. It wasn't in his eyes.

'Remember me? I'm the fireboy.' He waited until she opened the door, followed her. The fire was ash. He built it professionally again, kneeling awkwardly until the kindling caught. He rose, dusted his hands.

'Thank you very much,' she said without expression.

He looked down from his height. 'You were with Maxl.' She didn't move.

'I saw you together. There at Bert's beer garden. You left together. At one o'clock. By two, he was dead.'

Her lips alone moved. 'Who are you?'

'A partner in crime. A deserter from the R.A.F. They're on my heels. That's why I had to reach Popin. I have to get away.' The smile was carved across his face, 'In war times desertion from the force is as bad, or worse, than murder.'

It came as a slap across the face. She cried out, 'I didn't murder him.'

He looked over his shoulder. No one was behind him in the doorway. He said, 'Earlier and with the same verity you said you didn't know him.'

She repeated with violence, 'I didn't murder him.'

'The police are looking for you. You came to Popin for the same reason as I, for his help in running away. There's one thing you didn't count on. Neither did I. This storm.'

She was uncertain. 'The storm.'

'Planes can't fly without a ceiling. The Blackbirder won't fly again until the storm lifts.'

She hadn't thought of that.

'You'll have to be careful until then. Very careful.'

There was ice, a lump, within her. He seemed to be speaking out of certain knowledge. He knew why Schein was here. She knew one thing only. Schein was a Nazi. She was an animal, she could smell the Nazi spoor. She asked passionately now, 'Why was Maxl killed?'

'You don't know?'

'How could I? I didn't know him well in Paris. I didn't know he was in New York until I met him that night. Why was he killed?'

'I don't know.'

'Why?' she demanded.

'I honestly don't know. I know two things. He was a minor Nazi agent.'

Her nails cut into her palms.

'And he was a Blackbirder.'

'No!' But it was what she had been formulating below: an organization of Blackbirders couldn't be certain of every man they must trust within their ranks. Which side was Maxl selling out? Whichever had killed him. She wondered again now, 'Who are you?'

'I told you that.' He had turned. 'Your door hasn't a key. Do you know how to balk a latch?'

'Yes.' She knew most of the makeshifts of protection. She had learned that one the night the Nazi officer had tried to get into her room. After she had maimed him. That had been somewhere north of Vichy. A long time ago when she was very young. She said, 'I think my toothbrush will do it.' And she looked at him swiftly. But he hadn't noticed it: that she had come prepared to stay.

He had picked up a bit of kindling. He broke a piece to fit. 'Don't forget to use it. Good night.'

She closed the door after him. He didn't know she wouldn't need it. Nearing eleven-thirty now. She listened to his uneven descent of the stairs. She would wait at least ten minutes, perhaps fifteen. Not too long. It must be done before the three men went to bed. Before any one of them would separate himself, be prowling the halls. Blaike knew that Schein menaced her. He knew the waiter was a Nazi. He knew or he sensed that the Gestapo was after her. It was proven now. First Maxl. The meeting at Carnegie had not been accidental.

She felt no terror of it at this moment, only a great weariness. She had run so far and so long, she was winded. That was despair. She had had a respite. She could run again. Schein had killed Maxl. He had left the restaurant before them, put a greasy cap on his head, counted on the customary disinterest of passengers in a cab driver. He had killed Maxl when Maxl returned to the cab. But why, if they were on the same side? Now he had come after her. Whatever reason there was to kill Maxl, he thought she had guilty knowledge of it. She had run away; he had sensed that she would run to the blackbirders. It was the only quick means of escape for a foreigner in a country at war.

Ten minutes. She wouldn't wait longer. If anyone was below she had her excuse, her coat in the hall closet. She carried her purse with her as she went softly down the staircase. Halfway she looked into the living-room, empty, the hall below empty. She finished her descent, turned toward the closet at the rear. And she stopped short. She had heard a sound, a possible sound. She had on the blue pullover as well as her jacket. There at the foot of the stairs she was within two steps of the front door. She made a dash for it.

She hadn't counted on the fury of the storm. It flung itself on her. She huddled close to the house, rounded it, and fought her way into the wind, past the dark curtained windows, living-room, dining-room, kitchen. It was farther than she thought to the guest house, in the unprotected stretch she was battered by scratching flakes, maniac wind. The ground snow was above her ankles. She pushed on, stumbling, pausing over and again to push her heels into the slippers.

The little house was dark. She rapped. Above the wind could she be heard? She pounded. He might be asleep. She couldn't stand here freezing. She wouldn't return to the house from which she had escaped. She put her hand on the latch. It moved. Quickly she shoved inside, shot the bolt after her. Her breath was coming fast. She was wet with snow, shivering with cold. She stood there a moment before she could move. The inevitable Indian fireplace gave only faint red ashes, no warmth. She went to it, laid kindling, blew softly on the ash, pushed in two logs. Jacques wouldn't care. The fire caught and she stood to it, thawing, melting. Only when the warmth ran through her blood did she turn again to the room seeking a lamp.

She didn't need light. The fire was enough. She saw the mad disorder, the smashed radio, the broken chair. She saw the dark shape face down under the chair. With hopeless fatality she walked to him. She knew it was Jacques. The waiter had reached him first.

She bent down over him. It hadn't been a clean kill. She set her face away from grief. She hadn't smelled the blood. The room had been too cold. Not cold enough. There had been remnants of a fire. An hour at most. He had been killed since dinner. Blaike hadn't wanted her to talk with Jacques last night.

Terror shook her in its teeth. She must get away from here. The coincidence of her presence at one murder might be explained away, not at a second. Not with Schein waiting to accuse her. Not with Blaike and his self-centered wisdom and his granite eyes. Not to little fear-ridden Popin. No, she couldn't go inside, announce, 'I've found Jacques. He's dead.'

There was only one thing to do. Chance getting back to town, to the hotel, be gone on the bus to Albuquerque before the men arose in the morning. From Albuquerque on to the border. Chancey, yes. But possible. If she could make it to the hotel it was more than possible. She didn't believe the roads would be patrolled. The storm warnings had been insistent, emphatic, all through the evening. Even if anyone missed the radio warnings, he wouldn't set out at night with the storm still battering, not unless there were reasons more vital than his own safety. She could handle a car. If she could get away unobserved she could take it easy, not more than a mile to the highway, about four miles to Tesuque, five or six miles to Santa Fe.

No one would be disturbing her room early in the morning. She was a guest. By the time Popin learned she had departed, she would be en route to El Paso. There was another risk. If Schein came to her room tonight or if Blaike returned to it, her absence would be noted. That chance would have to be taken. One thing, this murder was not meant to be discovered as yet. She must get away fast before the time for discovery.

She couldn't start out in the storm without a coat. Jacques must have one she could borrow. She was afraid to leave this front room, enter the bedroom. It might be blind alley. There on the floor was the dark plaid of his mackinaw. She caught it up. It wasn't blood-stained. She enveloped herself in its weight, buttoned it high, clutched her purse under her arm. Her eyes gave one brief eulogy to the man crumpled there. He couldn't have died for her. It couldn't be Tanya's pattern repeated. But bitterly, she knew it could be.

The wind was moaning against the door. She stood inside for a last moment, dreading the plunge into the vicious night. Already there might be someone waiting outside. She opened the door, stepped through, pulled it tight against the wind's struggle to push it wide again. She saw no one, no shadows. The main house was dark. The shortest way to the garage was across the back of the house, past the kitchen and the studio. She stumbled and pushed through the deepening snow to the kitchen wall. She hugged it for a moment before daring the screaming temper of the blizzard again. Past the kitchen, protecting her face from the whiplash with one arm. The studio outer wall to encompass. The blackout curtain made it blank, inscrutable. If she could only know the three were yet about the fire. She had stood between curtain and window tonight, another could do the same.

She didn't hesitate. Before she reached the window she dropped on all fours, snaked her way in the snow to the end of the room. She stood up then, not attempting to brush away the snow that froze to her skirt, to her legs under the thin mesh stockings. A straight line now back to the garage. She couldn't run for it, snow was furry about her ankles, wind flung ice pellets on her face to impede her. She could only push, stagger on, hoping, praying to reach her goal. If only the night were dark. But the luminosity of snow, sky and the white grayness of fallen snow carved her stark and black against the landscape. Her breath was whimpering, no one could hear that, not above the wind. No one could hear the garage doors open.

Exhausted she stood inside. There were two cars, the one Popin had sent to meet the bus and a light pickup truck. She switched the ignition on both. Either one had enough gas to carry her to Santa Fe. The sedan would be warmer and there were chains on its rear tires, none on the truck wheels. She brushed some of the snow from the mackinaw before climbing behind the wheel. Her skirt was a thin sheet of ice from below her hips. She had lost one slipper somewhere between Jacques' house and here. It was unimportant. She kicked off the other.

She would run without lights until she was well out of sight. There would be no danger of collision, no one would be abroad on the side lane. The old car was noisy. Would the sound of wind drown out the rattle and chug? Would a fire, a punch bowl, conversation, obliterate unexpected sound? She warmed the car in the garage, backed it, turned its slippery, shifting wheels still by the garage, far enough from the house. No one had heard. No curious hand pulled aside the curtains. Now!

There was no road. She headed through unprospected snow to the front of the house, away from it. She was in the lane, turned right, toward the highway. She was so cold, so uncomfortably cold. Soon the engine would warm the car, thaw her a little. She brushed back her hair. It was stiff to touch. She adjusted the rear-view mirror. No one behind her. It was difficult holding the car, the snow was unbroken by so much as a rabbit paw. So cold. Her hands were too cold to clutch the cold wheel. She blew on the left fingers, thrust them into the pocket. No gloves. She slowed, holding with the left now, wedged her right hand into the other pocket. It touched something colder than snow. It touched steel. She knew what it was. The gun Jacques had held last night.

For a moment her eyes stung. If she'd wanted a gun, there'd have been gloves. Because she needed gloves— With

116

her knuckles she dug out the moisture. Frozen eyes wouldn't help. Had she seen a gleam of light already? She couldn't tell. If the snow packed too heavily on the rear window she wouldn't be able to watch the road behind. It was caked on the windshield, the wiper worked sluggishly, the triangle of clear view became smaller. The floorboard was warming now, her foot was wet, not stiff. But she had to open the window to the cold, her breath was misting the windshield. She saw in the mirror the gleam again. It wasn't a star. There were no stars visible on the overcast sky. She had been discovered. Wearily the thought lay on her, perhaps she was meant to find Jacques. This might be their move to take power over her. But why did these men want to harm her? She had no wish to harm them.

She knew by what evil they moved. Paul. Paul who hated her, hated her enough to kill Tanya, to kill Jacques. He had sent them for her. He would not rest until she was destroyed. And not until he was destroyed would she ever escape.

She could stop the car now, wait for those bits of light to catch up with her. She had Jacques' gun. But she feared the risk. If she missed, there were two of them against her. She must get away this time, wait for certain opportunity. The highway was beyond. Careful at the turn. The wheels whirred and she cried out. They must compass the drift. Frantically she dug her foot into the gas pedal, maneuvered the wheel. Breath broke from her as the car made a perilous lurch, cleared the mound, and she was headed to Sante Fe. The highway was empty, a long, straight, white treadmill, beneath its snow the slick of ice shivering the wheels. No pin-points showed behind her now. She had the head start. Whoever followed in the truck couldn't hope to better her time on these roads; he must be more careful without chains on his wheels. She didn't dare increase speed. It was difficult enough holding the car with her numb hands. She was heading into falling snow again, the wind hurled fistfulls against the windshield. The lights reappeared. How far behind her? Were they closing in?

Whatever man held the other wheel held also the greater strength to pack the car over the treacherous road. She swung perilously from the ditch; watch the road, not pursuing lights. She wouldn't be able to outdistance them all the way to Santa Fe. There was nothing but road in her eyes, no refuge along its emptiness. Her foot pushed down on the gas, muffling the panting in her throat. Faster, faster. Faster wasn't safer. She touched the gun again. Was it loaded? She couldn't investigate. The wheel needed both hands.

Almost too late she saw the side road. She swung the turn. The car skidded dangerously but with aching fingers she managed to right it. A side road in this open country could mean but one thing, habitation at the end of it. The road itself was heavy with unbroken snow. Will alone forced the wheels through the drifts. Her whimpering was audible, she didn't try to control it. If only the refuge she sought wasn't too far away. She didn't expect the pursuing car to overlook her turn off the road; there were no other headlights in the whiteness to confuse the issue. She would be followed here, followed more quickly than she could lead. She was breaking path. If only one house would emerge out of the shadowy whiteness. The lights again glared her mirror. This then was the end of flight. She was to be taken, returned, killed. And then the shadows ahead became small mounds, homes. She didn't hesitate. She skidded the tires, turned her car a barrier across the road. She slipped from under the wheel, plowed forward, stumbling. The snow was too heavy for moving quickly. But the first house wasn't far. Her fists beat against the primitive door, beat harder. Those other lights were closing in on the road. And the door swung open.

Julie saw nothing in the room, not shapes, not shadows in the firelight. Her choked voice alone had function, crying hoarsely, 'Please help me. Don't let them get me! Please, please! Help me!'

She heard the door close behind her, heard the bolt fall while her voice babbled frantically, 'Please, please help me. Don't let them in. They'll take me back! They'll kill me!'

The figures closed in on her. She shrank back. Only then did she actually see the man who had admitted her, his faded blue jeans, his faded blue shirt, the weary hat on his head, the inscrutable black eyes in the face like an Aztec mask. The two black braids over his shoulders were twined with red rag. She was in the Tesuque Indian pueblo.

She said brokenly only to herself, 'You don't understand. You can't save me.' She leaned back against the door to keep from falling.

The voice was quiet. 'You are in some trouble.' He came into the circle then, a younger Indian, blue-jeaned like the older man, his hair cut short. There were two women coming nearer, fat, black-banged, curious. There were children with sleepy, black-bead eyes slanted at her. There was no expression on any face.

She heard a motor cut. She broke in whispering, her eyes

begging all of them, 'Don't let them take me. Help me. Please, help me.' She didn't realize how she must appear, shoeless, stockings frozen to her legs, her wild hair frozen above her face, the man's mackinaw wrapping her. She didn't even realize that fear was livid on her face and that fear transcended language barriers.

The braided man said, 'Soledad.' He pointed. One woman came forward, took her hand, led her like a child to the wall. She draped a blanket over Julie's head, about her shoulders, pointed to the floor. Julie sank down. She could hear a voice shouting outside. The woman spoke, evidently in Tewa. The children scuttled to their positions by the hearth. The woman squatted beside Julie, pulled a blanket about herself, rested her head against the banco. The guttural shout was outside the door. 'Open up, in there. Open up, I say.' Julie shivered. The woman laid a quiet brown hand against her shoulder.

The door shuddered. 'I say, in there.' That was Blaike.

The braided Indian moved cat quiet to the door. His hands were deliberate on the bar. The opening was small. The lantern was held high to foreign faces. The young Indian stood behind the older man.

'Where is that girl what came in here?' Schein's voice was heavy.

The Indian shrugged. 'No girl. Nobody. Go way.'

The thick voice grew more guttural. 'Don't lie. She is here. I saw her come.'

'Nobody here. Go way.'

Blaike broke in pleasantly, trying to eradicate the hostility engendered by the German. 'My sister. She lost her way in the storm. We are searching for her. We thought we saw—'

The Indian repeated, 'Go way.'

'If we could but look—'

His ingratiation could succeed where Schein's arrogance failed. Blaike was pushing to the door opening. But he didn't enter. The two Indian men, young and old, blocked the way, with dignity, with more, with menace. 'This our house. You do not come in.'

The door closed implacably in his face. The bolt fell. The quiet brown hand stroked Julie's blanket. The braided man turned. Only his eyes were pleased. 'My house. He no come in.' He repeated in Tewa to the wide black eyes of the children. They giggled. Fists again beat the door. Schein's voice threatened. 'Open up there. Open up.' His voice was joined with others. Indian inflections. Not pleased at this. The older man took up the lantern, spoke to the boy. He went out and the bolt fell heavily in place. The boy came to Julie. He said, 'Do not be afraid. You are safe here.'

'Thank you.' She couldn't say more. She was still too terrorized to speak.

The woman, Soledad, murmured. He translated. 'Your clothes are wet. You are cold. My mother will bring you dry clothes to change into if you will.'

Again Julie said, 'Thank you.' But when she tried to rise fear held her. Her eyes scuttled to the door.

He said with pride, 'Do not fear. He does not enter my father's house.'

She rose then holding the blanket about her. She followed the woman to the fireplace. The boy pad-footed into the inner room. A little girl had warmed the calico dress, the black cotton stockings, the brown hide moccasins fastened above the ankles with silver star buttons. Julie changed quickly, gratefully. She retained the blanket. Another child brought her a tin cup of hot coffee. She shook her head. 'I can't take your coffee.'

The boy was in the doorway. 'You must not refuse a gift in the house of a friend. My mother would not understand if you did.'

Julie accepted the cup, swallowed gratefully.

He came in then. He said, 'I am Porfiro. I speak English. I go to the boarding school in Santa Fe. Those men would hurt you?'

She nodded. She realized then that the noise outside had ceased. She said, 'I don't know what they want. But I'm afraid. I'm terribly afraid.' She heard the turning of a motor. They were leaving. But they would lie in wait for her.

Porfiro said, 'Do not be afraid. We will help you.'

Someone was pushing at the door. She clutched the boy's arm.

He said, 'That is my father returning.' He went noiselessly, admitted the braided man, rebolted it. She could not understand what was said. There was soft laughter, mimicry of Schein's wild rage, of Blaike's politeness. Porfiro returned to her. 'The governor himself came forth. These men are warned not to enter again into our pueblo.'

She said it aloud then, soberly. 'They will wait for me.'

'They have driven away. One took your car.'

'It wasn't mine. I borrowed it.' She whispered, 'They'll lie in wait to catch me, to take me back, to kill me.'

Porfiro said, 'You are safe with us.'

'But I must get to Santa Fe. Could you help me reach Santa Fe?' Once there safely she could get a bus going south, going to the border.

'Tomorrow, yes. When the road is opened.'

Soledad spoke again.

Porfiro said, 'My mother says you are to sleep. We will watch. Tomorrow we will help you.'

Julie said, 'Thank you. All of you.' She curled in the blanket on the smooth dirt floor. She wouldn't be able to sleep. She said, 'I cannot thank you enough. If you had not opened your door—'

'No one would turn away a person in need. My father had just returned from the flocks.'

It was quiet in the room. These were good people, simple people. They cared for their flocks, they shared with a stranger at the gate, they helped the helpless, they dared stand up to the strength of evil. Their verities were untarnished by old and tired discussions, by neophilosophies of a blind present. She was safe for tonight.

Her eyes closed heavily. Exhaustion alone gave her sleep, exhaustion plus the certainty that no harm could befall her with Porfiro and his family on guard.

When she woke the others were already moving. It was only seven by her watch. A small girl brought her a basin of water and a towel, stood watching while she washed. Julie took out her comb, worked over her matted hair by her purse mirror. Several children watched her. She used her lipstick.

There was *pan* and strong coffee, a bowl of beans with chile gravy. She ate hungrily with the women and children, cross-legged before the fire. They watched her, speaking among themselves. The children tittered together, pointing at the fit of her Indian clothes. Not until Porfiro returned could she ask questions. Snow stomped from his boots. He said, 'Hello.'

'Has the storm ended?'

'It is not snowing. But there is no sun.'

'The roads—'

He was confident. 'We will go to Santa Fe at noon. It will not be difficult.'

She had to ask. 'Those men—'

He measured her. He said, 'A truck waits on the highway. The fat one is in it.'

Her lips closed tightly.

Porfiro asked, 'Are you afraid to go?'

'There is no other way to Santa Fe?'

'No.' He assured her, 'You are welcome in our home.'

'I must go.' Go before they returned with the police. 'I must go,' she repeated more firmly. She must get away before she was taken and locked up. Get away. Communicate with Popin by phone. Fran must be released from prison. Fran helpless, while Paul took steps to thwart her. Her lips twisted. If Paul knew that his beloved son wasted in prison because of this evil. Some day he would know. She would tell him. But at present she must stay free to help Fran. She must get away.

Porfiro said, 'We will go as always. Many of us in the truck to Santa Fe for supplies. You will be one woman with many in the back of the truck. The blanket will cover you. Your skin is not too white. The man will not see you with us. If you are not afraid.'

'I am afraid,' she told him. 'I'm always afraid. But I'm not afraid to face what must be done. And I must get away before they can take me.'

He nodded his head slowly. And he asked, 'That man is not your brother?'

'No.'

'They are not police officers?'

'No. Did they say that?'

He said, 'First it was you were the sister of the tall gray man. Then the fat black one said he was an officer. The governor put them out of the pueblo.'

She said, 'I don't really know who they are. I only met them. One at La Fonda. One at Popin's.'

'My cousin he works for Mr Popin.'

'Qi'in Tse?'

'He is my cousin. And Reyes. She is my cousin.'

She said, 'I don't know what those men want of me. I only know they are dangerous. They are Nazis.'

For a moment he disbelieved her, a slow grin taking away the ancient mask, leaving a boy's face. 'You see too many movies, I think. There are no Nazis in Tesuque.'

She warned him. 'We are at war.'

He had pride now. 'When school is over this spring, I will join the navy. Many of my cousins are in the navy. Every man of our Indian school football team joined the navy this year, but they must wait to go until the school year closes.'

'You know then that there are enemy spies, fifth columnists, hidden in many places in this country. I am certain these men are Nazis.'

'Why then do they seek to harm you?'

'Because I escaped from them in France. I am a refugee.'

He accepted it. He was suddenly decisive. 'You must go to the F.B.I.'

She couldn't do that. But she dare not tell him. He understood cinema suggestion. 'First I must have proof. I do not dare accuse them without proof. They are too strong. No one would believe they were Nazis. If I can only get away from them now, I will find proof.'

'You do not worry about that. I get you away.' He went among the women and children now, spoke in their own tongue. The women brightened, the children scurried. The boy went out. She sat against the wall on the banco. Schein

126

would not recognize her, the blanket hiding her face, Indian woman fashion. The mackinaw lay folded there on the bench. Her hand slipped into the pocket, the gun was still within, reassuring. Under cover of the confusion and the coat, she transferred it to her purse.

It was after eleven when Porfiro returned. The women and children were ready. They carried bright calico bundles. There were others waiting outside, a baby in arms, fat, placid. Porfiro spoke to Julie. 'Wear the coat under your blanket. It will not be seen. You will need its warmth.' The open truck was outside the door. 'Climb in back with the others. Two of my primos are ahead on the road. If the man tries to stop us, they will delay him.' Two other Indians climbed into the front with him. She sat on the bare floor of the rear with the others. The day was bitter cold, the sky slate. It was not fear that pulled the blanket across her head, covering her mouth and nose, only her eyes visible. She saw the truck parked on the siding just below the turn. She saw the two blue-jeaned Indians loitering near it. Schein, bowler jammed to his ears, overcoat collar turned up, gloved hands on the wheel, looked half frozen. She knew he scanned every face in the truck, her face. She didn't look into his eyes.

The truck turned on the highway, chugged along. Schein didn't follow. She dared relax when they passed the few houses of Tesuque. The truck labored up the snowy hill, passed the crest, eased down toward Santa Fe. It was that easy.

Porfiro parked just off the Plaza. His two compadres stretched their legs. He came around to the back of the truck. He said, 'Here we are, miss.' He didn't seem to know what to do with her. She didn't know exactly what to do herself. Obviously she couldn't expect to enter her room unnoticed in this disguise. As if he had sensed her thoughts he said, 'Your clothes are in this bundle. My mother has wrapped them.'

Julie took the brown paper package, told the Indian woman, 'Thank you.' Soledad nodded, smiled, smiled wider. Julie slid to the street beside the boy. She said, 'You know how grateful I am to you.' Her fingers had removed the bills from her purse during the ride; she held them out now. 'Please take this. Not pay. A present for your mother.' He looked at her quietly. 'You cannot refuse a guest's present,' she said, 'no more than I could refuse yours.'

'Thank you, miss.'

She said, 'Your mother's clothes? How can I return them to her?'

He said, 'Next week I go back to school. I was needed to help at home in the storm. Send them to me at the Indian Club.'

She repeated after him, 'Porfiro Melones.'

He hesitated. 'You are not afraid?'

She repeated as before, 'I am always afraid.' She turned, started away, but his steps came after her.

'The truck will be here all afternoon. Always someone will be in it. If you need to return, you are welcome.' He nodded just once, turned again. 'An Indian woman walks slowly, little steps, no legs.' He grinned.

She would remember. She clutched the paper parcel, shuffled in the brown moccasins the length of the Palace portal. She saw no hostile face. She crossed, shuffled the east side of the Plaza, past the bank to the ticket office. On the corner over there was La Fonda. Could she carry it off? An Indian was no novelty in the hotel but could she reach her room as an Indian? She could try. She held the blanket across her face, held her nerves check-reined. Small steps up the walk, open the door, walk in. Schein was in a truck on the Tesuque highway. Small steps into the lobby. Blaike was on a couch facing the door. He was talking to a plump pink man who wore the hat of a hotel detective. Small careful steps now, past the news stand, down the side steps, out the door. No hurry.

She retraced her steps back to the truck. Only the mother and baby were in it. The woman looked at her. Her eyes spoke even if her tongue was sealed by language. Julie settled down again on the floor. The woman said something, pushed over a paper sack. Julie shook her head. She couldn't eat.

'No quiere?'

She repeated after her, 'No quiere. No thank you.' She sat there, the bundle on her lap, the purse tucked under the shawl. They had been hard to carry to the hotel but no one had noticed her awkwardness handling them and the shawl. What next? Take the bus dressed as she was? Did Indians ride the bus? Yes. Two women on the ride from Albuquerque. Others on the ride to Tesuque. Someone would be watching the bus station. She couldn't pass for Indian at close inspection. She might send Porfiro to buy the ticket. She recalled then. She had given the boy all of her money save for a little silver. She had counted on reaching the hotel before the enemy did; she had counted on their remaining on guard in Tesuque until they saw her leave. She couldn't ask the return of her free gift. The boy had been reluctant to accept it. She must have the money and package from the safe. She had been an idiot, lulled by momentary security into registering it. The diamonds wouldn't leave her body again, not until the peace was cemented and the horrors of this war a long-winded tale told by ancients at the fire. She must recover them. In person. The hotel wouldn't accept a note to turn them over to a young Indian boy. She would have to get back to her room some way. The risk was trebled if Blaike had asked the hotel detective to watch for her. If Blaike had told the man she was wanted for murder!

He wouldn't! He would if it were advisable. When Porfiro returned she'd ask him to buy the evening paper. She must get back into her room, change clothes there. Even if she had to wait until the hotel slept, until early hours of dawn, she must reach its haven. Wait where? On the street if need be. She had the gun if anyone came to shove her. She wouldn't use it to kill, only to threaten. And she would use it if anyone attempted to thwart her regaining her package, if anyone attempted to take her before she could get away. She shook her head. She wouldn't use it. She couldn't kill.

It was almost five when Porfiro returned to the truck. He wasn't surprised to see her. He asked, 'You were not safe?'

'No. One of the men was there before me.'

'Will you return with us?'

'No.' She found a coin. 'Can you get me the evening paper?' She must know what had been revealed.

He went to the corner of the Plaza, hailed a small dirty boy, returned with the local news sheet. She spread her eyes over it. There were only six pages to search. There was no mention of Jacques. There wouldn't be. The blackbirders couldn't risk investigation of Popin's house. Nor would Blaike or Schein wish to be exposed to the police. Blaike couldn't have been accusing her of murder to the detective. There was no murder as yet. The tale he told might be as dangerous to her but the city police wouldn't be watching for her. Only Schein, Blaike and the detective. One must watch in Tesuque. Only two here.

She said, 'I'll go now. I'll be all right.' She was without hope but she smiled. She carried the package in front of her, the purse under her arm, as she walked away from the Plaza, up to a bakery. She bought ten cents' worth of rolls. In the connecting grocery store she examined her purse. There was exactly sixty-two cents remaining there. Two oranges. A pint of milk. Less than fifty cents now. A brick schoolhouse stood on the opposite corner. She went into the shadows between it and the larger adobe schoolhouse next. She was protected from sight, protected a little from the cold. She ate the dry bread, drank the milk, and ate one orange. The other she put in her pocket. Darkness was increasing when she emerged and with the darkness the cold deepened. She must get indoors.

Remembering the slow walk she returned to the hotel. This time she used the side door. At the head of the stairs she saw the detective sitting at the far end of the lobby. She didn't see Blaike. She shuffled to the steps leading to the women's room, followed that corridor. Possibly she could find a staircase leading to third. She couldn't dare the elevator, questioning. Indian women weren't seen in the upper corridors. The steps descended again, turned to the elevator cage. Julie reclimbed, retraced the corridor, descended the other flight and left the hotel. Indians were not welcome in many places. She had not seen one in a restaurant; they had brought their food for the day in paper sacks. There was the bus waiting-room. It would be heated. She found the way and she sat there on a bench. Suddenly panic swept her. If she had found the stairs at the hotel, how could she hope to reach her room unnoted? It was the first place

Blaike would guard. She would have to pass his door. The Indian blanket wouldn't fool him. She must wait until later, far later. She sat there unmoving.

At eleven o'clock, the porter gestured, 'Get going now.' She didn't speak, didn't look at him. She rose and went out again into the bitter night. Back to the hotel. She circled it. She could see her room at the rear, the small balcony, another below it. Unhampered by these clothes she could climb to it. If she could get inside the surrounding wall. If she could do it unnoticed. Two men hard-heeled around the corner. She shrank against the wall. They didn't look at her. She walked the opposite way, past the side door, up to the corner. She didn't glance at the two couples who passed her, entering the hotel. She followed them, slipped inside, and quickly slipped out again. Albert Schein sat on the couch watching the door. He hadn't seen the Indian. His eyes were on the women who had entered in front of her.

She wandered aimlessly on up the street. The Cathedral. She could go in there to wait. No one would say, 'Get going' in there. There were cars passing, others at the post office across. She wandered on following the walk past the Cathedral, past walled old Spanish houses. There was an open parkway after the road turned. She crossed to it. It lay deep in snow, the tall trees throwing black grotesques on the gray. The little river it followed was frozen. She plodded on. The headlights of a car blazoned her as she crossed the bridge. She heard the drunken laughter as it passed, the rough jabber, a derogatory word, 'Squaw.' She was suddenly terrified. The brakes squealed farther up the road. The car could turn back. That could be the meaning of the sound. She ran directly toward the great dark house, fell across the low wall, ran to the small portico and flattened herself against the door. Her shaking hand drew the gun from her purse, held it pointed. But no one came. She saw then at her feet the litter of advertising papers, throwaways. This house was empty. It would not present a shiftless doorway if it were not. It was a well-groomed house.

She tried the door. It was of course locked. She began a slow circle of the house then, window by window. Everything locked. Back door locked. If she could but hide here a few days until the first clamor of the hunt died. She had no compunctions. She took the barrel of the gun, broke the glass above the lock on the back window. Her hand reached in, twisted the lock, raised the window. She climbed through awkwardly, pulled the window down after her.

The luminosity of the out-of-doors showed a kitchen. Suddenly her knees buckled. It might have been a house to let. It wasn't. The dim blue of a pilot light was on the stove. Whoever lived here was temporarily away, that was all. There was furniture, the gas was on, the house was faintly warm, enough to keep pipes from freezing in an unseasonable spell. She found newspapers in a box, stuffed the hole of the window. She didn't dare make a light. She left the blanket on a chair. The gun she pushed back into her pocket, the purse she clutched under her arm. She moved through into the dining-room, living-room, hall. Somewhere there must be an electric torch, usually in a hall. She searched drawers and chest, found it where she should have looked first, on the closet shelf. It worked. She dimmed it with her hand, climbed the stairs without sound. Her heart was louder than her footfall. If this house was not unoccupied, those who lived here wouldn't believe anything a strange Indian-dressed girl told them in the night. There would be one answer, the police.

Bedroom doors were open. Three of them. One at the head of the stairs, the two others off the hall to the right. No one was in them. Each room, each bath was in precise beautiful order. She turned on the water in the center room bath, jumped a little at its sound. It ran warm. Suddenly she didn't care. There were no houses near on this side, only the stretch of parkland. She pulled the shade, hung the mackinaw over it. A black cotton stocking dimmed the light. She pulled off her clothes, ran a hot tub, luxuriated in it. Her head jerked; she mustn't fall asleep here. She turned on the shower then, even scrubbed her hair. It wakened her. She folded towels neatly, turned off the light, used the torch in the bedrooms. She was only borrowing. She found clean underthings; she took those most worn. She made a notation in her little book. She would send money to this house to pay for all she took. She folded Soledad's clothes, borrowed a bathrobe and slippers and went down again to the kitchen. She wasn't afraid now.

The bundle. It wasn't here. She must have left it on the waiting-room bench. For a moment hollowness sucked at her. She straightened her shoulders. It didn't matter. It might be better this way. If it were found, opened, reported, even printed in the little newspaper, Blaike would believe she'd got away. The hunt would roar on to Albuquerque. She put Soledad's clothes in the blanket, left it neatly on a chair. There would be food here. She opened the cabinet doors, used the torch. Canned goods. Staples. Something hot. Soup. She brewed it, ate it with crackers, washed up the traces and returned to the upstairs. She noted what she had taken. By torchlight she examined all the closets now. Two women alone lived here, one older, the best front room; one younger, this room. The one at the head of the stairs was for a maid or guest. The younger hostess wouldn't mind if she borrowed the blue jeans, a clean but old shirt. The girl was taller than Julie but she could fold up the pants legs. Most did in these parts. The shoes were too large; she would have to continue wearing those of Soledad. The bed waited, a heavy blanketed bed. She needn't dress now. No one was coming here tonight. If anyone did—If anyone did it would be three brown bears and she'd say, 'I'm Goldilocks and I was so very tired.' Julie took her purse and her gun and went to bed.

2

There was no sound in the house, no sound in the white world outside. The silence of snow was falling again outside the window. She'd slept late, past nine o'clock. For a moment on awakening panic touched her, realizing last night, where she was. But the silence of house and snow reassured her. She got up, dressed in the levis and shirt, borrowed socks. Before she left the room no one could know without examining the bed that anyone had entered it. She carried the mackinaw over her arm, the gun was inside her purse. Cautiously she crept downstairs, made the rounds of the windows. There was nothing to see but unbroken snow. Even her footprints of the night before were covered. She turned the furnace up a bit before fixing breakfast for herself. There were a few eggs, a bit of butter in the box. The two women hadn't planned to be gone long. No bread but crackers. Tea.

She took out the moccasins from the blanket, buttoned them, returned to the living-room. She had half a package of cigarettes left in her purse. She smoked one. It was a little time before the presence of the radio impressed itself.

News. She tuned in softly, barely a whisper, tried for wavelength. She could get only two stations, one had records, the other a soap opera. The records, interspersed with advertising, identified the source as Santa Fe. She sat there all morning until an eventual news broadcast. There was no mention of a missing girl nor of a murder.

She was comforted but apprehensive. Unless someone intruded she would do as she planned, remain here for two or three days. She wouldn't starve, she wouldn't freeze. Once so long ago she had waited seven days in an empty house in occupied France. Part of that time with only a few cabbage leaves to gnaw. Luck had returned to her. There were even books here. She took one about the southwest, pushed a chair near the window but out of sight if anyone came to peer. Nothing broke the stillness of all the day save the muffled radio. At the evening news broadcast she listened but nothing of local import was given. When night fell she knew more about the territory between this village and El Paso. She had studied the map. She returned to her bedroom after supper, hooded the bed light with a blue bandanna from her hostess' drawer, read until she was sleepy.

The second day was without falling snow. A watery sun fell through the sky for an hour's interlude before leaden clouds engulfed it. Her nerves were unreasonably taut. Once the phone rang. She counted slowly until the sound ceased, leaving a greater void of silence. And once someone came whistling to the front door. She heard him coming. She was in the coat closet before he rang the bell, until a long time after he had gone away. She ate early, cleaned up after her. She didn't go upstairs until after the nine-thirty news broadcast. There was still no mention of her or of Jacques. In her bedroom she looked out the window at snow and darkness. She even went into the front room where she could see the road. She counted two cars at intervals. Across on the corner there was golden lamplight in a room, a child sprawled in a chair with a school book.

She returned to her own bedroom. Tomorrow she'd better leave, not push her fortune longer. Wait for darkness, make her way into town. The bandanna over her head, the levis, the mackinaw. She'd have an easier time getting into the hotel than in the blanket. Watch the lobby for a safe moment, get her parcel, leave. She wouldn't need to return to her room. She undressed, folded her clothes over the chair, ran water for a bath. It relaxed her. Her own underthings were clean and dry now, she put the young girl's down the laundry chute. Her unknown fairy godmother would never realize that she herself hadn't dropped them there. Julie Guille in ancient times wouldn't have known.

She slipped into the bathrobe, brushed her hair before the dressing-table mirror in the almost blacked-out light. Only a person who had lived with silence these days would have heard the sound. Someone outside the house below. She turned off the light swiftly, stood, ears pointed for sound. It came. Someone circling the house. More than one person. At the rear now. Voices muffled. She snatched up her clothes, fled into the closet, dressed there. She even put on the mackinaw, tied the bandanna about her head. Gun in right pocket, torch in left. The purse was a hazard. She emptied it, stuffing its contents into the deep pockets of her levis.

The sounds were in the house now. She knew who made them. Not the women of the house. The rightful occupants wouldn't murmur, wouldn't walk softly.

There were no back stairs. The windows were high above the ground, too high for escape. She was trapped. Unless she could make it down the front stairs before the intruders started up. She couldn't. She knew by rustle they were even now in the living-room. She could wait until they came, hold them at bay with Jacques' gun. To what avail? To run with this pack biting her heels? She couldn't escape them that way. There was only one chance now of escape. It was ancient; in the time of Euripides it couldn't have been new. Sometimes it worked; that was why it was remembered. More often it didn't. If it didn't, she would submit. They weren't using the lights below, no reflection shone on the snow outside. They planned to take her unawares. Without sound she opened her bedroom door, the full way, the way the other two bedroom doors stood. She flattened herself not behind it but against the wall on the other side of the opening. Normally they would search first in the guest room, the one at the head of the stairs, not in her center room. They would hunt together because they must know she was armed. She waited. She heard the step on the stairs, saw the faint glimmer of a torch. She listened to the plush of their steps at the head of the stairs. They did enter the first bedroom. She waited further, until they were inside that room, advancing to the inner bath. Now! In that moment she moved, moccasin-footed, softer than they, a dark shadow in a dark corridor. Soundless, rapid, down the stairs. The front door at the left. She opened it. And she heard the thick voice, 'My gun is pointing at your spine. Close the door quickly and do not move.'

She hesitated. One eel-like twist and she could be outside, running. She couldn't run fast enough. Not with two, no, three of them now. They hadn't come on foot. And Schein would welcome a chance to use that gun. A suspected murderess attempting to escape. Killed by the real murderer.

Because she had ridden behind his bull neck on the night he killed. He might shoot her now before the others could come downstairs. She put full force into her closing of the door. The bang echoed like a shot in the quiet house. She didn't turn, she stood rigid.

The cry 'What—' came from the upper hall. Running steps now. No attempt at quietness. Blaike and whoever was with him. The torch a pond of light on the stair carpet. 'Turn on the lights.' It was Blaike who called as he ran. And it was Albert Schein who said with grisly satisfaction, 'It is all right. I have her covered with my gun.'

She didn't turn until Blaike snapped on the hall light, said, 'So you were here.'

'Isn't that why you came?'

It wasn't Popin with him. Popin wasn't in this. It was a member of the police department, ugly gun in ugly holster, a dark bewildered face. 'I wouldn't have believed it. Mrs Anstey, she never would have believed it.'

Julie said, 'I haven't hurt anything. I'll pay back everything I've borrowed. I've kept a list. I'll have the window fixed.'

Blaike told the policeman. 'You check it over with these people. We'll see they suffer no loss. And thanks for your cooperation, Sena.'

'Wait a minute.' Her voice didn't come out strong, demanding. It quivered. She appealed to Patrolman Sena. 'You aren't going to arrest me?'

He said, 'If it was me alone I'd have to arrest you. But the F.B.I. has first call these days.'

'F.B.I.?' She looked at Blaike's amused smile. She looked at the gloat on Schein's face. 'They aren't F.B.I.'

Blaike said, 'I'm afraid we are, Julie.'

Sena believed them. The implications of his belief covered

his simple face. He was more than a little proud of helping the secret service. She couldn't prove to him that they were impostors, foreign agents masquerading as government men. Their credentials must be perfect; they had passed muster of the police. She risked an answer scornfully, 'Why would the F.B.I. want me?'

'Merely for questioning,' Blaike stated. 'Come on.'

Schein said, 'First we take her gun.'

She handed it to Blaike, said, still scornfully, 'You needn't check. It hasn't been fired.'

He put it in his overcoat pocket. 'This way.' His hand was strong under her elbow. She walked proudly, head erect, as if she weren't bludgeoned by defeat. An officer waited in a police car outside the wall.

La Fonda lobby was as always sedentary. The hatted house detective raised a knowing smile. Flanked by Blaike and Schein, Julie walked to faint music back to the elevator. The same pretty Spanish girl, uncurious. Up to third. The death walk to Blaike's room. She wouldn't be detained long in this hotel. Held for questioning. Not by the F.B.I. By the Gestapo. She knew that sort of questioning. How long before death would be a boon, how long before she would be screaming for its release? What did they want to know? But of course they didn't want to know anything. They didn't even want to kill her. They wanted to return her to Paul Guille.

Blaike held open the door. She stood motionless. 'Enter,' Schein barked. She walked inside.

'Your coat?' Blaike took it. 'Sit down.' He pushed forward the arm chair. Schein took the straight one by the desk.

'Drink?'

'I am not a drinking man,' Schein repeated.

She said, 'No.' The percussion of fear beat over every inch of her. She was colder than she had been that night in the snow. Begin. Get it over with.

He poured a small Scotch from a bottle. 'You'd better take it. You need it.'

She swallowed it slowly. It put a false warmth into her. She asked, 'How did you find me?'

'Someone reported a window broken at the Ansteys'. I have been working in close cooperation with the police. The fact that it was stuffed with newspapers from the inside meant something. And some neighbors mentioned they thought they'd seen a bit of light.'

She asked, 'You aren't of the F.B.I.?'

'I assure you I am. If you want to examine my papers, go ahead.' He took them from his inner pocket, held them out. She ignored them. He replaced them. 'Schein has been working for us as a counter-espionage agent in Yorkville. Both of us after one thing.' His eyes narrowed on her. 'You know what that is.'

She shook her head.

'The Blackbirder.'

'I know nothing of that. Only what you yourself told me.'

Schein said, 'You were with Maximilian Adlebrecht the night he died.'

She turned to him, looked him up and down slowly from the pasted toupee to the black box toes. Distastefully. Then she said, 'You killed him.'

He was as motionless, as potbellied, as a plaster Buddha. He said, 'The police send me after you. They have found a brown coat in a locker. A coat like that one worn by the girl with Maxl. There is much blood on it. They have found a pair of gloves, the palms covered with blood. Brown gloves. In a trash can. They have found out a Juliet Marlebone is missing from an apartment on West 78th Street. There is a postcard sent from Chicago by Juliet Marlebone. If you did not kill him, they wish you to answer questions.'

She repeated, 'You killed him.'

Blaike broke in harshly, 'Did you see who killed him? Did you see him die?'

'No. Certainly not. I said good-by to him at my door. When I was upstairs at my window I saw him lying on the pavement. Dead.'

'You heard the shot?'

'I heard nothing. Not even a backfire.'

'Yet you knew he was dead?' Schein asked heavily.

'I knew. He wouldn't have been lying on the walk—' She could see him as if he lay at her feet now. 'Not in his good coat. Not unless he was dead.'

'You knew he was going to be killed,' Schein stated.

'No. How could I know that? What are you trying to say?'

He said it heavily, chunkily. 'Your appearance with him in that suspect pro-Nazi rathskeller was for him the kiss of death.'

'Oh no!' The horror of it spread over her face. He didn't mean an accidental betrayal; he meant a deliberate signal: this man is to die. She appealed to Blaike, 'You don't believe that, do you? You can't believe that. Why would I do that?'

'That's one thing we want to find out,' Blaike said. 'Why Maxl was killed.'

She closed her eyes. What if they were truly of the F.B.I., actually believed that? What could she say? She knew nothing.

'Jacques,' Schein's voice accused. 'Did you kill Jacques Michet?'

She shook her head, kept shaking it.

'If you did not, why did you not report to us what you found? Why did you run away? Why have you been hiding? Why was Jacques killed? Who is the Blackbirder?'

She didn't say a word.

Blaike took over. 'What did Maxl tell you that caused him to die? What did Jacques tell you? Why did you come to Santa Fe?'

She broke in, 'I don't know. I don't know anything about this.'

'You don't know why you came here?'

'Yes. Of course I know that. I don't know about those deaths.'

'Who is the Blackbirder?' Schein thudded.

Why did you come here? Why did you meet Maxl? Who ordered it? Who is the Blackbirder? What did Jacques tell you? What did Maxl tell you? Why did you kill Jacques? Why did you run away? Why? Why? Who is the Blackbirder?

She had stopped trying to answer. The questions were darts hurled harder and faster at her, the target. She wasn't wearied. She wasn't frightened. She was angry but she controlled it now. Once on the outskirts of Lille she had been questioned for two days. At the end of that time her questioners had been more exhausted than she. She had shut her mind, sealed it in an inner compartment of her consciousness. Even as she had it shut away now. In that far-away other world she had known the purpose of the questioners. She didn't now. Within the closed box she tried to understand. She couldn't. Not without knowing who these men were. She could figure out something more important, escape. For of course she must escape from them. When she had the blueprint she closed her eyes, leaned weakly against the back of the chair.

Blaike believed it. At once his voice was kind. 'Here, Julie. Drink this.' She opened her eyes child-wide, took the glass of water. 'Thank you.' She didn't know if Schein also believed. He was biting the end from a cigar. She finished the water. She said, 'I'll tell you what I know. It isn't much.'

'That's the girl.' Blaike's smile was human. He took the glass, passed a cigarette, lit it.

She kept that wide innocent look in her eyes. 'I've told you most of it already. I knew Maxl in Paris. Not well. I don't remember where I met him. He was at the Sorbonne—I don't know whether a refugee or a fifth columnist. He never discussed politics with me. I met him by chance that night—a week ago last night, wasn't it?—at Carnegie. After the Russian Relief Benefit. I thought it was chance. Maybe it wasn't. Maybe he had been looking for me.'

'Why do you think that?' Schein's pig eyes horned at her.

She shook her head. 'I didn't until you F.B.I. agents insisted he had something to tell me. Actually he didn't.'

'Nothing about blackbirders?' Blaike asked.

'No, nothing.'

'He didn't speak of the Blackbirder?' Schein demanded.

He knew. He had heard; an underling waiter had reported scraps of conversation.

She said, 'Oh, yes, we spoke of him. All refugees do.'

'And why do all refugees speak of him?' Blaike asked.

'Because'—she lifted her head—'because when a refugee runs away from torture or death he can't always make arrangements to reach a place of safety. He hasn't time. Nor influence, nor money. And even if it is against that just but merciless thing called the law, the Blackbirder is doing something that refugees consider above the law. He is helping the helpless.'

'For a price,' Schein sneered.

'Perhaps,' she defended hotly. 'There's bound to be great expense in a venture of this sort.'

'You do know something about it.'

She looked quickly, startled, at Blaike's slant smile. 'But I don't. Only it's logical. He'd do it for nothing if he could, but he can't.'

'Who is the Blackbirder?' It was Blaike saying it this time.

'I don't know.' At his skepticism she repeated, 'I don't know. I thought from something you said that it was Popin but I don't believe a man who knows nothing of mechanics could fly a plane. Do you? It might have been Jacques. But who would kill him? Not those he helped. The F.B.I.?'

'That isn't the American way of solving lawlessness,' Blaike stated.

'I don't know who the Blackbirder is. You can ask me that over and over but I can't tell you. I don't know.' She listened to their silence, still skeptical but not denying her. 'Shall I continue?'

'Yes. Go on.' Blaike walked to the table. 'I'm going to fix a drink. Will you?'

'No, thank you.' She repeated what she had said before concerning Maxl's death. 'I ran away because I was afraid. I was afraid the police would think I did it. Because I had been with him.'

'And why did you choose Santa Fe?'

She would not mention Fran. She would not mention her fear of government investigation. Her hesitation was only momentary. 'I told you I was afraid. I didn't want to

be locked up. I couldn't stand it. Once I was locked up—'
She broke off, wet her lips. 'I came here because I thought
I might need the Blackbirder's help.'

'You knew he was here,' Schein pounced. Smoke clouded
his heavy face.

'I didn't. I mean, I didn't have certain knowledge. Don't
you see?' She ignored him, turned to Blaike. 'I didn't even
know there was a Blackbirder, not really. It's all been whispers,
a legend, something a refugee believes in because he needs
to believe in it, because he might have a desperate need for
such a man some day.'

'To escape a murder charge?' Schein pointed.

Her mouth hardened. 'To escape Gestapo agents who
somehow manage to reach this country despite the F.B.I.'

Blaike's voice was quiet. 'Couldn't it be they enter by
such a method as blackbirding?'

This was why the F.B.I. was searching for the Blackbirder.
They couldn't chance the entrance of dangerous aliens
among honest refugees. Nor the escape of dangerous aliens
over the same route. Somehow she hadn't thought of it that
way. The Blackbirder to her had been only a shadowy figure
of refuge. He was still that but a sinister blackness darkened
his shadow. His helping wings could be abused. She shook
away the tremor.

Blaike went on casually, 'So you came to find the
Blackbirder. You didn't know about him, only so vague
rumors'—suddenly he whirled on her—'yet you knew
whom to seek! Popin!'

She must walk softly. Whatever these men were she mustn't
jeopardize Popin. He was her one link with Fran; with
Jacques gone, he was the one hope of escape for her and
Fran. If she said Maxl told her of Popin, it couldn't hurt

Maxl. But possibly it could endanger the bearded artist. She remembered what she had told Blaike on Tuesday night. 'He was kind to a friend of mine. I thought he would help me if I needed help.'

'And you didn't know he was part of this blackbirding?' he mocked.

'Not until you said it,' she retorted.

'What did Jacques tell you?' he countered.

'He didn't have the chance to tell me anything.' She was truly bitter for that. 'You interrupted.'

'He was in your room at least thirty minutes before I interrupted. You didn't just sit and look at each other for that time.'

'No.' Her eyes closed. 'No, we talked. We talked of his wife, Tanya.' She looked him full in the face. 'She was my friend. She died in a concentration camp. Because she was my friend.' She stood up then. 'We didn't mention the Blackbirder. You can believe me or not. I'm very tired. I'd like to go to my room if I may. Surely you can wait until morning for anything more. I've told you all I know.'

She swayed while he probed her face, steadily, searchingly. She endured the scrutiny. And he accepted her weariness, her honesty, her innocence. He said, 'I'll be right back, Schein. I'll see Julie to her room.' She didn't refuse him. Nor did he question her using her own room. They went up the corridor. 'You have your key?'

'Yes. I carried it with me.'

The corridor was silent. 'You were in the Indian's home at Tesuque?'

She didn't reply. She remembered Soledad's borrowed clothes left at the Ansteys'. She couldn't involve Porfiro and his family in the danger of Gestapo interrogation or of F.B.I.

Later she would evolve some way to retrieve the blanket bundle. Perhaps Popin would see to it. After the Ansteys returned.

Blaike said, 'Give me your key.'

She dug into her blue jeans, handed it over. He opened the door, returned it to her, preceded her into the room, switching the lights, examining bathroom, coat closet, balcony. He looked at the bed but not under it, no one could hide under a bed set that near flush to the floor. 'Seems to be shipshape.'

She wondered. From whom did he think she was in danger other than himself and Schein?

He started back to the door but stopped m front of her. 'Why did you accuse Schein of murdering Maximilian Adlebrecht?'

'I know that he did.'

'But you didn't see the killing?'

'No. But I know. There was no one in the street but Maxl and I and the taxi driver. Schein was the taxi driver. I saw his ears.'

He almost laughed at her.

'I rode behind him from Yorkville to 78th Street. I know his back. There was no one else around.'

'Did it ever occur to you that your cab might have been followed?'

'It might have been.' It would have occurred to her if she hadn't sat at a table while the waiter watched her and Maxl.

'I'd be careful of accusing anyone of murder without proof. I'd be careful even if I felt certain of my beliefs.' It was deliberate warning. She accepted it without comment. At the door he said, 'I wouldn't try to run away again if I were you. The police have your description. Two of them have had a good look at you. And you know you'd be in the local hoosegow tonight if I hadn't insisted on custody for my own purposes.'

She said nothing.

He turned again, shot the question. 'What do you know of Coral Bly?'

Her bewilderment was entire. He didn't even wait for the obvious answer. He closed her into the room.

4

She hadn't dared look at her wrist before. She didn't want to appear interested in the time. They must believe her beaten. A little past eleven-thirty. The endless questioning hadn't consumed two hours. And they'd learned nothing that could help or harm whether they were F.B.I. agents or the Gestapo. They couldn't be F.B.I. No matter how expert in their roles. Not even with their omission of Gestapo questioning methods. There were questions she could ask of each of them. Why did you pretend to be an R.A.F. flyer? Why did you serve as a waiter? She knew the answers: the better to go about our actual affairs, my dear. As an R.A.F. deserter, meet the Blackbirder face to face. As a waiter listen in on suspicious conversations. But the same replies would be valid if they were Gestapo. They could not act openly in a country at war with theirs.

Why hadn't she asked them: Do the police know of Jacques' death? Because she had feared the answer, feared that it had been suppressed for their own purposes. She was afraid to be curious. They might toss her to the law for punishment.

Would the F.B.I. leave her in her own room, alone, unguarded? Possibly. If the exits were closed, the outgoing roads patrolled, few in a small town; the means of transportation watched. Yes, they might do just that. Because they believed she knew the Blackbirder, and, given hemp enough, might lead them to the man. She smiled at her watch. They didn't realize she would lead them to no one. Not even if she knew the Blackbirder. She would return to Popin. And she wouldn't be followed. The artist would not deny her the information which evidently he had denied to Blaike and Schein. He could trust her. He would bring her to the Blackbirder. Because of Fran.

She hung Jacques' coat over the chair, removed the bandanna. She brushed her hair, put on lipstick. Boldly she opened her door, closed it with normal sound. Blaike was in his doorway before she reached it. She said defiantly, 'I'm hungry. And I'm going downstairs to get something to eat. Do you object?'

'Not in the least.' He smiled. 'Mind if I go along?'

'If there's no choice, I don't.' She smiled to herself waiting in the corridor while he spoke to Schein, rejoined her. She walked almost gayly to the elevator, rang for it. She slapped her dungarees. 'I've seen girls in these in this town who in Paris wouldn't be caught in a blackout without their Mainbochers and real pearls. It's a strange place, isn't it?' That was what the woman on the train had told her. They entered the elevator. 'I'll have to shop in the morning—with your permission. Or will you join me? I can't live forever in a borrowed shirt and pants even if it is the vogue. I seem to have mislaid my other clothes.' She wondered about that parcel at the bus station. Did the police have it? It didn't matter now.

They walked up the portal to the lobby. She said, 'I'm

stopping at the desk for some money. I gave what I had away.' She went directly to the gray-haired woman. He didn't follow too closely. He was there but he was dividing interest with persons in the lobby.

She said, 'I'd like to get my belongings.' She dug into the jeans for her coin purse, removed the receipt, passed it across.

The woman brought the envelope while Julie signed for it. She tore it open, boldly took out the money belt and removed some bills, rolled it again and thrust it into a pocket. Blaike was watching now but it didn't matter. She prattled blithely, 'I always divide my money when I travel. Once I didn't. On the way to Ostend. I had to walk the streets until I could get word through to Paris. La Cantina? They advertise a supper.' It was twenty minutes to midnight. 'My rations have been pretty scant the last few days. I'll buy you supper, too. I've never been tailed before. Isn't that the word? Not openly, I mean. I have been followed.'

He asked, 'How old are you, Julie?'

'I was twenty-two in June.'

'So young?'

She said quietly, 'Not so young. Some things make you grow old quickly—death is one. The death of your country. And your friends.' La Cantina was scarcely a quarter filled. They found a table. She said, 'If you don't mind shall we eat without question, as if we were friends? I'm really very tired. Tomorrow—tomorrow you may start all over again.'

'All right, Julie.' He gave the order, two suppers. 'We'll pretend we've just met. We're two normal, healthy, happy—'

'Americans,' she finished. 'Only Americans are even a part of that today.'

'You're in college. I'm training at Kirtland Field. Or is there a war?'

'There's no war. Not anywhere in the world. No one wants war. There aren't even madmen or greedy opportunists who want war. We're both in college. I have on a pink sweater and a blue skirt and those brown and white oxfords American college girls wear. Like the girl I saw in here the night I arrived. She was young and pretty and—and safe.'

He said, 'Watch it. You're forgetting.'

'I'm sorry. I won't again.'

'You will.' He spoke soberly. 'You can't help it. We are in a war. We can't forget. It's better that way. Until we can finish the job. We'll talk of after the war. What do you plan then? Back to Paris?'

'I'll never go back. I couldn't. It died for me. I wouldn't want to live with ghosts.' She began to eat. 'I'd like to stay here. I'm not really French, you know. My name is Marlebone. My father and mother were Americans.'

His fork touched the plate. 'Not—not Prentiss Marlebone?' His face was wondering.

'Yes. I used my uncle's name, Guille, because it simplified matters. He and Aunt Lily were my guardians. I lived in their house. Aunt Lily was my mother's sister. Both my parents died in an accident when I was very young. I don't remember them.'

'Prentiss Marlebone,' he repeated. 'No wonder you were Ritz Bar.'

She apologized. 'I know. My father was a wealthy man. Enormously wealthy, I believe.'

'One of the great American fortunes. You're the only heir?'

She nodded. 'My father was an only child, son of an only child. I don't know of any others.'

'No wonder—' He broke off suddenly. He said, 'No wonder, your uncle didn't want you to escape him. He was your guardian, you say?'

'Until my twenty-first birthday. But he didn't administer the Marlebone estate. The bank did that. I was sent an allowance each month. Paul administered the allowance.'

'I'll bet.' He attacked his steak. 'And if anything had happened to you, Aunt Lily would be your heir?'

She raised her eyes quickly. 'I don't know. I never thought of that. You mean if I'd been—' She shook her head. 'No. He wouldn't have done that. Just to get the money. It wouldn't have done any good anyway. Not with the Nazis in Paris. The bank wouldn't have sent American money to Nazi-controlled France.'

'You're pretty lucky that was the case,' he stated dryly. 'And that you had the guts to run away. Maybe you've illusions left about Paul, Duc de Guille. But five'll get you ten he'd turn his own mother over to the Gestapo for money.'

She said, 'You seem to know Paul.'

'Observation plus case history. I never met the old buzzard. I'd say you're lucky to be in America.'

'Yes. Lucky.' She should have been able to say it with heart. He didn't realize that although to all refugees America was the land of hope, to all the hope couldn't be fulfilled. Some were too deeply smeared by evil before they arrived. Some were Guilles. She had thought Fran lucky to be safe in this country. Now he was in an unknown prison. She herself was an uninvited visitor, deliberately, maliciously entangled in two murders. She and Fran wouldn't even be lucky if they could get away. They would still be hunted. They were among the lost wood children of the present debacle, doomed to wander on and on until the invading ants were exterminated.

She only half heard Blaike's remarks. Something about Midas. Something about not caring for anything unless it were made of gold. He was still talking of Paul. She answered without consciousness. 'He cares about only one other thing. His son.' It was out of her mouth. She had been determined not to mention Fran. Vaguely, intuitively she had known under pressure that Blaike and Schein had angled for that name.

Blaike's eyebrows were skeptical. 'That a fact?'

It was. Paul had two gods. Money and son. And because of his greed—greed alone had welcomed the Nazis—he had lost both. Her money. His son. She wanted him to know. Some day he would know what rewards he and his breed had reaped.

Blaike wasn't allowing the name to be flung aside now. He asked, 'Exactly what relation is Fran to you?'

She pretended not to understand the import of that. She hesitated. 'Blood relation? None at all. He was Uncle Paul's child by a first marriage.'

'You knew him well?'

'But of course.' Know him well? Know Fran well? She remembered the first time she had seen him, a slight, dark boy of about ten years. She couldn't have been more than three or four. His shining brown eyes. His laughter when she pressed on him the golden-haired doll, her cherished doll. She had fallen in love with him, blindly, totally, hopelessly from that baby moment. The Prince Charming of her little girl years. The hero of her school days. And the realization in those few years before war foreshadowed that she had grown up to him, could meet him on equal terms.

He was the only one of that family whom she knew at all. Not Aunt Lily, living only to preserve her own exquisite shell. Not Paul with nothing in his vain, mean face but the coddling of his own expensive whims. Not those two who had deliberately welcomed the conqueror as a preservation of their own decadent ways of life. She knew Fran, yes. She knew his answer to the Nazis who had come to him in American refuge, demanded he join with his father. One answer, the acceptance of prison instead.

She was wasting time here. She yawned. 'Sorry. I'm falling asleep in your face.' She put out her hand. 'I invited you to dine with me, sir. And I still owe you bus fare.'

He held the check. 'You can pay another time. You're under my care tonight.'

They left the room, started back to the elevator. He said, 'How did you come to know Fran so well?'

'We grew up together.'

'He didn't live with his father.'

'Not after he was older.' She raised her eyes. 'Did you truly know him?'

He nodded. 'Believe it or not, I did, Julie. I lived in Paris a good many years.' He laughed. 'I even met you once. And you don't remember. You were a regular Conover queen. If you don't understand that, I'll say it this way. You were one of the loveliest youngsters I ever laid eyes on.'

She flushed. She was embarrassed at her embarrassment. It had been three years since anyone had remembered the Julie who was young and lovely. She said somberly, 'I don't look the same. I'm not the same. I'm surprised you remembered her in me.' And she asked, 'That's why you were on the train, isn't it? Because you remembered. And that's why you came into my compartment. Because I'd changed so. Because you weren't certain.'

'That's about it.'

They passed his door, went on to hers. She asked, 'How did you know I'd be on that particular train?'

'I didn't.' He took her key from her, opened the door, repeated his earlier search. 'All trains, buses, the airports were being watched. I hunched Grand Central. Those who don't know New York well usually gravitate to it. It's better publicized.'

'But you were on the train.'

'Only just before you, when I saw you approaching the gate.'

'How did you get a ticket?'

'I didn't need one. A place would be made for me on any train I wanted to take.'

He must be a government agent. And was it because he wanted her on that train that she too had been able to procure a ticket? And why did he allow her to set out on this journey? She knew but she wanted statement. 'Why were you following me?'

He looked long at her before he answered. 'I hoped you would lead me to the Blackbirder.' He didn't appear disappointed in his hope. He went away jauntily despite his limp.

6

She had everything now to leave for good. It had been so simple. She unloosed her belt, fastened the money bag about her waist. The necklace shimmered safely in its compartment. Her pockets held all necessities, even the flashlight she'd inadvertently carried from Ansteys'. She sat down on the bed, consulted her watch. Ten past midnight. Plan a half hour to get to bed, to sleep. No longer than that. He still believed she would lead him to the Blackbirder. But not tonight. He believed she would go to bed tonight.

At twenty minutes past she turned out her lamp. There was no sound in the corridor outside. Unfortunately no keyholes or transom. Perhaps fortunately. She couldn't look out but no one could look in. She opened the windows. The balcony below hers was dark, the small courtyard darker. If Dame Fortuna held the wheel, it was safe. By easy stages. Thirty minutes past. She put on the mackinaw, fastened it, bound her hair in the bandanna, climbed through the windows onto her tiny balcony. No one in sight below. Blaike's windows were on the other side of the corridor overlooking the patio. She straddled the rail, clung to it with her hands, lowered herself to the one below. All quiet. Another drop, not too far to the ground. In the darkness here she couldn't be seen. A padlock and chain fastened the gate leading to the street. Danger now. She moved wirily, boosting herself up on the chain, climbing over, dropped rapidly to the street. The normally deserted back street. Deserted now. She didn't hesitate; she turned left, up the narrow pavement, past the convent, walking quickly, quietly, purposefully. Around the corner, the Cathedral shadowy across. She met no one. There were cars, not many. She looked in each as she passed. No one seemed to lock a car in this town. She tried the third. Keys in the ignition. Enough gas registered. Calmly she drove away.

No one tried to stop her. Around the Plaza, up the wide street past the City Hall, the police headquarters. Round the Federal building, out on the Tesuque highway. The road was passable now. Mountains lowering on either side. They couldn't hurt her. She didn't think failure; she was certain of success. Blaike wouldn't try to reach her until morning. The trip downstairs had accomplished both planned purposes. Retrieval of her possessions, lulling of any suspicion Blaike might have of her this night. Over the crest of the hill, no lights following.

In the morning he'd waste time looking for her, checking with the desk, the bus, the airport, the highway patrol. He wouldn't believe she dared run back to the place from which she'd fled. Before he checked on Popin she would be hidden. Popin must have hidden other refugees. He would keep her out of sight until the Blackbirder could fly.

Tesuque. Such a short journey now. And on. She wasn't certain of the turnoff. She clocked it, about four miles. It was there. This side road was still snow-packed but without danger. No one was hunting her tonight. A mile and she turned in to the lightless house. Popin might be sleeping.

She knew his bedroom window. If she couldn't rouse him otherwise, she'd rap on it.

She went up to the front door, let the heavy knocker thud. She waited, watching the road. It remained quiescent, dark. The door opened just a little and she saw his face peering into the night. He didn't recognize her when she pushed inside. She suddenly realized. The bandanna hiding her hair, the work jacket, the pants. She cried softly, 'Popin, it's me. I got away from them,' and then she saw over his shoulder by the firelight into the living-room.

Without volition she began to tremble. Her knees turned to water. Within her there was a wrench of physical pain. She moved one step, another. It was true. Her cry was broken. 'Fran—oh, my dear—Fran!'

He rose uncertainly when she pushed past Popin, stumbled down the step, across to him. He didn't know her, not at first. His voice came wondering, disbelieving. 'Julie—it's Julie.'

She was in his arms tightly, never to leave them again. She couldn't speak, she couldn't move. She kept whispering his name as if it had been lost from her as he had been. 'Fran—Fran—Fran—'

He spoke at last. 'Why, darling, you're shaking all over.' He set her away. 'Sit here. You're frozen, poor child. Popin, bring some wine quickly. Let me help you.'

Fran here. It was Fran. Free. Removing her bandanna, pulling off the jacket, instilling strength and courage and love into her again. She clung to his hand, 'Don't go away.'

His brown eyes were laughing. 'Silly little goose. I'm just going to put these things aside. Here, drink this.'

Popin held out the glass to her. But it was Fran who took it, brought it to her lips. Fran.

She cried to the small bearded man, 'You helped him escape! Why didn't you tell me you had planned this? I've been so worried.' She explained to Fran. 'He couldn't tell me. They were always here. I didn't Lave a chance to talk to him. And I had to leave. Jacques—'

His sensitive mouth moved. 'Popin told me.'

'The others.' She started up. 'Bolt the door. They might discover I've gone.' Fran didn't understand. Nor Popin. 'They found me. Blaike and Schein. I ran away from them. I couldn't be locked up. I had to stay free. I had to get back here to ask Popin to help you escape. But he'd already done it.' She smiled at the artist. 'If I'd known—' She stroked Fran's sleeve. Prison hadn't broken him. It must have been a western one where he could work out of doors. He was tanned and strong. He'd grown bigger. The muscles under his coat sleeve were hard.

He said, 'Haven't I often told you, do not worry for me, Julie?'

She nodded. She loved him so much, the ache of it burned hot. 'But always I do, Fran darling. You were locked up so long. And I was afraid you would be hurt. But you aren't.' She smiled a little. 'I think it agreed with you.'

His face darkened. 'Let's not talk about that, Julie.'

'No.' She didn't want to see his anger, not tonight. 'We must get away, Fran. As quickly as possible. Those men— Blaike and Schein—say they're from the F.B.I. I don't know. I think they're Nazis. I know one thing. Whatever they pretend they're after, I think they're looking for you. They've questioned me and questioned me tonight—'

'About what?'

'About the Blackbirder. But underneath I knew there was something else. They wanted me to talk of you. And I didn't. I didn't mention your name.' Only that lapse with Blaike. Nothing dangerous. She sat very straight suddenly. 'I understand now. They know you've escaped. That's what it is. They're looking for you because you've escaped. To send you back to prison. Nazis or F.B.I.—either way—they don't want you free.'

His hand smoothed her hair. 'I believe that's about it, my sweet.'

'You know them?'

'Popin told me. They came here asking questions.'

'They killed Jacques.'

'I'm afraid so'

'Because he wouldn't talk. Because he wouldn't betray you. Oh, Fran.' She turned in the chair, looked up at him. 'We must get away. Before it's too late. If we can get in touch with the Blackbirder.' She appealed to Popin. 'You know. You must ask him to take us out of the country quickly. I have the money to pay for it. Whatever he wants.'

'You have…? But of course.' Fran stood away from the chair, looked down at her. His eyes were bright. 'It hadn't occurred to me. The estate—'

'It isn't the estate. I couldn't go to the bank.' She laughed. 'I didn't know what bank to go to. You can't imagine how many banks there are in New York, Fran. Paul never told me which it was. He wanted to manage my affairs without interference.' The bitterness tasted in her mouth.

'How have you lived?'

'I've worked. I've learned how to work. And—' She savored the surprise. 'I have the necklace.'

He didn't seem to understand. 'The necklace?' The import of it reached him. 'You have the de Guille necklace?'

She nodded.

'How?'

'I took it, Fran. Before I left. Because I wouldn't leave it for the Nazis.' She shut her lips. She must be careful. She couldn't tell him, not yet, that his own father was one of them. Give him time for peace first.

'Where is the necklace, Julie?'

'Here. I'm wearing it.' She laughed up into his puzzled face. 'Not where it shows, silly.'

He shook his head, unbelieving. 'You're an incredible child, Julie.'

'Not a child now, Fran.'

'No, no longer.' His thoughts were years away. His eyes turned back to her. 'But you are tired. And I keep you here talking.'

'There is so much to say, Fran. I have so much to tell you.'

'Not all in one evening. We will have time.' He smiled. 'The rest of our lives to talk. You must sleep now. Popin.'

She had forgotten the bearded man nodding by the fire. His head perched awake at the call.

'Julie may remain here?'

'Anyway you wish it to be, Fran.'

'Upstairs?'

'Yes.'

'There's a fire laid?'

Popin nodded.

Fran turned to her. 'Come along. I'll go up with you.'

Popin bowed. 'Good night, Miss Julie. Pleasant dreams.'

'Good night and thank you. Thank you so much more than I can say.'

She went hand in hand with Fran to the upper room. He lighted the fire. 'You'll be safe here.' He stood above her, bent suddenly and kissed her mouth. 'Good-by, dear.'

'You're not going?' She was seized with sudden panic. 'Where are you going?'

'I don't dare stay here, Julie. Don't you understand the danger I am in? Escaped from internment. I would be shot if I were found.' He put his arm about her. 'Don't be frightened. Popin has a hiding place for me back in the hills. I must stay there until we can get away.'

'You aren't coming here again?' She clung to him.

'If I can, yes. If Popin thinks it safe. Tonight he believed it was. Yet I don't know. Suppose it had not been you at the door. Suppose it had been Schein and Blaike?'

She whispered, 'Suppose they come for me.'

'Popin will take care of you. Do as he says. He knows the ways of these affairs better than we. We can trust him.'

'Yes.' But Popin could not stand up against the gray man and the waiter. Fran didn't understand. He didn't know the ruthlessness of these men. She asked, 'If he weren't here and they came?'

'He'll leave Quincy, the Indian boy, on guard. I'll warn him. You will be safe. I would not leave you unless I were certain of that.'

In his arms she believed in safety. She closed her eyes. 'I have been so alone without you, Fran.'

'We'll be together again soon.'

'For always.'

He said solemnly, 'Until death do us part.'

She spoke with simplicity, 'You know I have always loved you. All my life.'

He held her silently for a moment. 'Now I must depart. You will go quickly, to bed and to sleep. You have no luggage.

There are pajamas in the bureau. I know. I have slept here. A little large for you. But they must fit all sizes. Popin has many calls. Goodnight, dear one. Until soon.'

She wanted to cling but she let him go, listened until his footsteps descending were soundless. She closed the door, leaned against it peacefully. This was a dream. She'd wake in the morning in the West 78th Street hovel, in the empty Anstey house, in La Fonda with Schein and Blaike across the hall. A dream, yes, but it could be held as long as she was in this blessed sleep.

It was a dream but she blocked the door as Blaike had demonstrated. The windows were inaccessible, a sheer wall to the ground below. She would be safe tonight. The diamonds—she'd meant to give them to Fran. But it was better that she retain them for the present. His danger was the greater. If he were taken again, she'd still need them to help him.

2

She was awakened by rapping at the door. The windows showed morning, the sun filtering through a gray flannel sky. Panic gulped in her. Not this soon! She slipped from bed; the bright blue pajamas fell over her hands, crumpled at her ankles, as she approached the door. Her voice was atonal. 'Yes?'

'It is I, Popin. And Reyes with your tray.'

She opened to his bright voice.

'Good morning, Miss Julie. Reyes, you will put the tray there.' He might have been an innkeeper, the posture of his hands, the round of his brown corduroy shoulders. The Indian girl was already placing the tray. She knelt to the fire. When thin smoke arose, she pushed to her feet, padded out without looking back. Popin waited until she had gone. 'I thought it better that you remain here until after our friends pay us a visit.'

'Won't they search?'

'Search my home?' It was incredible.

'But they are F.B.I. They say they are that.'

Popin said, 'I believe I can handle them. If not, there will be ample opportunity for you to move.'

She doubted. This room was isolated. The only way out was down the front staircase. Fran had said trust Popin. There was nothing better that she could do now.

'Very well.' She smiled at him. 'Fran is safe?'

'Yes, indeed. I will leave you to breakfast now. It is wise you lock your door as you have. Do not worry.' He closed the door after him. She blocked it.

She didn't dress until after breakfast. The sun was truly breaking through. If watery, it was good to see after these days of monotony. She realized quickly it was more than good; it meant ceiling, and ceiling meant the Blackbirder would fly again. She was restless for action this near the end of the journey.

She readmitted Quincy with an armload of piñon logs, Reyes to collect the tray. The girl said, 'I bring you the paper. Anything more you will ask me.'

'Thank you. There's nothing I want now.' Nothing but Fran. And she must wait. After waiting so long it shouldn't be hard. It was. It was more grueling than before. Because he was so near. Why couldn't she be with him in his hideout? Perhaps if she asked Popin. She must do as told. It wouldn't be for long.

She again bolted the door. The paper was Friday night's

from Santa Fe. She sat down to read it. War news with more hope in it. Local news. A paragraph. Jacques Michet, Tesuque workman, found dead. Believed he had been attempting to repair telephone lines at the home of Yosif Popin. Tesuque artist. Lines down by storm. Dead several days.

She pushed the paper away. No police investigation. No suspicion of violence. Simple accident. Who had suppressed murder? Who could but Blaike, Schein, cooperating with the police. But why? Too obvious. One of those men was the murderer. He had taken in the other as well as the small-town police. That wouldn't be difficult. What connection had Popin with the suppression? Was he—could he be a third in their plan? Fran said trust. She must trust.

She heard the car, the thump of the knocker. She crept to her door, listened. She couldn't hear voices. Too far away. She went back to the chair, lifted the paper again, reading unrelated items with eye not mind. An hour. Two hours. She hadn't heard the car go away. She remembered only then the car she'd taken last night. Where was it now? Were the police searching for it? She jumped to the knock at the door. Her voice wasn't her own. 'Yes?'

'It is Reyes.'

Fearfully she opened the door. The girl was alone, again with a tray. She said, 'It is early for lunch. Popin say bring it now while they are not in the house.'

'Who is here?'

'The man in gray. The fat one came earlier.'

She hadn't heard his arrival. 'The car—the one I came in—'

'Qi'in Tse took it away early.'

She nodded. She need not have been disturbed. Popin

took care of things. Of persons. Of Jacques. She said it aloud. 'Jacques?'

The girl's eyes were without feeling. 'He died.'

'I know.'

'He was buried yesterday. There was no one to mourn.'

I mourn. I, helpless, mourn. 'Reyes, he didn't fall.'

'Popin said so.'

'Who told him to say that? Who came?'

Reyes walked to the door. 'Is there anything more you want, you ask me.'

'Jacques?'

'I do not know nothing what happens here.'

Julie quickly bolted the door after her. Reyes saw nothing, said nothing. For that reason she continued to work here. Julie ate, waited long. There were books but she couldn't read. At long last she thought she heard a car. Popin did not come. Reyes did not return. Julie walked the room. She sat quietly lest her steps be heard below. She walked again. It was early dusk. No one came. At five she could endure the silent tension no longer. She opened the door a silent crack. The hall was in darkness. She couldn't be seen. She heard the muffle of voices from the living-room. Her ears ached with listening. She took one step, another, and suddenly she recognized the voice. Fran's! It was safe to go on. Fran wouldn't be here if it were not safe. She started down quickly. Halfway she saw into the lighted living-room. Yes, Fran. Fran and a girl. An exquisite girl, copper hair ruffed about her small face, a beautifully curved leg, a silken leg, pointed to the gray whipcord leg of Fran's.

The girl's voice was precise. 'I see nothing ridiculous about it.'

'But darling.' He said darling. His thin brown hand was

under her hair. Julie didn't move, didn't take breath. 'It is so ridiculous.' He spoke with an accent; he had no accent.

'Ridiculous? That you take this girl with you to Mexico and refuse to take me?'

'Listen, my sweet. I take her to Mexico. It is the least I can do. She is in trouble. She is so distant a cousin but she is that. I cannot refuse to aid her. She is young, helpless.'

'Why can't I go along?'

'Coral, please. Have not I told you? There is so much freight I must bring back for your father. There will be room only for myself on the return. Why must you be so unreasonable? I have told you this girl means nothing whatever to me. I take her to Mexico. That is that. I pick up the freight. I return here. Two days' time. Can you not give me two days' time?'

Julie stood rigid. The sickness was all through her, in her lungs, in her knees, in her mind and heart. She watched his hand turn the face of the lovely girl to his, watched him bend to her. Julie didn't close her eyes. She watched the kiss.

The girl pushed him away, not soon, not with impact. 'You can't get around me this way, Spike. Experienced as you are at that sort of thing. If this girl means nothing to you—'

'I have sworn it, Coral. Shall I swear it again?'

'Don't bother.' The copper of her sweater was against his sandy tweed coat, pressed hard even if the voice was cool with hidden laughter. 'I know very well if she did mean something to you, you'd swear it just as fondly.' The cigarette between her scarlet lips was thin and white as a stiletto. 'I can't see that she is. A poor cousin throwing herself on your doubtful mercy. And for some reason you're willing to help her out. She must have something on you.' The girl's scarlet pointed finger touched his cheek sharply. 'You see, darling, I have no illusions about you, none at all. I know you'd dispense with me without regret if something came your way that equaled me in looks, in willingness, and in fortune, And knowing all that, Spike, I still'—the word cracked like a whip—'want you, and intend to have you.'

'There's only one thing wrong in that, Coral. I would dispense with you only with great regret.' His voice held that bantering tenderness Julie knew so well. Eye to eye now, suddenly shattering the tension with laughter, moving together. Julie closed her eyes. She mustn't watch again. She'd been a fool, an utter, hopeless fool. This was the kind of woman he'd known always in Paris. She had believed he could turn from one like this to her gaucherie, her inexperience, to her who had nothing to offer but blind adoration. Fran didn't want devotion, undying love; he wanted something to whet his skill. She stepped softly, upward one step, another. She kept backing up with that clear amused voice following her.

'You are a devil, Spike. All the trips you make to Mexico but you won't ever take me. Always an excuse.'

'Your father has told you.'

Julie was backing up to what? To isolation of a room again. She'd been tricked into staying there. Not because of danger for Fran—the girl called him Spike—but because she must stay out of the way, leave the house to Spike and his woman. The gray man had asked, 'What do you know of Coral Bly?' He had known of her. He had known of Julie's betrayal.

She couldn't return to that upstairs cell. She couldn't wait there for Fran to call, 'Ready.' To believe his lies. To believe they were escaping to Mexico together, would remain together. To pretend to accept the plausible tale he would have for her when he left her there. But she had to get to Mexico. Her danger hadn't diminished even if Fran was safe. She would accept no favors here, none from him. She would find her own way to safety. She could trust no one here, not again. Jacques had been murdered and the newspaper reported accidental death. Someone was evil here. Blaike and Schein weren't strangers to Popin. All had worked together to keep her from embarrassing Fran in his new life.

There would be no escape from that upper room. What must be done must be boldly, chancily. She was at the top of the stairs now. She drew breath, breath that hurt all through her. She ran down again quickly, turned into the living-room, stopped short. She said, 'Oh Fran. I didn't know you were here. I'll be back in a minute. I left something in the studio.' She too could lie in her face, in her throat. She went on past them. She didn't look at Coral Bly but she saw every particle of the exquisite copper girl. Without turning back she went on into the dining-room, through the kitchen where Reyes prepared dinner. The Indian girl raised black eyes to her and returned them to the vegetables. Julie went on, out the kitchen door into the dark dusk. She shivered. Jacques' coat was upstairs. She rounded the house. There was a lean low touring car in the drive. Coral's car. There were keys in it. Only mechanically did she move. She touched the handle of the front door, refused it. She opened the back door, got down on the floor and pulled the heavy lap robe over her. If she were discovered she had no resources. She didn't care. Fran would get rid of the girl quickly now. He wouldn't accompany her; he'd remain to force his lies on Julie. She wouldn't be there to listen. She would be riding to the highway with Coral. To reach the highway, that was why she was huddled here, prone on the cold floor. She knew better. She was here to talk to Coral Bly.

She heard their voices now. She couldn't see but they were approaching the car. Coral said, 'I think you're making a mountain, Spike. What if she did see me?'

'I promised her. No one would see her. I must explain.'

'You'll be up right after dinner?'

'Absolutely, darling. You explain to Kent why I can't make dinner tonight.'

'An old friend.' Her laughter and a decision. 'If you're lying to me, Spike, I'll cut your heart out.'

'I adore you.'

The whir of the engine, the car leaving the drive. Julie lay there, bracing herself so no sound of her body could be heard. She waited long enough before cautiously rising. Speak not too soon, not too late. Her head lifted to the top of the seat. Higher—until she was mirrored.

Even then Coral didn't notice at first. She must have sensed before she saw. Her voice was hostile but there was fright underlying it. 'Who are you back there? What are you doing?' She was pulling to the side of the road, slowing the car, obviously not knowing what she should do.

Julie said, 'I just wanted a lift.'

'You'll have to get out—' Her voice broke. 'You're—'

'Yes, I'm the girl.'

'Why?'

'I wanted to ask you something.'

Coral was brusque. 'Well, ask it.' But she was nervous. She fumbled for a cigarette, half turned in the seat, let the match lift to Julie's face. She wasn't so nervous then. She must have seen in it hopelessness, gullibility, an idiot child. 'Ask it. And then you'd better get back. Spike will be looking for you.'

'How long have you known Fran—Spike?'

The girl was puzzled. 'About two years.'

'Has he been in prison any of that time?'

'Certainly not. How absurd!' Her eyebrows lifted.

'I mean—interned.'

'He is French. Why under the sun would he be interned? He was here before the war started.'

'You're certain of this?'

'Of course, I'm certain. He's been working for my father for almost two years.'

Julie knew. She had known it on the steps. She should have known last night. He didn't have the prison look.

'Is that all?' Coral Bly asked. 'If so, you'd better get back. Spike can't protect you if you're trailing about the country. I'd take you. But I'm late as it is.'

'Does he want to marry you?'

'I don't see that it concerns you. But as you ask—' She was brittle. 'We will be married soon. We'd be married now if it weren't for his foolish pride. He has the old-fashioned idea that a husband should be able to support his wife, after her own fashion. When his Parisian estate is released—and it doesn't look as if it would be long now—we will be married. Now, if you'll please get out—'

Julie's hands clenched in her jeans pockets. Clenched on the flashlight still there. She opened the left-hand door. Coral had her hands on the wheel again, the engine running. Julie didn't plan. She opened the door of the car and she brought the flash down hard on top of the copper head.

Coral weaved and Julie hit her again, not too hard, but correctly, behind the ear. The girl slumped in the seat. She was out. She'd be out for at least half an hour. Julie tugged the coat from her, heavy beaver, laid it on the seat. She went to the other side of the car, took the lap rug, laid it on the ground there at the side of the road. Coral was taller than she and dead weight. But Julie pulled, tugged, edged, supported her until she was out of the car, rolled in the blanket. She wouldn't freeze. She'd come to. It was she who would walk back to Popin's.

Julie slipped into the fur coat. It smelled of mimosa. She shut her teeth. The Riviera and mimosa blooming. Fran beside her. She sat behind the wheel and drove away. She hadn't wanted to hurt Coral. She needed this car.

She had wanted to hurt her. She had wanted to hurt her the way Coral had made her hurt. She'd wanted to kill the beautiful, arrogant girl. She hadn't killed her. She hadn't touched her. Coral would go back to Fran's arms. She mustn't think of Fran, of Coral. A half hour and a little longer and the alarm would be given. She drove straight to Santa Fe. She didn't stop. She went through the town and out on the Albuquerque highway. South. To the border. She'd been alone before. She'd been alone a long time. Not this way. Not in desolation. Before she'd had the dream of Fran.

The road went on and on endlessly over the deserted mesa. The moon was out now, misted but shining. It wasn't until then that she realized. The ceiling had lifted. And Fran was the Blackbirder.

Even now the alarm for her return might be given. The police sent to patrol the road. On and on. Not many cars but each one a menace. Through a town, a gaudy and drab

Mexican town. Go on. She switched the radio. She knew the Albuquerque station from the Anstey radio. There was music, no police bulletins. The sky glow of Albuquerque. She took the cut off road into town. On and on. The gas gauge was low, almost empty. She couldn't press on without gas. She couldn't buy rationed gas. She saw a parking lot, drove in. The attendant took the car, gave her a little stub. She walked away, one block to the main street. There were buses, a few cars. There were soldiers idling, laughing girls. Two M.P.'s swinging their clubs. Men and women. There were voices in English, voices in Spanish. There were picture theaters and restaurants, drug stores, shop windows, everything bright. For the moment she was covered by the city. She selected a larger restaurant, ordered coffee and a roll. She wouldn't take time for more. She must get away before they caught her. She'd added another crime: assault on an innocent girl. She was afraid to ask about the Greyhound station; she looked in the telephone booth, Fifth and Copper. She didn't know where Copper was but she wouldn't forget the street. The color of the girl's hair. She found Fifth, standing on the corner she saw the station a block away. She walked quickly to its doors. She didn't enter. The bus station would be the first place watched. She turned, crossed to the dark corner opposite. She was helpless, hopeless. She couldn't run any farther. She was caught. This was the end of flight. She couldn't have endured it this long, all the violence and despair, the loneliness and terror, but that at the end of endurance Fran was waiting. He was waiting no longer. The spirit in her had died.

This shadow where she cowered was a spired church. Marked with the cross. It would be open to the weary, the oppressed. She could rest a little before they came to take her. She went inside. There was scent of incense, she remembered then it was Sunday night, vespers must just be over. She slipped into a back pew, lowered her forehead to the cold, unyielding wood. If she could but remain here, if she could sleep until they came. If she could sleep forever. It didn't happen that way in life. You had to go on, you had to endure the ordeal. To be taken, to be returned, to face Paul's thin cruel mind, to be at his mercy—not have him at hers, as she had planned. She couldn't endure that. Yet she must.

She couldn't. She lifted her head slowly. She needn't. She would go to the F.B.I., the real F.B.I., tell them everything. All about Maxl's death, what she knew of Jacques' death. She could give them the necklace, she didn't know what they would do with it but it would never be returned to Paul. She could tell everything from the very beginning. Everything but Fran. She needn't mention Fran. If she confessed to entering the United States without permission, if she confessed that was why she'd run and stolen and broken into houses and hit a girl on the head, they wouldn't ask about the Blackbirder. There was enough without the Blackbirder. She mustn't close that door of hope to other refugees. Whatever Fran had done to her personally, he was helping others.

She would be locked up. The F.B.I. would intern her. That was the price of breaking the law. You must pay for breakage. It was so little. It couldn't be so bad to be locked up. Not in America. She wouldn't be ill used. There wouldn't be marching gray ants below the prison window. She didn't know she'd been crying until she left the church. She wiped her face, the handkerchief smelled of mimosa. It didn't matter now. Come to me all you who are weary and oppressed. The words were as true as when He said them. Her burden was lifted. There was peace in capitulation.

There was a hotel on the next corner but she didn't enter. She must avoid recognition, avoid the police, until she reached the F.B.I. She chose a bright crowded drug store. The number was in the front of the book. She dialed it. Ring upon ring. No answer. She replaced the phone. No one at the office on Sunday night. She went out on the street. She must hide until morning. Hide where? She wouldn't be defeated now. She started walking, her hands dug into the pockets of her jeans, touching the few bills, the flashlight, the small black book. And out of what seemed a dim faraway she heard the whistle of a lonely train, she smelled the coal soot, she remembered a harsh but kindly voice, 'If you should want to look me up.'

She scuttled to the corner street light to find the address. Professor Otis Alberle, 417 North Hermosa. A taxi, no. She mustn't mark herself, she must remain a part of the crowd. She was shaking now lest she be taken before she could ask directions, reach North Hermosa. She braved another drug store, spoke to the cashier. 'What bus do I take to Hermosa?'

The girl was friendly. 'Monte Vista-Sawmill. Going east.' She pointed. 'Across the street on that corner.'

Julie crossed, stood in the shadow of the cigar store. She wasn't alone waiting. There were four or five others. University girls, uniformed boys, a woman and a small boy. The bus came slowly. Julie climbed on in the midst of the others. She spoke softly to the driver. 'Will you tell me where to get off to reach the four hundred block of North Hermosa?'

'Sure.'

She sat behind him, her back to the other passengers. The mimosa-scented coat collar half covered her face from the window. The wheels crawled under the pass by the

Alvarado, up the hill, past schools, past hospitals, past the wide blocks of the University, on and on into dark residential streets. She was the last one on board. And her eyes were uncertain on the driver. 'You didn't forget Hermosa?'

'No, ma'am.' He was young. He chewed gum. He couldn't be one of theirs. 'You a stranger here?'

'Yes.' She didn't want to talk but he was talkative. It would be more suspicious if she were silent.

'Army?'

'No. University.'

She let him ramble on about the football team, the coach, the war. He said finally, 'Here you are. End of the line.' The bus stopped. 'Up that way. This is Hermosa.' There was one young girl waiting on the corner. She and the driver exchanged 'Hello.'

Julie started up the street. 417. She used the torch. Not this. A few more. This was it. A clipped hedge, leafless now, a small white stucco house, gray in the darkness; a red-tiled roof, black now. There was a wide path, an evergreen garnishing either side of the door. A studio arched window, shades half drawn, the amber comfort of a lamp shining through. Julie took one breath. She walked up and rang the bell.

The porch light beamed. She held her fists clenched. A man opened the door, the same young rumpled professor she'd seen at the station. She asked, 'Professor Otis Alberle?'

'Yes?'

She saw beyond standing in the living-room the grizzled woman, in a housedress now. Julie called, 'Please. It's I.'

The man's puzzled head turned toward the older woman. She came into the hall.

Julie said, 'Don't you remember? You told me should I need—'

The man didn't stop her. She stepped into the hall.

The woman said, 'Why, it's the girl I told you about. The one from the train, Otis.'

Julie said, 'I do need help.' Her voice faded. 'I need it terribly.'

3

The woman's name was Mrs Helm. She said, 'Now whatever you have to tell us can wait until you've had this hot milk. I know when a person's used up. I haven't been a settlement nurse for years in Chicago for nothing. I can tell a person's condition quick enough.'

Her son-in-law had a mild smile. 'I'm sorry we've no extra coffee.'

'Hot milk's better,' Mrs Helm stated. 'Time like this it's better. You drink it up then you can tell us anything you want. I spotted you on the train. I told Otis, didn't I, Otis? I said, "That girl's in trouble. She doesn't want anyone to know but she's in trouble." Cool as you please but every time that man—you remember the one?—looked at you, you shivered. Inside you. I know. I've seen people in trouble.' She broke off proudly. 'I'm a grandmother.'

'I'm a father,' the professor twinkled. 'Don't forget that, Mother Helm.'

'Your daughter?'

'A boy. Three days ago. Both of them fine. I'm staying to help out when Margie—that's my daughter—gets home from the hospital. She'll need me. You can't get help these days. The war. Feel better now?'

'Much better,' Julie said.

The two watched her, waiting, trying not to be curious,

trying to ignore the unprecedented intrusion of something strange in their nice normal existence.

'I'm in trouble,' she began.

'That man?'

'Partly. I want to talk to the F.B.I. They aren't at the office tonight, Sunday, you know. I was afraid to stay alone until tomorrow, afraid if I did I wouldn't get a chance to talk to them then.'

It was like a movie, a cheap book. They were amazed to stupefaction but they pretended they weren't.

'I feel—I feel ashamed coming to you this way. You don't know me. You don't know anything about me. But I didn't know what to do.'

'You did right,' Mother Helm decided. 'And what good are any of us if we can't tell when a person's in trouble and give them a hand?' She looked defiance at Otis.

He said, 'We'll do anything we can, Miss—'

'Juliet Marlebone.'

'Well now, Juliet,' Mrs Helm began, 'you want to stay here tonight. No, it's no trouble at all. There's twin beds in the guest room. I can only sleep in one of them at a time. There's a bassinet, too—that room's going to be the nursery—but you won't crowd me and I won't crowd you. If Otis doesn't mind. It's Otis' house.'

The mild man couldn't have refused the dominant mother-in-law if he'd wished. But he didn't wish. He was undeniably enjoying this vicarious entrance into raw life. It wasn't something that normally dared invade the University cloister. He said, 'Miss Marlebone is welcome.'

'Then tomorrow—' Mrs Helm looked down her nose. 'Are those all the clothes you have?'

Julie nodded. 'I lost mine. I borrowed these.' She took a

deep breath. 'I can't let you do this without knowing that it might make trouble for you.'

Mrs Helm bristled. 'Trouble? Because a friend stays the night?'

Otis was a little dubious. 'You're not an escaped Nazi?'

'Look at her!' Mrs Helm snorted. 'Just look at her and ask that!'

'I'm not,' Julie told him honestly. 'I'm running away from the Nazis. I've been running from them for three years. But I've done things I shouldn't in getting away. There's probably a police alarm out for me now. I hit a woman and took her coat—this one. I only borrowed it but that's hard to prove. And I stole her car—borrowed that too. It's downtown in a parking lot. I'll mail her the stub tomorrow but that won't excuse what I've done. There've been worse things than that—'

'You've not murdered anyone?' Otis was more dubious.

'No, I haven't. But I've seen two men murdered because they spoke with me. You see, I'm not talking about little trouble when I say trouble. I haven't any right to involve you. I hadn't any right to come here. I came because I was desperate. I haven't a friend.' Her eyes were empty. 'Those I thought were friends—aren't.' She held her hands tightly together. 'I don't want you to be in trouble. I don't want you to treat me as a guest. If you'd only let me hide tonight in your attic or your basement. Then you could pretend you didn't know I was there. I wouldn't ask that only I must stay safe until I can talk with the F.B.I.'

Mrs Helm was subdued now. 'You can't have done anything really bad or you wouldn't be trying to reach the F.B.I.'

'I have to tell you the truth. In normal times, under

normal conditions, some of the things I've done would be really bad. Nor am I trying to excuse them. It is only that when you are fighting for your life, and for the life of someone dear to you, you forget values. You do things you know are wrong because you must. No one dies easily.'

Otis' eyes were quiet, understanding. He said, 'We have no attic, no basement. Few southwestern homes do, Miss Marlebone. If we did, we would still offer you a bedroom. And if trouble comes, we'll stand by you, helpless as we will be in the face of real trouble. We can't do otherwise. We wouldn't know how to turn a beggar into the snow.'

'Thank you.' She raised her eyes. 'I want you to know that I was as helpless as you when I left France three years ago. I learned because I had to. To live.'

'We could be forewarned. Who might come?'

Julie said, 'I know I wasn't followed. But the police will have my description. If they can trace me, they might come. Or those men—the ones I believe to be Gestapo agents— they might come. I don't believe anyone will. There's only the driver of the bus to remember me, if it occurred to anyone I might stay in Albuquerque. But no one knows I have'—her smile was small—'friends here.'

'Tomorrow you will see the F.B.I.?'

'If I remain free until then. Do you think they would be willing to come to me? They do go around to investigate tips. In New York they once called on a woman I knew. I'm afraid to appear on the street. By tomorrow the police will all be waiting for me. If the police get to me first, I won't reach the F.B.I.'

Otis was dubious again.

'Because the police in Santa Fe believe that Blaike—the man in gray—and his friend are members of the F.B.I. They believe it so entirely that they released me in the custody of those men last night. I know them to be connected with the Nazis.'

Professor Alberle wound his watch. 'I have a class at nine and one at ten. If you like, I'll get in touch with the F.B.I. for you after that. I think I can explain to them. And you will remain here with Mother Helm tomorrow morning? Shell take care of you. I vouch for that.'

'I'd just like to see that man in gray turn up.' She nodded ill cess to him. 'I'd just like to lay eyes on him—'

Julie's eyes filled. 'You are very good. Both of you. Perhaps some day I can thank you.'

'Nonsense! Come along to bed now. You can have one of Margie's gowns. She's about your size—'

'She was,' Otis grinned. 'Nine months ago. It's a wonderful baby. Eight pounds, eleven ounces.' He held out his hand. 'Don't try to say thank you, Miss Marlebone. When it's all over won't I make the faculty senate pop out their eyes telling them about this!' He was a little wistful. 'Of course, they'll never believe me.'

7

Otis phoned before noon. 'I talked to one of the F.B.I. men. Jimmie Moriarity. Either he or Duke Palmer will be out sometime today to see you. I hope you don't mind'—she could see the apologetic smile—'I'm afraid they think you're a little cracked. But they promised to come today. I told them it was something about spies.'

She thanked him, handed the phone over to Mrs Helm. She returned to the ironing board in the kitchen. It had been a good morning. She and Mother Helm had cleaned the house like dynamos. She ironed now while the woman made apple pies. This was what she'd have some day. A small and friendly house in a young city. A city where the sun was bright. Where the people were nice people, the kind who made pies and ironed shirts. She'd have dresses like this yellow print of Margie's which she was wearing and she'd sing while she ironed. She didn't sing now. She listened to Mrs Helm talk. She followed Margie from the day she was born until her child was born. She followed Mrs Helm, widowed early, raising a child and helping other women to raise their children. Mrs Helm was neither cheerful nor uncheerful. She was matter-of-fact. She talked and she worked.

She returned to the kitchen. 'Otis eats lunch on the

campus now with gas rationing on. War!' She clacked plates on the kitchen table. 'Some day we women will get hold of this world and there won't be any more war. Women can settle each other's hash without slugging it out with fists or bombers. You wait!' She asked again, 'You actually lived in Paris? You saw those dirty Nazis?'

'Yes.' Julie didn't want to talk about it any more. She folded the shirt. 'There. Not as good as you'd do it. But I've learned pretty well. I worked in a laundry for a while. In Havana.'

'You've been about everywhere.'

Only the beaten track of a refugee. It wasn't romantic. It was dread.

They lunched. They washed up after. And they sat in the living-room under the pall of waiting, listening to the news on the radio: no description of a hunted girl. Reading desultory items in the morning paper: no mention of Julie. There was no more housework to be done, nothing to busy the hands. Mrs Helm pawed with a piece of blue-gray knitting but her needles were spasmodic. There was nothing to do but wait. The older woman said frankly, 'Any other day the phone would be ringing its head off. Kept me running to tell about Margie's baby. Not today.' She sighed. 'It would be something to do.'

No phone calls. No door chimes. And then they sounded, musical, muted. Julie jerked in her chair. Mrs Helm whispered, 'Let me go. It might be them. It might be—it might be a snoopy neighbor.' After two o'clock.

Julie remained out of sight listening.

A man's voice. 'Miss Marlebone is here?'

'You're from the F.B.I.?'

'Yes.'

No! The cry stuck in her throat. She had recognized the voice too late. Mrs Helm had him in the little house, at the living-room arch, before Julie could rise and flee.

'Here he is at last, Juliet.'

She backed away. 'No. Don't you see, Mrs Helm? It's the gray man!'

There was fright on the woman but it wasn't flabby. It was bolstered with decision. She advanced. 'I didn't remember your face. You get out of here. Right now. Before I call the police.'

'I'm not leaving.' Blaike told her. 'Not without Julie.' He stood there, close enough to bar the way if Julie leaped.

'You'd better go if you know what's good for you, young man. The F.B.I. are on their way here now to protect Juliet.'

'I am from the F.B.I.'

'No, he isn't,' Julie said tensely. 'He isn't, Mrs Helm.'

'And don't I know that! Don't worry, Juliet.' Bravely she moved to Julie's side, stood arm in arm with her. 'I'm not going to let him do anything to you.' She attacked again. 'You'd better get out while you can, mister. If you wait for the F.B.I., we'll turn you over to them.'

Blaike laid his hat on the chair, removed his overcoat, smiled the old smile. 'Julie—or you, Mrs Helm—would you mind calling the F.B.I. office? Ask for Moriarity or Palmer. They're the two head men in this territory. I've been with them since noon. Let me speak to them. I'm asking you to put in the call so you won't look for treachery.'

Mrs Helm decided. 'You stay beside me, Juliet.' The phone was in the hall. They had to pass him. He stepped back, still smiling. Julie looked up the number, read it off. Mrs Helm dialed. Waiting was silent. 'Mr Moriarity or Mr Palmer.' Her eyes brandished Blaike in the doorway. Julie's head was a pinwheel. If Blaike were actually F.B.I., where did the pieces fall? Schein and Popin? Fran? Jacques and Maxl? If he were F.B.I., would that office believe her lack of complicity in all that had happened? 'Hello, wait a minute, please.' She thrust the phone at Blaike, pushed Julie away from him.

'Hello. Oh, hello, Jimmie. Blaike speaking. I've located the girl. You'll have to get out here and vouch for me.' He laughed. 'Afraid a phone introduction wouldn't do. She wouldn't believe it. You get out here fast before she changes her mind about talking. Yeah, it's the same girl. The one the Professor called about. Step on it, Jimmie.' He replaced the phone. 'Now, ladies, shall we return to the front room and wait for Jimmie? Because I'm staying right here until he comes. And I'm not letting you out of my sight, Julie.' He bowed them past him. Mrs Helm was reduced to silence, more frightened now. The knitting needles clicked raggedly. Julie sat on the edge of a chair.

'You are of the F.B.I.?'

'I am.'

'How did you find me here? Did they call you?'

'No. The police located Coral Bly's car this morning. I flew here at once; fifteen minutes it takes. I had Professor Alberle's name before I came down.'

'But how?'

'Everyone you spoke to on your trip west was checked, Julie. Even porters, railroad conductors. The woman with whom you had many conversations on the train was, shall we say, double-checked? The F.B.I. is thorough, Mrs Helm. We learned that you were visiting a daughter and a son-in-law here, that your daughter was going to have a baby, that there was no possible connection between you and Julie Guille.' To her puzzled frown he amended, 'Juliet Marlebone.'

Julie said nothing.

'With Coral's car located here and no further trace, it was worth taking an outside chance on inquiring your whereabouts from Mrs Helm. Particularly since she passed an address to you on the Belen train.'

'You noticed that?'

'Julie, believe me, I could relate to you every breath you took from New York to Santa Fe. It'd be a pretty dull performance but I could do it.'

'What you said was true, you were following me?'

'Yes. I've been on the Blackbirder case for almost two years. When I saw you with Maxl, I knew I'd struck pay dirt. You'd lead me the rest of the way.'

He had been wrong yet right. The Dame had favored him.

'You know why. You know who the Blackbirder is.'

'I know now. I didn't last night—night before last.' She thought of the weary wait this afternoon. 'Why didn't you come sooner?'

'I had a good many things to check over with the boys before I came. You wouldn't run out this time. You'd given up.'

She said, 'I couldn't run any farther.'

'You understand that now? You can't escape your destiny no matter how fast, how far you run. Eventually you've got to face it. It's better to meet it before you've depleted yourself, while you're still strong. You'll never win by retreat unless it has meaning and purpose, it's to gather up strength and take a stand.'

There had been meaning and purpose when she fled Paris. There hadn't been in these latter days. Selfish fear wasn't good enough. She'd rationalized but she'd been rudderless even before she knew of Fran's defection. She hadn't had enough knowledge for planning; ignorance had weakened her, and in her weakness she'd hidden away in New York, excusing inaction as circumspection, caution; her only shield, flight. She should have attacked; she should have forced knowledge of Fran's whereabouts. Not waited for the letter to the Ritz, his last known address, to be forwarded and answered. She should have asked questions, demanded answers. She had been afraid. For her personal safety. Afraid that what had happened, would happen? She'd been running even while standing still. She should have known Fran wasn't in prison. He wouldn't have had to smuggle out an innocent letter, and the letter, as far as governments were concerned, had been harmless. He could have given an address. She knew that American concentration camps weren't bastilles of horror as in brutalized Europe. Yet she had believed, waited, too tired from flight to think straight. She would have waited forever. He didn't intend her to turn up to spoil his game with Coral, more important, his Blackbirding. He would never have written again. Only by accident would they ever have met in this vast country. He would exercise care about accidents. Just as when he knew she was in Santa Fe, he remained out of sight. It was sheer accident that she had escaped and returned to Popin's. No one would have expected her to return to the scene of the crime.

The doorbell sounded. Blaike said, 'I'll get it.'

Julie nodded. 'He's what he says he is, Mrs Helm. I was wrong.'

Jimmie Moriarity was tall and sandy, a little stooped, without illusions. 'Here I am, Blaike. Where's the girl?'

Blaike made introductions. 'Jimmie knew me in

Washington before he was transferred here, Julie. I want you to examine his credentials as well as mine. I want you to talk without fear. We are members of the Federal Bureau of Investigation.'

She looked over the papers. She didn't need the reassurance. She knew. Mrs Helm held out her hand, studied the sheets, returned them.

Moriarity asked, 'You're the same girl Professor Alberle phoned about?'

'Yes.'

'What's the dope?'

She said, 'I want to give myself up. I came into this country on a false passport.'

'Blackbirding?' Blaike asked.

'No. By way of Havana. Even if I'd believed your credentials in Santa Fe, I'd have run again, Blaike. Because the F.B.I. was after me just as much as the Gestapo. But last night'—she shrugged—'I decided to turn myself over to the F.B.I. I'll tell my story.'

Blaike said, 'That's not important now. We have to get back to Santa Fe.'

The residue of doubt of him remained although she had certain knowledge. He had had Jacques' death suppressed. She said, 'Not until I say what I'm going to say. I want it all on record, on F.B.I. record.'

Blaike told her, 'I know most of it. I've told Jimmie most of it.'

She repeated stubbornly, 'I want to tell it.'

Moriarity looked at Blaike for orders. She saw that. The Santa Fe police had done the same. She wouldn't leave until she'd said it. After that, if Moriarity wanted to let her go with Blaike, she'd go. She couldn't do otherwise.

Blaike said, 'Go ahead,' and she heard the click of the front door. She stiffened.

It was only Professor Alberle entering the hall. He apologized. 'I thought I might be needed. I hurried home.'

Mrs Helm said, 'These are the F.B.I. men, Otis. Only this one'—her hand jabbed at Blaike—'is the gray man too. You come in and keep quiet. Juliet's going to tell about it.'

His eyes quickened. That was why he had come. He was on time for the show. He faded into a chair.

'I'll try to be brief as I can. My father was Prentiss Marlebone. He and my mother died when I was a baby. My mother's sister and her husband, Paul Guille, raised me. Perhaps you don't recognize that name. Your State Department would. He is a friend of Laval's. I escaped from his house the night the Nazis entered Paris. I took with me a fabulous diamond necklace, the de Guille necklace. It had been in the family from the time of Louis the Twelfth. I didn't want the Nazis to have it. Uncle Paul was a traitor. When I was stealing out of the house, I saw him and Aunt Lily drinking toasts with the Nazis, toasts to the fall of France.' She went on. 'It took me more than a year to get out of France. As soon as Paul knew I had escaped, he sent the Gestapo after me. Because of the necklace.'

'And because of your money,' Blaike said. 'He was your legal guardian until you were of age. You were only—'

'I was nineteen. I could never have escaped without Tanya, the maid, and her friends. She wouldn't leave with me. She stayed behind to help others. They found her—and they killed her.'

The scratch of Moriarity's match was livid.

'It took me almost another year to reach Havana. I was there a long time. I had no visa.'

'An American wouldn't need one,' Moriarity said.

'I don't know what I am. I was born in Persia. I lived in France for sixteen years. I had never been in America. From Cuba I wrote to the one person who could help me reach the United States.' She held her lips firm. 'My cousin, Francis Guille. I wrote him where he'd last been, a New York hotel. It was months before I heard. He was in an American internment camp as a dangerous alien.'

Blaike leaned forward, eyes crackling.

'Nazi sympathizers had—had framed him—because he wouldn't collaborate. The letter was smuggled out of prison, mailed from Mexico by a friend of Fran's, a man named Popin.'

Blaike's mouth was open.

She ignored him. 'I knew then I had to get to America. I had to free Fran. I also knew I couldn't hope for a passport. If I told who I was, a member of the Guille family, I'd be returned to France or interned. I bought a false passport and I came to the United States, to New York. I wrote Fran again, to the same hotel, to be forwarded. I knew eventually it would reach him as my first letter had. I found work. The good jobs—defense jobs—were closed to me. Because I was an alien. I waited. Months. And months. And then one night—' She broke off. It wasn't months ago, it was only ten days past. 'I was at Carnegie Hall. I saw a boy I used to know in Paris. I didn't want him to see me. But he did.'

'That's Maximilian Adlebrecht,' Blaike interpreted.

Moriarity nodded.

'Yes. Because I didn't want to make him suspicious, I went with him to a beer garden in Yorkville.' Her eyes widened. 'I noticed a waiter watching me. He didn't move.

He just stood there and watched. He looked like a Nazi. I know what a Nazi looks like. I've known them. I was taken by them many times while I was trying to escape from France.'

'Steady,' Blaike said.

She swallowed. 'You know what happened. After I left Maxl, he was killed. In front of my house. I ran away. I knew if I were questioned, the police would find out about how I came into the country. I knew the F.B.I. would be in the case because Maxl was a German refugee.'

'He was a German agent,' Blaike said.

'He may have been.' She sat straight. 'Before I ran I took a notebook from his body. It had my name and address in it. I spent that night in the subway.'

'All night?'

'Yes. The next day I left for Santa Fe.'

'And why did you choose Santa Fe?' Blaike's voice was easy. She lied. She wouldn't talk about the Blackbirder. 'Popin's name was in that notebook. He was a friend of Fran's. I wanted to find Fran.'

Moriarity said, 'You didn't know the F.B.I. was looking for Fran Guille as hard as you were?'

'I believed Fran was in prison.'

'O.K.'

'That first night in Santa Fe I saw another friend of Fran's. Jacques Michet. He pretended not to know me. Somehow even talking with me meant danger to two men. Jacques came to my room that night, secretly. He told me I was in danger. He didn't get to tell me why. Blaike interrupted.'

'Get this straight,' Blaike charged. 'I was following you. As far as I was concerned that made me responsible for your safety. I didn't want you liquidated under my nose. I didn't know Jacques from Adam. I only knew he was part of Popin's outfit. Why did you skip out of Popin's?'

'Because Albert Schein was the man who had watched me in Yorkville. I knew he'd kill me that night.'

'What made you think that?'

'Because I knew he'd killed Maxl. And he knew that I knew. I went out to Jacques' house. Jacques would protect me.' She faltered only a little. 'Jacques had been murdered.' She turned to Blaike, accused. 'You saw Jacques that night.'

'I saw his body.'

'You let them call it accident.'

Blaike said, 'I was posing as an R.A.F. deserter. You know that. To get at the Blackbirder. Popin decided if the police investigated a murder the blackbirding activities would come out. He persuaded Schein and me it would be wiser to make an accident of it.'

'You let them do that to Jacques?'

'Temporarily, yes. The most important thing has been to get Fran Guille, the Blackbirder. The murder can be taken care of later.'

Professor Alberle said, 'Some of this I don't understand.'

'Shshsh.' His mother-in-law's eye fixed him.

Julie turned to Moriarity. 'I don't know what I should have done when I found Jacques. I ran. Again. That's all I've done for three years. The Indians hid me that night. Later Blaike and Schein found me. I got away from them and went back to Popin's. Fran was there.'

'You saw him then?' Blaike asked.

'Yes. I thought he'd just escaped from prison. I didn't know he'd never been in prison. Not until yesterday. I heard him talking to Coral Bly.' She said wearily, 'I couldn't take help from him—the way things were. I hid in her car. And then I bopped her. I borrowed her coat and her car and started for Mexico. When I reached here I realized I couldn't make it. I hadn't enough gas.' She looked at him. 'I wasn't going to tell about Fran. Only about the passport. Being locked up didn't matter any more, not much anyway, not as much as getting to rest and being safe from the Gestapo.'

'That's your story?' Blaike asked.

'That's all.'

'You're satisfied I'm bona-fide F.B.I.?'

'Yes.'

'If you aren't, we'll get Washington on the phone and have the big chief o.k. me. I don't want you to have any doubt when you go with me.'

She said, 'I haven't any doubt now. Only Schein—'

'He isn't. I played his game to keep him quiet while I worked on Popin to get at the Blackbirder. There are no records. There's nothing but word-of-mouth transactions and his bank account. I have to get Fran flying someone in or out, someone who can't travel any other route. I hoped he'd take me. But Schein has become suspicious of me. I don't know if I can work it. You can. No one is afraid of you. That's why we're going back.'

'Going back to them?' She shook her head. 'No. I can't do that.'

'Why not?'

'Don't you see?' He must see. 'I know what it is to be hunted, not able to reach a place of refuge. I can't close up any channel of escape to refugees, even if it isn't legal.' She was weak but firm. 'I simply can't do it.'

'My dear Julie, do you still believe the Blackbirder helps honest-to-God refugees?' He was exasperated. 'From the beginning he's flown for one purpose only, to bring into this country those men and women whom Paul Guille and his bosses want brought in—saboteurs, fifth columnists, Gestapo agents, spies. My God, you don't think any true refugee could afford to pay from one to ten thousand for a blackbirding seat, do you? Those are Fran's prices.'

She begged, 'Are you sure?'

'She asks am I sure!' Blaike appealed to Moriarity. The latter grunted. 'Listen, child, it's so sure a thing that I was smuggled out of a French concentration camp in a dead horse for one purpose alone, to catch the bird.'

'You were imprisoned too?' She couldn't keep horror from her voice.

His was steady. 'I didn't get the bum knee—yeah, it's legitimate—following pretty girls to Santa Fe. Nor from a Channel crackup either. I was on duty in France for five years before the war. My front job was in a news service. Matter of fact, I actually was a reporter before I decided that snooping for Uncle Sam was more important. I didn't run out of Paris after the fall. No one was supposed to know about my extracurricular work but someone with a Boche haircut did. It takes a good many able-bodied men to effect a rescue from a concentration camp, Julie. Do you think any government would have risked that to release one small employee if it weren't important? It was important for one reason. I knew Fran Guille. He didn't know me but I knew him. I'd been keeping my eye on him for a long time. Our government found out it was Fran smuggling Nazis into the country. How? Well, we've spies in the inner circles too. But we didn't know where he was, what disguise he'd adopted, and the U.S. is a darn big country to scour. All of our information came from

Paris. We didn't even know what name he was using, or where he operated.'

She said, 'The Gestapo runs the blackbirding.'

'No. It's a funny thing but they don't. Fran runs it. It's a business. It's made him a rich man, by the way. I don't know how it started, may have been strictly accidental, say he ran into some old friend in Mexico who wanted a lift to the U. S. and was willing to pay a price. Fran wouldn't bother about politics if the money was handy. There's never been a Guille in history who turned down easy money. Fran couldn't help but see the opportunity for a juicy racket. He was piloting Kent Bly's plane, started doing that a bit over two years ago. Down to the Bly copper mines in Mexico and back again. Essential transportation. Cleared by the War Department over the border and through all channels. I found this out since coming here, of course. Kent Bly doesn't know what's been going on. He gave Fran the job to help out a refugee.'

'And because of Coral,' Julie said.

Blaike ignored that. 'Bly has been too busy on government contracts to make many trips himself. Naturally if he did go along, blackbirding was out. No, the Gestapo hasn't run things. They didn't dare muscle in. There'd be too much risk of closing the whole thing that way. They couldn't get to Bly; Fran was already there. It's Fran's own baby and he's played it smart. He knew the Nazis would spend big money on what they deemed important Fran communicated with his father as soon as he'd made his first accidental blackbirding trip. Paul sent lists of men that the Axis wanted inside, and what their purpose was to be in this country. Fran's orders. The price was scaled to the worth of the traveler. We know. We've seen the lists which the Axis sent to Paul. Fran doesn't have a scrap of paper that incriminates him. A smart lad. But we have him now, or we will, with your help.'

She was calm. 'What help?'

'I'll tell you all about it when we're under way. First thing is some clothes for you.' He eyed Margie's housedress. 'You're going back looking like a million bucks. The way you used to look in Paris when a million was big money.'

'Back to Fran?'

'Yes, back to Fran.'

She shook her head suddenly. 'I can't. Lock me up. Do anything, but I can't.'

'You'll be safe. I'll explain all that.'

'It isn't that I'm afraid.' She repeated. 'It isn't that.'

Moriarity said, 'If you're going to buy the girl some duds, Blaike, you better get going. It's after four. I know how long it takes my wife.'

'I can't do it.'

'You will do it.' The little professor spoke mildly from his chair. 'It won't be easy. It isn't easy to be brave. Not for people like us. We don't know how. We don't ever have to be, not actually. We call it bravery if we go to a doctor or dentist to have him stop a pain. You believe you have been brave in these past years, Miss Juliet. But everything you've endured has been for your own eventual happiness. Now you're asked to do something in itself repellent, to betray someone you love. Not for the reason that totalitarian nations have taught their people to betray each other, not from fear nor for personal gain nor for frenzy over a false god. You're not even asked to do this thing to help yourself. It won't help you. It will scar you. But you will always know it had to be done. It had to be done in order that the hunted

197

ones, the helpless ones who have managed to escape to a new land, may be safe in it. I haven't any right to say these things to you. To betray your instincts takes more courage than I would have.'

She spoke at last into the silence. 'I will go.'
To betray someone you love.

2

The plan was sharp as a bayonet in her brain. She metronomed it as they winged to Santa Fe. Blaike had outlined it at dinner. No one in the Alvarado dining-room would have dreamed that he was offering not devotion as he bent toward her, but a trap for Fran. She was to go direct to Popin's.

'Fran will be there. The hangar is about a quarter of a mile in back of Popin's place. We've held him up this long with storm warnings below Albuquerque and the border. Now we've given him release to take off after nine o'clock this evening. I don't think it will be difficult to convince him that you should go along. He hasn't any fear of you trapping him. And he's been losing money every day of this storm. Don't worry, you aren't actually flying with him. I'll be there before you leave. And he'll either agree to take both of us or neither. Once he's committed, I'll see that neither of us flies.'

'You won't be alone?' There were too many against the gray man.

'I'll have my men in Teṣuque ready to come when I call. I can't take chances bringing them with me to Popin's. Don't be afraid. I've handled other cases alone, Julie.'

'There's Schein.'

'Schein in his F.B.I. role will be helping the state police find you tonight. I've given them enough dossiers to go over to keep them engaged as long as necessary.' He had smiled at her across the table. 'And don't be disturbed about facing Coral's wrath. She and her father are to be held here in Albuquerque—naturally they don't know they're held, they are merely helping—until I release them. She hasn't seen Fran. She was picked up by a trucker, thought it was hit and run. He took her to the hospital in Santa Fe, then reported to the police. When she came to she was hysterical. I was there before her father. I made certain she didn't get in touch with Fran.'

'And Popin?'

'Popin is a wily little Bulgar, Julie. In his previous incarnation he was a minor artist who stooled for the reigning politicos as a sideline. There may have been compulsion that forced him into blackbirding, family in occupied territory or such. But neither Fran nor the Gestapo would have needed that wedge. Not with money to offer. Popin is an opportunist. When he sees which way the straws point he'll save his skin. Just don't worry about the details. All you have to do is honey up to Fran and buy that seat on the black plane.'

All, that was all. And it wouldn't be hard. She looked now the way Fran would want her to look, the way he would have remembered her from Paris if he had remembered. The French-cut, pearl-gray wool, the scarlet spectator coat, the scarlet sandals, the flare of scarlet hat, warm scarlet lips. His eyes would flicker over her. *So long as I was in your sight . . . Burning in flames beyond all measure . . . Untrue Love, untrue Love, adieu, Love!* He would never, not as long as he lived, believe that her betrayal was for any reason but a woman scorned. Nor could there be for her the release of explanation. Otis Alberle had understood.

The private plane landed them at the airport after seven. A cab waited. The man at the wheel was placed there by the F.B.I. Blaike slid from the car at a darkened corner of the village. The car went on toward Tesuque. Her fingertips in the gray doeskin gloves were cold. She didn't think about what lay ahead.

She watched the rush of dark landscape. The driver slowed, dropped her in the road. She walked the few yards, turned toward the house. She laid the knocker staccato on the door.

Reyes opened it. Julie pushed in. 'Is Popin at home?' Her words were clear, bright. She went into the living-room, raising her voice. 'Tell him it's Julie.' She didn't have to continue. Popin and Fran came through the archway, the artist faintly surprised, Fran striding toward her in amazement.

'For God's sake, Julie, where have you been?'

She stripped off her gloves in front of the fire. 'But darling, getting ready to go to Mexico, of course. You didn't expect me to leave looking as I did? In those dreadful overalls?' She laughed. 'I've been shopping. And then I had to get some money.' Her bag was an oblong of scarlet. She opened it, took out the fold of bills. 'Will fifteen hundred be enough to get us started?'

He was suspicious. 'You still have the necklace?'

'Certainly.' She flung her hat and gloves to the table, laid the purse on top of them, handed him her coat. 'You don't think I'd sell the Guille necklace for fifteen hundred dollars, do you? It's worth—'

'Half a million.'

He welcomed her return because she had neglected to

hand over to him the necklace. Only that. She tossed her hand. 'You were at dinner. I've had mine. Go finish.' She curled into a corner of the sofa.

'I've finished.' He sat beside her. He didn't understand her. 'I'll have coffee in here, Popin.'

Popin bowed. The subservient one. 'You will join us, Miss Julie?'

'Yes, if you've plenty.'

'It comes direct from Mexico,' he explained.

Play the game. She mustn't delay. She took his hand. 'Fran, I'm so happy. When do we go?'

He was still puzzled. 'But how could you go in boldly, attend to shopping? Blaike and Schein—'

She laughed. 'As soon as I read in the paper that Jacques' death was an accident, I knew they couldn't hurt me. That's what I'd been afraid of, that the police would question me and find out about the passport. When there was no danger of that, I decided to go to town. I didn't want to bother you. You seemed busy.' Her eyebrows arched. 'So I just went.'

'How did you get there?'

'Walked to the highway and hitch-hiked. That's an Americanism for begged a ride. I hitch-hiked out here tonight too. A doctor at the hotel was driving this way and he brought me along. When can we leave, Fran?'

He began to play up at last. And her fingers were more cold against his warm ones. 'Tonight.'

'Really, Fran?'

'Yes. We are clear after nine o'clock. You see, Julie, that girl you saw me with yesterday afternoon was here on business. She is the daughter of the man I have been working for.'

'You've been working?'

He remembered. 'Since I was released, yes. He's a big mine owner. I've been piloting his plane for him. A five-passenger cruiser.'

She mustn't appear suspicious. 'This man has hidden you?'

'Yes. Hidden me and given me something useful to do. I've had to be careful. I don't use my own name. You may have heard me called Spike. It's an American nickname. And I use Guild, not Guille. The Germans would return me to Paris if they could locate me.'

She looked directly at him. 'You know then about Paul?'

'Yes, I know.' His face was sad. 'I can't explain it. I knew he wasn't in sympathy with the government we had, but to sell out to the Boche—' He shuddered, lighted a cigarette.

If he would only speak the truth to her, she could forgive. It wasn't his fault that he couldn't love her. She began, 'But Fran, you don't want to leave all this, your new work, just because I must get away. You don't want that.'

His eyes were tender. His hands touched her expertly. He knew how to quiet a woman's fears. 'Dear one, I don't want to be here without you. If you must go, I will go with you.' He smiled. 'And perhaps I'm not as altruistic as I would believe. This Blaike and Schein—Popin and I feel you are correct in believing them to be Nazis. If so, they are here looking for me through you. It may be wise I go while there is time.'

If it could be true, if they were actually leaving together, to remain together. No matter how you wanted to believe a dream, it wasn't reality. She held his hand against her cheek for a moment. 'Darling—darling—' It was her good-by to the dream. She turned away, opened her purse, took a cigarette. He held his lighter to it. A thin platinum toy, initialed in emeralds. A Danish countess had given it to him.

Fran had not fled without his possessions.

She asked, 'What will you do about the plane?'

'I'll get someone at the mine to bring it back to Kent. Several men have pilot licenses.'

If he knew what she had heard, he couldn't lie so blandly. But she could appear trusting. He didn't know she too had learned to act a part. She accepted coffee from Popin. She said to Fran, 'I was almost jealous when I saw you with that girl. She was so attractive.'

'You needn't ever be jealous of me, Julie.' His hand on her dark hair, yesterday his hand on copper hair.

'I am though. I've always been.' Whatever she said the hurt couldn't cut any more deeply. 'It's the way women—all women—sort of perk if you so much as walk across the room.' If she could just think of him that way until Blaike arrived, a man, any casual man, whose physical presence made a room electric. Not think of a thin dark boy with gentle eyes who had sailed boats on the pond for a little girl, not really a cousin. Always the best boats. Everything always the best for Fran. He didn't have to ask; it was given him. When war conditions emptied the golden horn, could he be blamed that he chose his own way to refill it? Blaike was right. There was a core of his father in Fran. The elegance of life was too important to the Guilles to allow the means of its attainment to act as deterrent. She had been the means of Paul's riches, of his playing the leader in the Croix de Feu, of his epicurean dinners, his streamlined horses, his platinum wife, his rich man's son. He wouldn't have sent after her if she could have left behind her the fortune for which she, to him, alone existed. He wouldn't have cared if she had starved in a ditch if her departure hadn't meant also the departure of luxuriant living. She was valuable to

Paul alive not dead, to that alone did she owe her escape from the Gestapo twice in France, again here at the hands of Schein. She had been willing to be Fran's means of elegance. But he didn't need her now. He had blackbirding. If that were taken from him he still had Coral Bly, daughter of a millionaire, waiting. He could flick Julie aside.

Dread suddenly plunged into her heart. But he wouldn't do that. He wouldn't get rid of her by the permanent means, by death. He didn't have to do that. She'd give him up. He had never really belonged to her anyway. She saw that with electric clarity. Without having watched him with Coral Bly, she would know it. She wasn't wise enough in the way of men for Fran.

If Blaike would only come, come quickly, end this farce. Blaike hadn't known that her life might be endangered here. She hadn't known it. Even the soft beard of Popin was sinister now. His sleepy eyes were waiting only for Fran's word to open wide. No. It wouldn't be here. Not with Reyes in the house, and doubtless Quincy. Jacques had been killed. Who had killed Jacques? The Indians had been here when the deed was done. They saw nothing, heard nothing, spoke nothing. Jacques was an accident. There wouldn't be a repetition. Why risk discovery, investigation of Popin's house, when so soon she, unprotected, would go willingly into a land where she was a stranger? Where she could so easily disappear. *No!*

Fran wouldn't do it. He loved her. Not as he loved other women, the sleek, sophisticated animals who arched at his touch, but she had been his little sister. He had had love for her. It could not be eradicated by expediency. She would tell him on the plane, he was free to return to Coral. She wouldn't attempt to hold him by any artificial thread that might once have bound them. But there wasn't to be any plane.

Why didn't Blaike come? Fran's fingers stroking the nape of her neck, touching her throat. She shivered not as once she had but in horror. They were sinewy fingers, they might be flexing for strength. Popin's cat eyes blinking at the fire. What had Blaike said? An opportunist. Would he blink at murder if the loot were sufficient? Fran's voice came softly, 'Where is the necklace, Julie? I want to see it.'

Her laughter sounded silly. There was nothing at which to laugh. But she spattered it. 'I wear it. I can't show it to you now, darling. It's safe.'

'But where?' He was insistent. He didn't want to waste time after on a dead body.

Her teeth were chattering. She countered, 'Where do you think?'

'I want to know.' There was an evil strength in him that had been there before, but she hadn't recognized what it was then. She had dismissed it as temper, taken care always not to anger him.

She glanced at Popin, spoke rapidly under her breath, 'In a money belt, of course.' She lifted her voice. 'Fran, how did it happen you sailed to America when you did? Was it that Paul knew then what was coming, didn't want you subjected to it?'

'No, it was business. I told you at Cherbourg that day, remember? Business for the Bank of France. That was why I couldn't take you with me. It was state business.'

'You told me that.' She couldn't be in worse danger than she was. 'But if Paul wanted France overthrown, why was he attempting to save it?'

'Why bother your head?' He kissed her; she didn't allow

her rigidity to be sensed. 'My father didn't want France overthrown, merely the corrupt government of those days. He wished her returned to her hereditary rulers. He took what he considered the best way to achieve that purpose.'

She said, 'I wonder if he believes now that it was best.'

Fran didn't answer at once. Had he heard a car? His reply was soft. 'I wonder. I'm thankful you and I are out of it, Julie. Let's have another drink, Popin.'

She jumped a little as the cat eyes opened. 'Yes, Fran.' He started back to the far table.

Fran said wondering, 'And you never once made contact with your bank, Julie?'

'I couldn't. I didn't know how. Which is it?'

'Manhattan National.' Where she'd held a deposit box. 'A man named Tyler takes care of your properties. Until I talked with him—'

'You talked with him?'

His eyes lidded. 'Yes.' Suddenly he laughed outright. 'That was one reason for the trip, Julie. My father wanted a bigger hand in directing your affairs. Tyler said—but it would not interest you what Tyler said. He was outraged at the idea.' He frowned. 'And outrageous, I must add.' He turned to her gently. 'But you are no longer nineteen, are you, my Julie? You have come of age. You have passed into your heritage.' His fingers touched her again and she was as frozen as if they were angered. And he laughed.

Where was Popin? Had the request for a drink been signal? She half turned on the couch where she might see behind her. She wouldn't be taken unawares. The little man was approaching, bearing three glasses on a tray. She was afraid to take the drink. She put it to her lips and she did not swallow.

Popin sat again by the fire. His voice sounded strange. 'What time is it now, Fran?'

'Only fifteen minutes.' He drank. He said, 'Fifteen minutes, Julie, and we may fly away.'

The knocker pounded against his words. Julie quivered back into the corner of the couch. Blaike hadn't returned her here to die. Fran set down his glass. He was on his feet. He spoke to Popin, 'We are at home to no one.'

The knocker was hullabaloo. If they didn't answer it, she would. She'd leap, run, fling open the door before either man could restrain her.

'To no one,' Fran repeated. His head tilted to Popin. 'Look out.'

Popin crept to the window. He peered between the curtains. 'I can see no one.'

The pounding rose; a voice was heard, distorted by the night.

Popin was uneasy. 'We cannot have disturbance. It is not wise. Someone might be passing.'

Fran hesitated. Julie listened for the knocker. It would come again. He wouldn't have gone without entry. She had to speak. She urged casually, 'Answer it, Fran. We can't listen to that racket longer.' But there was no racket. It had ceased.

Fran's hand was in his pocket. He brought out a small automatic. It lay in his palm. He said, 'I will answer it.'

She didn't move, she didn't scream. She was schooled to wait. Blaike had surely faced a gun before. It wasn't essential to warn him. Fran's feet were jungle silent, approaching the door. He opened it a small space, his hand in his jacket pocket. He opened wider, looked out, closed it. Within her there was anguish. Blaike couldn't believe they were elsewhere; he wouldn't have gone away. He had.

Fran returned alone. 'Whoever it was has gone now.' He reached for his drink. He lounged beside her again. 'Finish your drink, sweet. Warm you up before we leave.'

From behind them the voice spoke. 'Here I am.'

Fran was up and turned, a few drops from his glass splashing on her skirt. She didn't have to turn. She knew the British accent. Popin didn't stir. His eyes were wide.

Fran demanded, 'How did you get in?'

Blaike came forward. He set his small bag by the hearth. 'The back door was open. I pounded at the front but no answer. Figured you must be in the studio. Hello, Popin.' Mild surprise came over his mouth. 'Miss Guille. I didn't expect to find you here.'

She answered with the irritation he had requested. 'I am here.' She turned her shoulder to him, watched Fran.

Popin said, 'Spike, this is Roderick Blaike. Mr Blaike, Mr Guild.' He was nervous.

Blaike wasn't. 'I figured you must be Spike Guild. What time do we take off?'

'What makes you believe I'm flying?'

'Heard it in town.'

'He couldn't have, Spike,' Popin said quickly.

'I did,' Blaike repeated.

'Who told you?'

'Schein.'

'Schein didn't know!' Popin's voice cracked.

'He told me.' Blaike spoke directly to Fran. 'He'll be along too if he can make it. We're both ready. Here's my fare.' He opened a billfold, counted down ten one hundred dollar bills. He held them out to Fran.

Fran eyed them. He picked up his drink. 'I can't take you tonight.'

'Why not?' He ruffed the money. 'It's all here.'

'You'll have to wait. I haven't room tonight.'

'Who else?' Blaike looked at each one in turn. 'There are five seats.'

'I'm carrying freight.'

He had told Coral he was picking up freight below the border. Fran didn't want another passenger. Julie was still as death. No witnesses.

'I haven't room for but one passenger. Julie was here first.'

'I have to go tonight.' Blaike was quiet but unyielding. 'There are British agents in Santa Fe. They arrived this afternoon. I must get away tonight. Leave the girl behind.'

Fran's hesitation was diminutive, while his eyes flicked from the bills to Julie. He said, 'I assured Julie she should go tonight.'

'Take her on the next load. It can't matter to her.'

She spoke thickly, 'It does matter. I am in danger here. I must go with Fran.' She hoped he would understand if anything went wrong, if Fran forced her to leave at the point of that gun.

'You'll go,' Fran stated. 'Blaike can wait. Popin will put him up.'

'You promised me,' Blaike was belligerent. 'I paid Popin a deposit the other evening. I was to go on the next trip. You can't put me off now. I must get away.' He paced to the window, turned. 'What's so important about the girl getting away tonight?'

'That is her affair,' Fran stated smoothly. He was at ease now in the face of Blaike's seeming upset. 'I am no more than the pilot, Mr Blaike. Nevertheless'—his brows arched—'it is I who make the decisions.'

'You are the Blackbirder?' Blaike demanded.

'I am the Blackbird?' Fran laughed. 'Because the plane I fly is black, I am the Blackbird?'

'Blackbirder,' Blaike corrected.

'Blackbird. Blackbirder.' Fran shrugged lightly. 'These English words. Come, Mr Blaike, you will have a drink. Popin will prepare it.' He consulted his watch. 'You will find it pleasant at Popin's. All of his guests do. And safe. It will not be long. A matter of a few days, I assure you.' His hand touched Julie's. It was meant to reassure her of the falsity of his statement. 'Julie and I must be on our way.'

She didn't know Blaike's next move. She sat tight. Did he realize that Fran was armed? Fran had her coat, was holding it to her. She rose, let him help her into it.

Blaike crossed to them. 'Wait a minute. You can throw off some of the freight. Your boss wouldn't know. Carry it on the next flight. Why toss good money away? I can't promise to sit here until you're back again. I may have to run, find another way across the border. If you're determined to take the girl, all right, but—'

The knocker was a thunderclap. The F.B.I. at last. But Blaike didn't expect this interruption. Obvious in the jerk of his head toward the hall, the breakoff of his sentence. Fran scowled, 'What now?' Popin opened his eyes, frightened. The knocker fell again.

Blaike demanded, 'Who can that be?'

Popin began, 'Perhaps I should answer—'

'I.' Fran's hand was in his pocket clenched. This time he strode.

He barely touched the latch and the door was pushed into his face. Schein followed. He blustered, 'Why was I not informed you fly tonight?'

Fran said curtly, 'Because I have room for no more passengers. You must wait.'

'You will take me. The others will wait.' Schein's black shoes were thuds into the room. When his near-sighted eyes saw Blaike, Julie, he halted. 'It is these for which I would have to wait?'

Fran had followed him. His hand remained in his pocket. 'I'm taking my cousin, Julie Guille. No one else. There is room for no one else.'

Schein said with slow menace, 'The police will be here tomorrow. You take me tonight. You got me into this; you will see I get out of it, or else—'

'Or else what?' Fran was insolent. 'Get your things on, Julie. We're leaving.' He faced Schein again. 'Or else what, Bertie? You'll talk? You'll have a hard time convincing the police I had anything to do with a death in New York while I was in New Mexico. In case you succeed, have them look for me in Old Mexico.'

Julie was buttoning, unbuttoning, buttoning the top button of her coat. She didn't know why, she only knew she was doing it. Blaike had pushed back his hat. He plumped down on the couch as if this were planned diversion. Popin watched cautiously from his chair the mottling of Schein's jowls, the apoplectic anger of his corded fists.

Schein choked, 'You are a fool. You are a fool.'

Fran brought out his hand. His mouth smiled. He pointed the automatic at the man's belly. He said, 'I'm running things here, Bertie. I've reminded you of that many times. Again I remind you. If you are good, Popin will put you up until I return for you. You and your friend Blaike. If you aren't—and I will find out so easily—it is the chair for murder in New York, is it not? You'll make a fine roast, my fat friend.

I will only be sorry that I cannot witness it. You are ready, Julie? Go to the back door.'

She moved like a china doll. Blaike didn't look at her. She backed to the hearth. Blaike couldn't mean to let her go like this, with a murderer. He didn't know she was to be murdered too. She hesitated there by the fire. She had to move again, retrieve her hat, gloves and bag from the table. She didn't. Her eyes were hypnotized by the cruel malice scimitared on Fran's lips, the rage on Schein's thick red face.

'I don't like you,' Fran was saying to the man. 'I've never liked you.' He spat. 'Fat Boche swine. You giving orders to me! Orders from that popeyed idiot you heil-squeak to. Fah! You turn my stomach. Both of you. I'm through with you—' His hand lifted slightly.

It happened then and she caught the edge of the mantel to steady herself. The thick fist crunched Fran's hand. Schein twisted the gun away, smashed it across Fran's face. Fran fell back. The hand which came away from his cheek was wet red. The sickened grunt was from her own lungs.

Horror was shaking the fat waiter. 'You were going to kill me! You were going to shoot me down like a Jew!' He shouted suddenly, 'Stand away!'

Fran didn't listen. His eyes were insane. He sprang, his sinewy fingers tensed. There were four shots. Automatically she counted them. And she moved slightly from the candelabra touching her hair. She put her hand to the singe. Fran lay on the floor twitching, face down. Schein held the gun steady. Popin's hands covered his eyes. Blaike was on his feet. Suddenly she started forward, anguish in her throat. 'Fran!' It welled, broke there, '*Fran!*'

Schein commanded, 'Everyone stay where you are.'

She shrank back as if she had felt the impact of the gun Schein turned on her.

'He is dead,' he stated coldly.

Blaike sank down again. 'Well.' He lit a cigarette.

Her eyes were scorched, blinded. 'Fran . . . dead . . .'

'Do not disturb yourself,' Popin pleaded.

She made simple statement. 'He was my husband.'

She sensed the turn of Blaike's head, Schein's scowl.

Popin said, 'Yes, I learned that. He meant to kill you. To inherit—' His hands apologized.

'I know.' Her voice was torn open. 'But he is dead.' She didn't know the new Fran. He had never been real. She could remember only someone tall and gallant and gay. Cherbourg. The secret marriage in the drab office, secret because Paul would object, object even to his own son controlling her fortune. Fran didn't say it that way, secret because she was young. Fran saying good-by to her that same night. 'I can't take you, Julie. This is a dangerous mission. And no one must know of us until I return.' No one had known. No one had ever known. She had waited with her secret. And he. *My love was false from hour of birth.* He hadn't married her to get control of the money! No! He had loved her then, that one night.

Blaike suggested, 'You'd better stop that mourning. He wasn't worth a damn. You'll make yourself sick.'

She said only, 'Death is so permanent.' She had loved him always, beyond need of forgiving.

Schein announced, 'We are going now. You'—the gun pointed at Blaike—'you, Mr R. A. F., will pilot the plane.'

'All of us?' Blaike asked carelessly.

'You, me. The girl?'

'She is very rich,' Popin whispered.

Schein decided. 'She may be of some use.'

'Popin?' Blaike raised an eyebrow.

'We do not need him.'

The beard shook in terror. 'I too am useful. See how useful I have been to Fran. See—I can help.' He quivered. 'I don't want to be left behind. Heil Hitler! I will help you in many ways.'

Schein pointed the gun.

Popin screamed, 'No!' He flung his arm up over his face.

Blaike said, 'Might as well take him along. He can be useful when he isn't too scared.'

Schein scorned but he turned the gun away, back to Blaike. 'Now,' he ordered.

Blaike leaned back against the couch. 'And suppose I refuse to pilot you. You needn't jab that gun in my direction, you can't frighten me. And if you kill me you won't ever get away. The Manhattan police will get you on Maxl's death. The F.B.I. will get you as the Blackbirder's receiver in New York. And for that pro-Nazi beer garden you ran, yes, and impersonating an officer of the government—'

Schein's face was fury. 'You did not fool me, not once. I knew you were of the F.B.I.'

'But you couldn't find out from any of your spies because I wasn't on the books, eh? I'm not on them. I'll tell you that much. So it's better you believe I'm from the R.A.F. and that you can bully me into taking the plane up. And once we're in the air with your gun at my spine, I'll protect my own life by flying the course you order, yes? It won't work, Bertie. The F.B.I. will be here at any moment. Even if you leave them four corpses you'll still be caught. But I don't believe you are going to shoot. The minute you do you'll cut off any chance, however faint, of convincing me I should perform as your pilot.'

'The F.B.I. will not be here,' Schein smiled slowly. 'They wait in Tesuque for a call from you. There will be no call. Because Papa Popin's telephone wires are not yet fixed.'

'That is so,' Popin spread his hands. 'The company it has too little help and it is very hard to get the materials. The storm did great damage.'

'So you are here, Mr Blaike,' Schein said, 'and I have the gun. It kills well. If you are F.B.I. or if you are R.A.F. makes no difference. You will choose to help me.'

'I don't,' Blaike said.

Schein was patient. 'You will now be patriotic, hein? It does not impress me.' There was cruelty deepening under his eyes. 'For each man his price. I do not offer you death. I offer you the girl to go free—or that she die. You know Maxl was following her in New York. You know why? There are those in Paris who would have her delivered. Perhaps if I kill you I do not go free. But I will make certain before I am captive that she is in the hands of those who will return her to Paris. To death in Paris. Not pleasantly.' His smile was animal. 'We know ways of death. Unpleasant ways.'

Blaike's words were choked back in his throat. He hesitated. She didn't. She lifted the candelabra and flung its burning flares into Schein's gross face. He howled, the gun falling as his hands went up to protect his eyes. It slid almost to her feet. She picked it up quickly, held it pointed at him. She kept it steady while Blaike stamped on the rug, Schein beat at his coat.

Only when she spoke did they look at her. 'I'm tired of violence.' There was no feeling in her voice nor in her spirit. Not even the ache of remembrance remained.

She was empty. 'I'm tired of violence and threats and bullying. Stay where you are.' She fired as she spoke, not to kill, to stay the burly man. The sudden pain that nauseated his face meant nothing to her. His hand clawed at his elbow. 'Sit down,' she said. He swayed back into the chair. The first drops of blood were already dripping from under the sleeve, past his wrist, onto his lifeless palm. She didn't care. She said, 'I'm tired of all the hate and the viciousness and the brutality that you and your kind have generated. I'm tired of the godness you have assumed, the death you have dared impose. You will die too, Schein. Many others like you will die. Not pleasantly. Because what you have done deserves neither justice nor mercy, only retribution.'

Blaike broke in quietly, 'The phone is actually out, Popin?'

'Yes, but—'

'I know. I saw him. Will you call?'

Popin raised up in the chair.

Julie ordered, 'Stay there. Is it Quincy?' At the nod her voice lifted his name. She waited until the Indian came to the door. The gun still covered the three men near her.

Blaike said, 'Quincy, there are men in Tesuque who must come here at once. They are from the F.B.I. You understand F.B.I.?'

Quincy looked to Popin.

Julie said, 'Do as this man says. Get there quickly.'

The Indian kept his eyes stolidly on Popin.

She urged, 'It's all right. If you doubt, ask your cousin Porfiro of the girl who stayed at his father's house. Say that she tells you it is right. There is a car?'

Popin capitulated. 'You may take the car, Quincy.' His eyes scuttled to Schein. He still didn't know who would win. 'Hurry.' He waited until the Indian went out. 'Quincy is on my side, to protect me. Never is he to leave me when strangers are here, not unless I say.' His words tumbled. 'I did not dare do other than what Fran said. He brought me to this country away from the Gestapo. I did not dare offend him or he would give me to the authorities. But always I have been on your side, the American side. I will show you. I have kept records of everyone who came here, the name, where they should go, what they should do. Fran did not know but these records I have kept.' There was the sound of a car whirring away. 'I knew the time would come. He ordered Maxl's death. Because Maxl wanted money. He killed Jacques because, after Julie came, Jacques refused to help longer. Jacques did not understand she had to die because she would spoil the business. And there was the money. He would kill me next because it was I who introduced to him Maxl. I must be protected, so I have kept the records for the F.B.I.—'

Julie interrupted quietly. 'You can tell him all about it while you're waiting for his men. I'm leaving now. Sit back, Blaike. I'm not afraid to use this again. I'm going. I've done what you wanted. I don't want to be locked up. I've changed my mind about that. There are too many important things that I, I alone, must see to.'

'Running away again?' Blaike's mouth twisted.

'No. I'm going back. I'm going to watch Paul pay.' Her mouth was bitter. 'I'm going to tell him Fran is dead—and how he died.' And after that, she too would kill. She would kill Paul. She had known for a long time that it was what must be done. She had tried to run from the knowledge but she had known always that she must return, to kill, and be killed. It was her right.

'You won't get far.'

'One thing you don't know. Fran taught me as well as Jacques how to pilot his plane. You've cleared the Blackbirder over the border. Once I'm there I'll find a way back to Paris. It can't be more difficult than escape was. You have a gun? Don't reach for it. If Schein rallies you may need it. Put your hands now above your shoulders. You too, Popin. Keep them there until I have gone. Don't follow, please. I shoot straight. Fran taught me that too.' She caught her bag, gloves, and hat in her left hand. 'There wouldn't be much point in our killing each other, Blaike. Schein and Popin are more important than I. You know that. There's no way I can help you now. And it couldn't help anyone much for me to be interned.'

She kept the gun trained on them as she backed to the door, continued backing through the dining-room and into the kitchen. She locked the kitchen door behind her, a slight delay if he were foolish enough to follow. Once outside she ran, up the path into the woods, not attempting to avoid clumps of snow. In the clearing beyond the plane glistened darkly under the moon. She climbed into the cockpit; there was an automatic starter. She turned the engine to warm. Fran's gloves, helmet and jacket lay on the seat. His papers were in the jacket pocket. She closed her eyes. She could not be weak now. She removed her coat, laid her things inside. She put on his. She stood outside the door, her gun trained on the blackness at the edge of the woods. There was no movement there. None of the three men back at the house would trust the other. This waiting was endless. But it would take Quincy at least twenty minutes to go to Tesuque and return.

When the motors throbbed reassurance, she climbed

inside, closed the door. She taxied the small cleared field. The stick was sure to her hand. The plane roared, rose skyward. She circled, set the automatic controls, headed south. Radio communication. She pulled off the helmet, put on the earphones.

She was passing over Albuquerque. Not more than fifteen minutes. Quincy and the F.B.I. assistants wouldn't be back at the house yet. But Blaike would still be in control. Popin had already turned his coat. Schein couldn't attack. One hour, two hours, the way seemed long. There was hatred to feed her mind. Hatred of the evil which had been loosed by a beast in an iniquitous land. Hatred of war. Hatred of Paul who had bequeathed decadence to a small dark boy. Fran had been given no stars, nothing but things. And the little boy grew up empty, without knowledge, without spirit. For that alone, Paul deserved death. Fran would have killed her. He didn't want to; he'd tried to keep her away. But after she found him, she had to die. Because she was his wife, because it was the only way to be rid of her—and retain the Marlebone fortune. Things. There was no hatred for him in her. Only grief. There hadn't yet been time for love to die; with the whole heart given, love couldn't die. *Whatsoever you are, my heart shall truly love you* . . . Words could say truths beyond truth. Three hours. She should be approaching El Paso, over the border then, not landing at the Bly field marked on Fran's course, flying uncharted on to Mexico City.

The radio crackled in her ears. It was directing her to land. Army orders. Her hand tightened at the controls. She could run for it. But there were anti-aircraft guns below, there were planes ready to take off, these were war times. She must be above the Army field. They wouldn't hesitate to shoot down an unidentified craft. Surely they must know the black plane of Kent Bly. Yet the orders continued. She must land. Blaike might have countermanded clearance but he couldn't be here. She'd brazened her way out of tighter places. She could convince. She looked at her watch, spoke automatically. 'One one seven—one one seven—approaching field to tower—landing clearance, please.' She listened to directions, circled the field. Her landing was easy. No indication of tensity. If they refused clearance, she would find another way once she was hidden in the city. On a border there were always ways. She sat quietly in the cockpit, waited until the men came to the door. They were two young soldiers. She opened, took her coat over her arm, her other belongings.

One of the soldiers was saying, 'Jeeze, it's a woman.'

She smiled a little. 'I don't understand. I took the pilot's place tonight at Mr Bly's request. I understood I had clearance. The papers are here.'

The one private said, 'I don't know about that, ma'am. All we had was orders to spot the black plane.'

'I'm sure there's a mistake. If you'll just speak to the commanding officer.'

The other one said, 'You'll have to speak to him. At HQ.'

She didn't want to leave the plane. She must get away before Blaike followed. Despite the gun still in her pocket, there was nothing to do but accompany these boys. Quietly. The wind wasn't cold but it blew dark and wild as they crossed the field. There was an army truck waiting.

'Might as well sit up front with us. More comfortable.'

One offered her a cigarette. They weren't suspicious.

HQ was dim, only the light over the sentry at the door, at one window. She walked with the soldiers into the building, into the office. A thin lieutenant was on duty. He asked, 'Julie Guille?'

She began patiently, 'I don't understand, Lieutenant. I had permission from the War Department to fly tonight.' Her mouth was dry. 'Spike wasn't able to make it.'

'I don't know anything about this, Miss Guille. You're to see Major Cochrane. This way.' He led her through another room, snapping on lights as he went, out and across a dim corridor, into yet another room. 'If you'll wait here.'

She smiled at him. He left and her smile thinned. There was a cot, a table with magazines, two chairs. She waited and then she tried the door. It was locked. She went quickly to the window, lifted the shade. A sentry, rifle on shoulder, paced below. She opened the window a little, redrew the shade. She walked to the center of the room, slowly removed the jacket. She was trapped again. The gun she transferred to the pocket of her red coat. The lieutenant had taken no chance that she would not be here to see Major Cochrane. Blaike had reached a phone, had transmitted orders. It was childish for her to have considered that he might let her go scot free. Blindly she had hoped. What she had done was so small a wrong in proportion to the greater wrongs he smashed against.

She started to a knock at the door. It was opened. The lieutenant was followed by a private. 'I thought you might care for something to eat while you're waiting.'

She said, 'Thank you.' She could not ask the favor of escape. He was under higher orders. She heard the door close, not lock. Again she waited, tried it. It was fast. There were coffee, sandwiches, a candy bar, and cigarettes on the tray. She hadn't realized her hunger. Nor her weariness. When she had finished eating, she lay on the cot, the folded jacket as a pillow, her coat over her. She didn't try to think. There were times when it was better not.

3

Blaike said, 'Sorry to keep you waiting.' She hadn't heard his entrance. She had been deep in sleep.

He stood beside the cot looking down at her. Even through sleep she saw the haggard lines of his face. Her watch said four-thirty. She pushed up. She said, 'I've not been waiting for you. Major Cochrane—'

He sat down on the chair. 'I'm Blaike Cochrane.' He managed a smile. 'The Roderick, as I told you, is never used. The Major isn't important.'

'I see.' Her feet were on the floor now. She pulled the red coat about her coldness. She said, 'I don't know why you couldn't let me go.'

His smile was wry. 'Maybe I didn't take to your one-man suicide-squad scheme. You didn't really believe you'd come through it unscathed?'

'It didn't matter.' She looked at him with a spark of unspent passion. 'There's more of us than of them. Many of us have died. Many more will. But some day we'll exterminate them, all of them, one by one. I want my share.'

He said, 'We have men trained for that, to fight, even to die. But not without weapons, not without a chance. We'll conquer them. When that's done you may share. The woman's way. Feeding and clothing, and helping the children to forget that once there was a world like today's. It won't be spectacular. No one will weep over your holy grave. It will be merely work, drab, everyday work. But it will be of more value than snuffing your life out to satisfy personal revenge.'

When she spoke it was in dull anger. 'I don't want praise. I don't want martyrdom. It's personal, yes, but it's more than that. It's repayment for all who have suffered for what Paul did, those who have suffered far more than I. I must kill him.'

He was silent. He turned his head at last. 'Paul is dead.'

She repeated as if she didn't understand. 'Paul is dead.'

'He's been dead for months. A bomb exploded in the car in which he was riding with important Nazi officials. All were killed.'

'Aunt Lily?'

'She was last heard from in Ankara. She's married again, a wealthy Turk. She'll come out on top.' He turned the subject deliberately. 'The Gestapo hasn't been after you since you left France. They don't know about the necklace. Do you think Paul would risk losing it to them? Schein knew only that you escaped them. But he wasn't after you. He had no time for that. He was running from the New York police. Nor have they been after you. Schein hoped they would be; that's why he killed Maxl in a place that could involve you. They do want your testimony, yes. But they've known it was Schein from the first night. The F.B.I. doesn't want you. You're an American citizen; you were registered as an infant. It was necessary because of the Marlebone estate. I've taken care of the Santa Fe police. You were helping me on the case.'

She said, 'Thank you.'

'Don't you get it?' he asked. 'You're free. To come and go as you please. You can leave now.'

'Then why did you stop me from going?' Her eyes held his.

'Because—' He jammed his hands into his pockets.

'Because I knew you didn't know what you were doing. You were blind with pain. No matter what you thought of him—you said it there at Popin's—"Death is so permanent."' He spoke with strength. 'I came here to prevent you from destroying yourself. That's the one thing none of us can afford to do now. We're all needed. I can use you. Popin has those lists. Incidentally they will save his neck from the firing squad. My job now is to track down every one of those men and women, hundreds of them. Every one a definite danger to our victory. You'll know some of them. You'll know other faces. It will be dangerous work but you're not afraid of danger. I'm asking your help. It is up to you. If you don't want to you can go. Free. Without restrictions. Think it over. I'll be across the way.' He stood up, shoved his hat forward again. 'I also came after you because I didn't want you to die. Not until you'd lived, Julie.' He went out.

She walked to the window. Pinpoints of light sharpened the darkness. There was the stir of awakening at the great Fort. Below her window the guard was changing. The bugles of reveille came blowing through the dark.

There was only one answer she could give Blaike. Fran was gone. It was better he should die. He could never have learned to live in a world dedicated to love of thy neighbor. Liberty, Equality, and Fraternity. Man is created free and equal. Not some men—Man. Little children, love one another. There could never be any answer but to help achieve that peace. Even if it took a million years for it to come to pass, her own small effort would speed that day. Her effort and the effort of all good people everywhere.

She gathered her things together. Her hand touched Fran's jacket. She withdrew it, left its leather there on the cot. He was gone. The ache too would go. The cutting away of a malignant growth left the body pain-racked. But no one would ask the return of the disease to heal that pain. She couldn't grieve. She could want him in every fiber, want her dream of him, but her face must be set away from grief. He had to die. He had been born too late. He had been born on the wrong side of the tracks.

She opened the unlocked door, crossed the silence of the corridor. She tapped softly on the door across. There was no answer. She opened it slightly. The room was like the one in which she had waited. Blaike lay asleep on the cot, the one leg stiff, the other relaxed. He didn't waste time talking about what had happened to him over there; he had left that behind. He was turned face forward to the fight.

His breathing was of exhausted sleep. She realized only then how after the ordeal at Popin's, after the mopping up, he had set out again to follow her. To save her from her own despair. To ask her to live. He was the first person in a long time who had cared about what happened to her. She laid her bright coat gently over him. She sat down to wait.

The End

penguin.co.uk/vintage